## Praise for *Stepping Into Sunlight*

"With emotional and spiritual honesty, *Stepping Into Sunlight* chronicles the rebirth of faith and courage in a young woman traumatized by the unthinkable. Sharon Hinck's authentic and endearing heroine is so convincing that I found myself praying for her! I laughed. I cried. I asked God a lot of questions. Hinck's concise yet poetic language ushered me into a worshipful place."

—Patti Hill, author of *The Queen of Sleepy Eye*

"Told with humor and lump-in-the-throat insight, *Stepping Into Sunlight* is a compelling story of learning to live again after trauma. This was my first Sharon Hinck novel, but it gathered her a permanent spot on my favorite authors list."

—Deborah Raney, author of *A Vow to Cherish* and The Clayburn Novels series

"For everyone who has ever been afraid of what life may hold (and who hasn't?), Sharon's novel is a beacon of hope and healing. Kudos!"

—Roxanne Henke, author of *After Anne* and *Learning to Fly*

"With a deft hand Hinck ushers the reader into the frustrating, inward world of the victim, challenging us to gauge the level of our compassion for those who walk a journey we can't adequately imagine and daring us to wonder if we, too, could flatten our fears and replace them with modest, indiscriminate kindness."

—Susan Meissner, author of *Blue Heart Blessed*

"A beautifully woven story of one woman's desperation, determination . . . and hope. A cast of oddball, but thoroughly charming, characters make this book a delightful read from start to finish. Highly recommended."

—Kathyrn Cushman, author of *A Promise to Remember* and *Waiting for Daybreak*

Books by

# Sharon Hinck

*The Secret Life of Becky Miller*

*Renovating Becky Miller*

*Symphony of Secrets*

SHARON HINCK

# Stepping into Sunlight

BETHANY HOUSE PUBLISHERS
*Minneapolis, Minnesota*

Cover design by Jennifer Parker



Published by Bethany House Publishers
11400 Hampshire Avenue South
Bloomington, Minnesota 55438

Bethany House Publishers is a division of
Baker Publishing Group, Grand Rapids, Michigan.

Printed in the United States of America

**Library of Congress Cataloging-in-Publication Data**

Hinck, Sharon.
Stepping into sunlight / Sharon Hinck.
p. cm.
ISBN 978-0-7642-0283-4 (pbk.)
1. Conduct of life—Fiction. 2. Kindness—Fiction. I. Title.

PS3608.I53S74 2008
813′.6—dc22

2008028096

To Flossie Marxen,
who has cared for so many of the hidden wounded

❃

*"The King will reply,*
*'I tell you the truth, whatever you did*
*for one of the least of these brothers of mine,*
*you did for me.' "*
*Matthew 25:40* NIV

SHARON HINCK writes "stories for the hero in all of us," comtemporary novels praised for their strong spiritual themes, emotional resonance, and unique blend of genres. She was named 2007 Writer of the Year at Mount Hermon Christian Writers Conference and has been a Christy Award finalist and an ACFW Book of the Year finalist. When she's not wrestling with words, she enjoys speaking at churches and conferences. Sharon earned a M.A. at Regent University, located in the Tidewater area of Virginia, the setting for *Stepping Into Sunlight*. A wife and mom of four, she now makes her home in Minneapolis, Minnesota. Visit her website at *www.sharonhinck.com* and check out the special Penny's Project blog at *http://pennysproject.blogspot.com*.

# chapter 1

TERROR IN THE SUPERMARKET. It sounded like a ridiculous headline from one of the tabloids on the rack near the checkout lane. Yet the only name for the pounding in my chest was that melodramatic word. *Terror.*

Gaudy detergent boxes leaned out from the shelves. Beneath fluorescent lights, the corridor stretched into eternity—as if the bakery counter were shrinking into the distance while the grocery store shelves rose up into towering cliffs that threatened to crash down on my head. I gripped my half-full shopping cart for support as its wheels squeaked and wobbled. Three cautious steps edged me closer to my goal. Blood pulsed a quickening tide across my eardrums. *Don't panic. You can do this.*

Last week I'd managed a quick run for milk, eggs, and bread. This week I had set a more ambitious goal. But the surreal menace hit me with even more force today. Breathing hard, I scanned my surroundings. A woman at the end of the aisle gave me a curious glance.

I hunched deeper into my zip-front sweatshirt and turned my back on her. What did she see? I was just another thirty-something woman dressed for the gym. If she detected the haggard lines of my face, maybe she'd write that off as the exhausted look of a normal mom.

And I *was* normal. I had to be. This errand would prove I was ready to cope with everyday life again.

Farther down the aisle, a loud crack cut through the piped-in Muzak. I jumped and lifted a hand to my temple. A vein pulsed against the skin with enough pressure to burst. A pudgy boy leaned down to retrieve his yo-yo.

*You're being ridiculous. Scared by a dropped yo-yo? What's next? Fear of Hula-Hoops?*

I pushed my shopping cart past the boy and his mother and forced my feet to keep a steady pace. Six more steps. Five. Four. My target stretched in front of me. The bakery counter.

Now all I had to do was order the cake.

"Can I help you?" The counter woman's voice creaked with age. I stared at the bear claws on the bottom shelf of the display case.

*Come on, Penny. Tell her. You need a small cake. Chocolate.*

"Ma'am? Can I help you?" Now she sounded concerned.

Why was this so hard? This store didn't look at all like—

*No! Don't go there.*

My fingertips tingled, and waves of nausea rose up to catch in my throat. Pastries and muffins filled my vision, but the space around them turned gray. Gray with little red sprinkles. Or maybe that was the decoration on the sugar cookies.

I bent forward to draw a deep breath, fighting off the sensation of falling. Who really needed a cake anyway? Too many carbs. This had been a bad idea. I released my grip on the shopping cart and ran.

Back up the aisle.

Past the mother who pulled her son close as I brushed by.

Past a mountain of paper towel rolls.

Past the pyramid of tangerines. My stomach lurched at their scent.

The automatic doors opened outward too slowly. I pressed my shoulder against one side and forced it to let me escape. A short sprint brought me to my car. The passenger side was closest, so I dove in that side, pulled the door closed behind me, and hit the lock. Curled up half on the floor and half on the seat, my body shuddered.

*Block it out.*

I squeezed my fists to my forehead.

*Get over it.*

But I was getting worse, not better.

September sun baked the air inside the car with another reminder that I was in a strange place. Back home in Wisconsin, the leaves were turning orange and the temperature had a bite. Today's heat made Chesapeake, Virginia, feel as foreign as Bangkok.

Someone tapped on the glass of my wagon's door. "Honey chile, you need help?"

I scrambled to pull myself up onto the passenger seat. A broad dark face peered through the window. The woman probably thought I was hot-wiring the car. Was that a shower cap on her head? One pink roller poked from beneath the cap, clinging to a lock near her temple.

I grabbed my sunglasses from the floor and held them up. "Just looking for these," I called through the glass.

She pursed her lips and braced a heavy arm against the car's roof. Her flowered muumuu filled my line of sight. "You ran outta there like lard on a hot skillet."

While my northern ears struggled to translate, she leaned down and studied my face. "Sure you're okay?"

I nodded vigorously enough to make my neck hurt. "I was shopping but changed my mind."

She looked puzzled but then flashed a broad white smile. "Well, chile, them prices can set me to runnin', too." Her eyes scanned me as if she were an experienced grandmother checking for injuries. Finally, she patted the roof of the car and waddled away.

I scooted over behind the wheel. Hysterical giggles freed from my throat. Running from high prices?

My smile died. If only my problems were that simple.

For a crazy moment I wanted to roll down the window and call the woman back. Cry on her ample shoulder. Tell her everything. "My husband left for three months at sea. I don't know anyone here. And a few days before he left—" Even in my imaginary conversation I couldn't finish that sentence, couldn't make myself explain why the simple act of buying groceries had become impossible.

Instead, I started the engine and aimed for home, pressing my hand against the ribs where my heart fluttered, as if I could soothe my circulation back into sanity. At the next stoplight, I fumbled in the glove compartment and pulled out a dog-eared business card. *Victim Support Services*. The policewoman who'd given it to me had been matter-of-fact when she'd told me I'd need help in the days to come. Shock had cocooned me in a blessed numbness for several days. Dazed and grateful to be alive, I counted on my faith, family, and inner strength to shelter me from delayed reactions. Even when the nightmares began, I tried to hide them from Tom. When that was impossible, I reassured him they were a brief aberration. I'd bounce back.

Or so I'd thought. Lately my confidence was as slouchy and battered as my old canvas purse on the passenger seat.

I tapped the card on the steering wheel. A left turn would take me to the Norfolk address.

As if in argument, the car stereo blinked the time at me. Bryan would be getting off the school bus soon. I needed to get home and be there to greet him. He was counting on me. Besides, I had good reason to distrust the benefits of counseling.

When the light turned green, I tossed the card into my purse and pulled ahead.

The heat brought prickles to my skin, but I didn't open the window. The air-conditioner made little impact on the superheated interior, so I pretended I was enjoying a sauna at the YMCA. Too bad I didn't have a towel.

It took full concentration to navigate the unfamiliar streets. Norfolk, Virginia Beach, Chesapeake—the cities ran together like an irregular puddle. In our Chesapeake neighborhood, modest brick ramblers lined up behind chain-link fences. Some tidy yards offered bursts of color from planters or a birdbath. Others were strewn with cigarette butts and crushed cans.

A mulberry tree, overripe fruit staining the neighbors' sidewalk, helped me identify our house in the middle of the block. Almost there.

As I emerged from the car, the pit bull next door yanked his chain and began a token round of barking. When the heat discouraged him, he lowered himself into the dirt that he'd clawed bare of grass. I knew exactly how he felt.

"Afta-noon."

My breath choked, and my hand flew to my neck. Laura-Beth Foley, owner of both the mulberry tree and the pit bull, sat on a paint-chipped chair in the shade cast by her house. She blotted her forehead with a tumbler that dripped condensation past the freckles on her cheeks.

Tantalizingly close, my house called to me. My nerve endings screamed for escape, but politeness glued me to the concrete. "Hello."

She smiled. The slight gap in her front teeth didn't mar the friendliness of her grin. She was probably only a few years older than I, but her bleached blond hair made her look even older. "Finally got the twins down for a nap. Hotter 'en blue blazes, and it makes 'em fretful."

"Mm-hmm." I hunched inside my long-sleeved hoodie. I probably looked ridiculous in this land of tank tops, but the soft cotton comforted me.

Laura-Beth had delivered a lopsided banana bread when we moved in several weeks ago. She'd told us about her girl in fifth grade, a boy in third, and twins who were two. I couldn't remember all their double names. Jim-Bob, Billie-Jo, Mary-Lou? It was as if southerners couldn't contain their personality in a single name.

"Come on over and have some iced tea." Laura-Beth lifted a magazine from her lap and fanned her face.

I looked at my front door. The lock gleamed—even through the shadows cast by the awning. "Oh. I . . . I can't. Maybe another time."

She shrugged. "All right. But I hope you don't mind a piece of advice. Try some chamomile tea for your nerves. You're gonna get an ulcer if you stay wound this tight."

"Thanks. I'll do that." I racewalked to my door and hurried inside, bolting it behind me.

Dropping my purse on the small table near the front door, I slumped onto the couch. Each second passed slowly while my heart searched for a normal rhythm.

Across from me in the blank television screen, a shadowed reflection revealed a stranger's face. A new Penny Sullivan. The old Penny used to live in the Midwest with her husband and son: Tom the youth pastor and Bryan the seven-year-old motormouth. *That* Penny hosted backyard barbeques for the youth group and volunteered in Bryan's classroom every Friday. *That* Penny enjoyed people and saw promise and potential in every face she looked into. *That* Penny would never avoid a friendly neighbor—or be told she needed to do something about her nerves. I squinted at my likeness in the television glass. The face was still heart-shaped with full lips. The hair was still long and auburn. But the eyes had changed. Flat, dull, frozen in a moment of shock, like a bad photograph.

I glared into the screen. "You are not giving up. Bryan deserves more than a can of alphabet soup for supper. We need groceries."

I pushed myself from the safety of the couch and marched to the kitchen for the phone book. Plenty of grocery stores delivered these days. If Penny couldn't go to the chocolate cake, the chocolate cake would come to Penny. For the second time that day, my lips flickered in a brief smile.

A quick call led to the promise of a grocery drop-off in time for supper—complete with chocolate cake and chamomile tea. Even better, I learned that Tidewater Groceries could take my weekly order via e-mail. I wouldn't have to drive to the store or even talk to anyone on the phone. Problem solved.

*See, Penny. You can do this. You can keep it together.*

Buoyed by my success, I walked down to the corner to meet Bryan's school bus. Someone had to make my son's life as secure and normal as possible while Tom was at sea. I would give Bryan back the mom he used to have. I decided not to look too closely at the fact that it took every ounce of my determination to accomplish the simple act of leaving the house to meet his bus—the kind of thing I used to do without a second thought.

The bus pulled up, the yellow doors folded open, and Bryan plunged down the stairs. The sun put copper glints in his brown mop of hair, and grape juice stains surrounded his lips. For a moment I remembered how it felt to be myself and grinned.

"Hey, Mom. Guess what?" Bryan handed me his backpack and marched past leaving me to follow as his pack mule. "We're doing a really cool play. It's for Thanksgiving, and I get to be a Pilgrim 'cause they came on a boat. Didja know it's close to here? And we get to have corn and squash and stuff. Mom, what's squash? And we get to invite our moms and dads."

"Sounds fun." But worry twisted under my skin. I tried to picture myself walking into the school gym full of kids and parents. Rows of tables decorated with crepe paper. All the strangers. The noise. The chaos. My chest tightened. What was my problem lately? I'd always loved Bryan's school events. Why did I feel dread instead of anticipation?

"Will Daddy be home by then? I get to sing a special song all by myself." He ran up the steps to our door and puffed his chest out.

"He's hoping he'll be home by Thanksgiving. We don't know yet. But I'll tell him all about it when I e-mail him tonight."

He twisted the door handle and kicked the door with more force than necessary to swing it open. "I want him to be home."

I took a slow breath. "Me too." Bryan's grumpy spells had begun the minute Tom's ship sailed toward the horizon. I should have hidden Bryan in Tom's kit bag, so my husband could deal with the cranky little stowaway.

"Don't forget to tell him about my field trip." He planted himself in our small entryway. "Hey, Jim-Bob told me that cool movie with the robots is on DVD now. Can we go rent it tonight? Can we?"

I hefted his schoolbag in his direction. "Take your backpack to your room."

"Mo-om. You said you wanted to see it."

"Your backpack?"

"The movie. Please?"

I shook my head. "Not tonight."

He pulled the bag from my hands and stomped off to his room. "You're no fun anymore."

Right. As if being fun was my biggest concern these days.

We were both prickly the rest of the evening. At bedtime, we marked our tenth big red X on the kitchen calendar with great ceremony, but the expanse of blank days ahead sneered at me.

After I tucked Bryan into bed, I padded out to the living room. The small room opened into an eating area overseen by a short kitchen counter. I missed our Victorian dining room and the built-in bookshelves of our generous, wood-floored front room. Here, the beige carpeting looked so mottled, I hated crossing it in my bare feet. Mini-blinds dangled from the windows, giving the house the feeling of a drab office, and instead of using a spare bedroom for a study as we had in Wisconsin, we now used a card table in one corner of the living room.

Tom and I had laughed as we set up our computer in its new home. I found a fabric remnant bright with blue irises, and he told me it was the perfect elegant touch for the home office and coordinated beautifully with our blue denim couch. I praised his bookshelf assembly, as he created the "library" on the wall next to the "desk."

It was all great fun settling in to our scaled-down home when we'd moved in a month ago, and we hadn't even felt as if we were making a sacrifice.

Had I been naïve? Had I forgotten to count the cost?

No. We were ready for this. I couldn't have known about what would happen.

*Stop. Don't think about it.*

I quickly booted up the computer. Tom's face grinned at me from the screen saver, warm and inviting in spite of the formal dress uniform he was so proud of. I touched the tiny scar under his left eye, leaving a smudge on the monitor.

Why was this separation so much worse than the weeks while he was at chaplaincy training? Each empty square on the calendar stretched ahead of me like the cold linoleum tiles of the grocery store aisle. *Tom, I don't know how to do this.* A weight sat on my lungs and squeezed my throat.

I slid the computer mouse and his face disappeared, letting me breathe again. Bryan would keep hounding me to see the latest animated DVD, so I searched for movie rental stores in the neighborhood. I jotted down the addresses and printed out MapQuest directions on our wheezy printer. Good errand for tomorrow. Maybe.

My pen doodled rain clouds next to the list of directions. Maybe not.

I scrolled past the Google list of movie stores and found Netflix. Even better. I quickly signed up and chose the movie Bryan wanted along with a few for me. God bless the Internet. Movies by mail.

When I opened my e-mail program, I found two brief notes from Tom, one for me and one for Bryan, which I flagged to show him tomorrow. What would Tom think if he knew I'd barely managed to leave the house in the ten days he'd been gone? That the night terrors were getting worse and not better? I flexed my fingers and attacked the keyboard.

*Hi back atcha!*

*Yes, we're fine. Bryan got a part in a school play for Thanksgiving, so we're hoping you'll be home by then. I don't know why my mom e-mailed you. I thought she was busy with Cindy's new baby. I wish she'd stop fussing about me. How many times do I have to tell everyone? I'm fine. Tell her that, too, okay? Maybe she'll listen to you. Today I tried a new grocery store. I splurged and bought a chocolate cake. Now don't feel bad. It's not as if we're celebrating your absence. We just deserved a treat after surviving our first full week without you. How's the food on your boat (sorry—your ship)? I miss you tons, but I know you're doing a great job. YES, you have what it takes. You're going to be a terrific chaplain. Want me to write it in a bigger font? You are exactly where God wants you. Love, your favorite wife. :-)*

After signing off, I wandered into the kitchen to try some of my new chamomile tea. It tasted as if I were chewing on a dandelion stem, and even after choking down the whole cup, I didn't feel an ounce more relaxed. That's what I got for listening to Laura-Beth.

My cup joined the sink full of supper dishes. They'd keep until tomorrow.

In the bedroom, I opened my dresser drawer and stared at a cheerful striped pajama set. To change, I'd have to take off my baggy shirt and the tank top beneath it. And I should probably wash up and brush my teeth.

Too much work. My outfit was all cotton knit anyway, as comfortable as sleepwear. I shoved the drawer shut and crawled into bed in my clothes.

Every one of the past sixteen nights, a dark companion had joined me the minute I stopped moving. In the days since Tom's deployment, it had advanced with even more arrogance, as if it could take up the room my husband had left vacant beside me. I curled into a tight ball and tensed against the familiar assault.

Fear crept up the edge of the bedspread, under the covers, and under the skin of my scalp.

All day I pushed back the memories. But they waited for this moment when I tried to sleep—for this time when I was alone, vulnerable. Frenetic, violent images on a horrible repeating loop attacked my mind. My body shook and I tried to pray. The whisper scraped in my throat.

"Make it stop. Please. Make it stop."

THE NEXT MORNING, I slouched at the kitchen table and nibbled the edge of my toast. Was it possible to have a chamomile tea hangover? I could barely hold my eyelids open.

*Come on, Penny. It's up to you to make something out of this new day.*

I focused my bleary gaze on my son. "Bryan, get your backpack. Time to catch the bus."

He pushed aside his bowl of soggy Cheerios. "Yea!" His smile nudged his cheeks into round chubs that proved he still had some of his baby fat. He bolted to his room and raced back with his school stuff. Was he more eager to see his friends or to get away from me?

For all of his seven years, Bryan had tagged along beside Tom or me, enjoying each person he met. The move to Virginia and a school full of strangers had thrilled him, and he'd adapted with enviable skill. I gulped a last swallow of lukewarm coffee and rose from the table. "Remember to give your teacher the permission slip."

Bryan plopped into the middle of the kitchen floor to tie his tennis shoes. "Do you think we'll see sharks? Is this the same ocean Daddy showed me? Are you gonna drive for the field trip? Know what? Martin's mommy put cookies in his lunch yesterday. Are you making cookies?"

I planted a kiss on top of Bryan's head and hoisted him to his feet. "I hope you don't see sharks. You're supposed to be studying seashells. It's the same ocean, but your class is going to a different beach." Bryan slipped his arms into the straps of his backpack with my help. Why did second graders need to drag around their weight in textbooks?

When I opened the front door, he stood at attention. I rested my hand on the top of his head. "Heavenly Father, bless Bryan today. Please protect him from accident or injury. Help him do his best in school to your glory. Let him draw close to you today and know that he is precious to you and to me and to his daddy. Let him share your love with the people around him. Amen."

He squeezed his eyes shut even tighter. "And my book report," he stage-whispered.

"And give him courage to read his book report when it's his turn. Amen."

"Amen." My son slalomed down the front steps, twisting his knees from side to side with happy, flat-footed jumps. He galloped to the corner where other children waited, while I stood guard from the doorway. Good thing our traditional blessing time distracted him from his other questions about field trips and cookies. My mothering skills had already dropped to remedial level. I didn't want to explain why I couldn't drive for the field trip. And baking?

Maybe that wasn't such a bad idea. As a new transplant to the area, I had a valid excuse for not driving for the field trip. No one wanted the kids to end up in North Carolina if I took a wrong turn. But cookies knew no boundaries and always scored great Mommy Points. The last few weeks I hadn't been very successful in being a perky, self-reliant chaplain's wife. I needed something to give me a sense of accomplishment—and something new to e-mail Tom about, to convince him I wasn't shriveling under the strain of his absence.

First, basic morning chores needed attention. I attacked the kitchen and cleaned up the remains of breakfast, then unpacked some stray boxes. It took most of the morning to figure out where to fit off-season and special-occasion clothes in our tiny closets. The physical labor of moving hadn't been as draining as the tedious decisions that had dragged out during the weeks of settling in.

Lunchtime came and went before I pulled out the sack of flour, sugar, salt, and my recipe box. A lengthy search finally revealed where I'd stowed the cookie sheets. The new kitchen still felt foreign and confusing. I stopped to jot a reminder on a sticky note: *Organize kitchen.*

I poured myself a glass of cranberry juice and shuffled through recipe cards, but none of them grabbed my interest. Gingersnap, snickerdoodle, chocolate chip, oatmeal raisin. My stomach soured with each recipe. Weariness poured over me in a sudden wave. I turned to put the box of cards back on the shelf, and my elbow bumped my half-empty glass.

The glass clattered against the counter, and red liquid spilled out and ran onto the tile floor.

In that second of startled clumsiness, I fell into an elevator shaft of horror. My kitchen disappeared. Images flashed around me like lightning. Blood pooling on cold linoleum. A gun swinging in my direction. The round shape of the old woman's lips.

I gasped and dropped to a crouch, as recipes fell around me. With my back pressed against a cabinet, I covered my head and squeezed my eyes closed.

Still, I fell. Deeper, deeper into darkness and fear and death. Paralysis grabbed my limbs.

My mouth opened in a scream, but only a harsh ringing sound came from my throat. The scene melted away as the ringing sounded again.

The shrill phone hauled me back into reality. I blinked several times while I struggled to remember who I was, where I was, and why recipe cards and juice were scattered around me.

The ringing from the kitchen phone stopped, then started again.

I staggered to my feet and fumbled for the receiver. "Hello?" I slurred.

"Penny? What's wrong? You sound funny." My mom's voice blared from thousands of miles away.

"Must be the connection."

"Have you been drinking?"

I tried for a laugh, but only managed a shaky breath. "I was doing some baking."

"Oh. Well, how hard is it to keep a dish towel handy to wipe your hands so you can pick up when I call?"

I couldn't think of anything to say, and an expectant silence stretched like a verbal staring contest.

She blinked first. "Tom says you're doing fine. Is that true? I didn't think you'd hold up once he left. Do you want me to fly out there?"

"Mom, I'm okay. I know Cindy needs your help with the new baby."

"But, honey, aren't you scared? Being there alone? I told you moving away was a bad idea." She was a classic mom with a wealth of skills in the fine art of worry. One day people would go to the Museum of Moms to study her greatest works.

"Tom and I prepared for this. I knew I'd have to be a single mom when he went to sea." And I'd had romantic visions of standing on a widow's walk staring out to sea, salt air blowing my hair, as I waited for his ship to return.

"But that was before. Before the . . . you know."

I hissed in a breath through my teeth. She'd broken the taboo. Brought up the denim-clad, pistol-waving elephant in the living room. The one I'd been trying to forget for more than two weeks. I grabbed a dish towel and blotted at the red juice.

"I still think you should move back here until Tom is done with this Navy thing. Did you go to the victim place?"

I forced a laugh. "Oh, come on. How will that help? I need to put it behind me, not talk to some stranger about it. Besides, psychologists always want to hear about how your mom messed up your life. You wouldn't want that, would you?"

Now the silence echoed with disapproval. She cleared her throat. "You don't want to end up like—"

"Mom, please." I couldn't let her take the conversation down that road.

She switched gears. "Well, Tom said you promised to go."

"I just didn't want him to worry. He hated leaving so soon after . . . Look, Mom. I'm fine."

"Well, call me more often, okay?"

"I'll try." I forced life into my voice. "I'm kind of busy. Getting settled in, new church, school activities, making friends. You know how it is."

She laughed—her first natural tone during this conversation. "Yeah, you and Tom always had a full calendar."

"Well, you take care. Thanks for calling."

"Give Bryan a big hug from his grandma."

"I will. And I'll e-mail you some pictures soon."

Regret tickled behind my sternum as I hung up. I should be glad I'd convinced her not to make a big deal of my . . . experience, but part of me wanted my mom to fly out for a visit, rescue me from myself, and convince me I wasn't going crazy. Another part of me wanted to pack up Bryan and run home to Wisconsin. I picked up the scattered recipe cards and tried to return some order to their box, but I was too muddle-headed to make sense of the categories. Did Grandma's meatball soup go under *Meat* or *Soups and Salads*? Why wasn't my brain working right?

Last night had been rough. First the nightmares had invaded. Then when those relented, the empty side of our double bed kept startling me into wakefulness. Maybe I shoud indulge in a little nap. Sleep would probably do more good for my parenting than baking cookies, anyway, and it would definitely be better for my waistline.

Deserting the baking supplies on the counter, I dragged myself to the bedroom. Tom's side of the bed welcomed me, so I crawled under the sheets and pressed my face into his pillow. The scent of Johnson's baby shampoo surrounded me—Tom's favorite for his fine blond hair. I never tired of the smell. Inertia weighted me to the mattress, and I let the world go away. My mother would be horrified. A nap in the middle of the day. No hardworking woman of Puritan stock would fritter time that way. Yet my willpower was broken—spilled out and scattered like recipe cards on the kitchen floor. I needed to escape.

I dozed, and my dreams brought me comfortingly to my old neighborhood in Wisconsin. Fall whirligigs spun from the tall trees. I sat on a bench in the park near our old house and sipped from a can of Coke, savoring Bryan's laughter from the playground. An elderly couple strolled across the grass. They held hands and smiled as they watched Bryan climb across the monkey bars. His green-striped shirt was frayed around the neckline, where he sometimes chewed the edge. The couple resumed their walk and approached my bench. I looked up to smile at them, but when the old woman saw me, her face contorted. "You! You didn't stop him."

Ice slid across my skin. A dirty corner of condemnation in my heart accepted her words, and I cringed. I wanted to run from her glare, but could only press my spine harder against the bench.

The man lifted a shaky arm and pointed to me. "Why are you still here?"

The woman wore the same lavender linen blouse that she was wearing when I'd last seen her.

"No." The word strangled in my chest. *Not again.*

Several cracks ruptured the air, and I jumped. Who had been shot? Someone was hit.

A boy in a green-striped T-shirt tumbled from the top of the jungle gym.

*Bryan!*

I pushed past the couple and ran to his body. Blood moistened the sand around his head.

*No! This isn't the way it happened. Not Bryan.*

"Mom? Where are you?" He called out to me as I cradled him in my arms.

"Shh. It's all right. I'm here."

"Mom? Mom?" The muffled voice reached into my dream and pulled me out. I stared at the pillow in my arms. Only a nightmare. I wasn't holding Bryan's bleeding body.

"Mom! I'm home." Bryan bellowed from the front steps. The doorbell joined his call, ringing over and over with schoolboy impatience.

My pulse roared into high gear like an Indy race car. I shot up and staggered for the door. How long had he been out there? Had he been scared when he got off the bus and I wasn't waiting?

When I yanked the door open, Bryan grinned up at me and hopped from one foot to the other. "Did you forget it was bus time?"

"I'm sorry. I took a nap and didn't wake up in time to walk down to the corner for you."

Bryan rolled his eyes. "Mom, I don't have to take naps anymore. Why do you?"

"Oh, you know. Mommies get tired sometimes."

"Wanna see my shells?" Bryan dropped to his knees, pulled out a paper sack, and upended shells and sand all over the carpet without waiting for my answer.

I knelt beside him, happy to sort treasures with him. I hadn't accomplished much else today.

"Oh, no." He held up a lifeless shape that had pincers and poked it. "The crab I found today. It looks dead. I was gonna make him a house with my Legos." He thrust the ugly carapace under my nose.

I scooted back. "Maybe you should take that outside."

He lit up. "Do you think if we water him he'll wake up?" His niblet teeth flashed around the gap waiting for his two permanent incisors. Bryan's mouth was half baby, half boy.

"Um, no. I just thought you might like to . . . bury him. That's what you do when a pet dies."

"Cool." He launched to his feet and raced for the back door.

Still groggy, I followed him to the kitchen and scrounged the cupboards for supper ideas while keeping watch on Bryan through the screen door. He used my gardening trowel to dig a hole, then collected rocks to create a headstone. He plucked dandelions from near the fence to decorate the grave. Should I be worried about how much fun he was having creating a funeral? I'd always pictured myself having tea parties with a tiny daughter in lace-edged socks and dress-up jewelry. Instead God had blessed me with snips and snails and puppy-dog tails. Hard to believe how much joy I'd found in watching my son collect bugs, crash toy trucks, or climb the doorjambs to play Spiderman.

Laura-Beth called a greeting from her backyard, and Bryan trotted over to the fence to chat. Her voice carried through the screens. "Tell your mom there's a great place to go crabbing in Portsmouth. You just use some chicken necks for bait."

I pulled away from the door, not wanting to hear any more. I didn't need any advice on crabbing. I'd been crabbing all the time lately.

With a kettle boiling for pasta, I found some aspirin and guzzled a tall glass of ice water. When Bryan tired of playing with his dead crab, he came inside and reached for a piece of the garlic bread I had pulled from the freezer.

I grabbed his grubby wrist. "Hold it, buster. Go wash your hands. I'll put out carrot sticks for a snack."

He brushed his hands off against his jeans and looked at me hopefully.

"No. That doesn't count. Go wash." Parenting standards weren't going to slip just because Tom was at sea.

With a heavy sigh, he trudged to the bathroom. The faucet ran for about five seconds. I winced as I pictured the condition of the towel after Bryan wiped his dirt-smeared hands.

He came back to the kitchen only slightly cleaner and hoisted himself onto a stool by the counter. "Are you feeling better, Mommy?"

I handed him a carrot stick. "What do you mean?"

"You know. 'Cause you've been so sad all the time."

*Ouch.* I thought my mommy façade had fooled him. "Maybe I'm just missing our old house."

He gave a sage nod. "Me too. But know what? I like the ocean. Can we go there again tomorrow? 'Cause know what? We're s'posed to get more shells. Mrs. Pimple says so."

"Mrs. Pimblott."

"Yeah. And I need a bucket to carry them. Can we go to the store?"

"Honey, you have school tomorrow—"

"I kno-ow." He blew his bangs upward with a huff. "But we can go after, right? It's a good idea, Mom."

I tweaked his nose. "You think everything is a good idea."

He missed the sarcasm and nodded. "Know what? If we go to the beach, I could find another pet."

*Oh, lovely.* "Hey, buddy, there's an e-mail here for you from Dad. Why don't you go read it..."

He'd already torn out of the kitchen. I smiled as I finished getting supper on the table. Before bedtime, Bryan dictated a long response to Tom, describing his new friends, his favorite teachers, and the sad demise of the latest pet attempt. I imagined the sound of Tom's deep-chested laugh as he finished a tough day of work and opened his e-mails from home.

---

Friday I spent most of the day on the couch while Bryan was at school. It wasn't like me to lie around all day. Some part of me knew I should be worried about the lassitude and heaviness throughout my body, and the foggy disinterest in life that had invaded my brain. But I wrote it off as a mysterious virus. That's probably what had hit me at the grocery store—the latest bug going around.

Still, I felt guilty for the sluggish day. When Bryan got home from school with a list of "Great Family Outings" from his teacher, and begged to do something fun, I promised him a quick Saturday trip to a nearby botanical garden, complete with boat ride.

The next morning, Bryan was almost jumping out of his Nikes with excitement, giving me no chance to back out. I still felt bloodless and weak. Tying my shoes took huge effort. Gathering my hair back in a ponytail nearly exhausted me. Even the car keys felt heavy in my hands. I picked up my purse, then hesitated in the doorway. Going outside suddenly felt like a bad idea. Bryan pushed past me and ran out to the car. I shook off the ripple of anxiety. We were going to have fun. Not just fun. We were going to have an amazing day so I could e-mail Tom all about it. I was sick of the careful, concerned questions he kept sending me and longed for the easy bantering we used to share. I needed to convince him that everything was fine.

Bryan filled the drive to the botanical garden with a running description of everything happening at school. The words lapped around my ears, soft and non-threatening. My occasional murmurs kept him going. He was a low-maintenance boy when he was buckled in and free to talk as much as he wanted. Now that I was out of the house and moving, my anxiety receded. Sunlight and shadow flickered in turns across the windshield and I had to keep blinking to stay alert.

When we reached the Norfolk Botanical Garden, we paid our entrance fee and grabbed a map. Bryan ran ahead, then back again, hooked to me by an invisible bungee cord. I strolled slowly, taking deep breaths. Tall loblolly pines reminded me of Wisconsin forests, but a display of pink butterfly bushes startled me with brilliant colors that would have faded by now back home.

"Mom, I'm thirsty."

Fallen petals wilted on the gravel path. I ground a few under the toe of my shoe as if they were cigarette butts. "We left the juice boxes in the car."

He clutched his throat. "But I'm dying. Can't we buy some pop?"

"Maybe on our way out. Come on. There's a fern garden up ahead."

"Then let's go." He tugged me along. The sunshine and vibrant shades of green gave me hope. The paths called for me to explore. My old self flickered to life, shaking off the strange, lifeless person who had abducted my body for the past weeks.

A group of retired ladies in red hats passed us on their way to the tropical garden. As our path opened out we saw young moms pushing strollers on the other side of a wide canal.

I took a deep breath. So far, so good. "You're right, bucko. This was a good idea."

A snowy egret posed on the edge of a pond, a perfect image to inspire stillness and peace. Maybe I'd be able to handle this after all. Not just today's outing, but also the weeks ahead.

"How come Dad quit his other job?" Bryan picked up a rock and skimmed it across the pond. The egret eyed him with disdain.

"He believed God wanted him to become a chaplain."

"But how did he know?"

"He talked to friends he trusted. He prayed. He listened to God."

There. I still had it in me. The Good Mom with the spiritually nurturing words to offer my child. It was important to keep showing my son a polished image of God—even if my own picture of Him had become matte and dull in recent days. "We always want to be ready to go where God asks us, right?"

He squinted out at the water. "I guess."

I ruffled his hair. "Don't sound so excited about it. Hey, the kids' vegetable garden is up ahead."

"When do we ride the boat?"

"After that. I promise."

We followed a wide walkway toward the next section of the garden. Pounding footsteps and a shout intruded over the sounds of fountains and birdcalls. Three young men burst from around a turn of the path.

One ran in front, laughing, a blur of denim under a black baseball cap. He brandished an iPod overhead. Another boy in a sweat-streaked T-shirt charged after, with a heavyset third friend on his heels. "Give that back. I'm gonna kill you." The second teen's voice was breathy with laughter. My rational mind heard that.

A deeper primal center of my brain didn't.

He lurched sideways in a misstep as he passed us, jostling against me. "Sorry, ma'am."

I stumbled back with a gasp. Then I couldn't breathe. Stark fear crashed into me, wiping out the sunlight and birds and trees.

*"I'm gonna kill you."*

The path came up to meet me and my knees hit a layer of woodchips. What would the red-hat ladies think if they saw me face down on the trail? I could always pretend I was searching for a contact lens. I tried to laugh, but my heart exploded like a pheasant's wings on the first day of hunting season.

"Mom?"

*Bryan.* I couldn't pass out. Bryan needed me. Then coherent thought fled.

"I'M SORRY. I'M SORRY. I'm so sorry." The mantra of the embarrassed and unstable. I chanted it as a park staffer helped me to my feet. Bryan's yells had brought her from a nearby garden with impressive speed.

"I'm sorry," I whispered between labored breaths. *Don't want to attract attention. Don't want to try to explain. Don't want this uniformed woman practicing her rusty CPR skills on me.*

"Should we call an ambulance?" The young staffer's voice rose in pitch, as if my panic was contagious.

"No, really. I'm fine. Just a little light-headed." I rested my hands on my thighs.

She frowned. "Can you walk? We can get you to our first-aid station."

"Some big guys crashed into her." Bryan skipped in place, apparently more intrigued than frightened by the spectacle of his mom hitting the deck.

"Do you want to file a report?"

"No." I panted. "An accident. My car?"

"Sure, I can help you to your car, but don't you want me to call someone?"

I shook my head.

She supported my elbow, and we began the long walk back to the entrance. Bryan chattered at the woman the whole way, but I didn't listen. Instead, I focused on holding back the dizziness that crowded my senses.

Maybe something was really wrong. I'd never felt this woozy and disoriented before. And my chest ached from my heart's crazy effort. Hadn't a morning talk show reported that women were often unaware when they were having a heart attack?

I led the way to our car. "Where's the closest urgent care?" I pressed my hands against my chest to keep my heart inside my rib cage.

Bryan glared at me. "But we didn't ride the boat yet."

The woman jotted directions on a piece of paper. "It's only a mile from here. But are you sure you're okay to drive?"

"I'm not used to the heat, that's all. I'm from Wisconsin."

"Oh." Her brows climbed as if that explained a lot.

I shooed Bryan into the car and grabbed the paper. "Thanks." Short breath. "For your." Gasp. "Help."

She pinched the bridge of her nose and was still shaking her head as she retreated to the visitor center.

I settled into the car, and dust motes floated up from the dashboard. Not a place I'd choose to die. Who wanted their last sight of planet Earth to be a tree-shaped air freshener and a crumpled juice box? *Hear that, heart-o-mine? You can't give out now.*

Somehow I kept moving—through the drive to urgent care, Bryan's nonstop questions, the explanation to the receptionist, and my quick-change into an ugly paper gown. Bryan explored every drawer in the room and pilfered a few wooden tongue depressors. Then he read a *Highlights* magazine while swinging his legs in annoyance.

Gradually, my heart stopped doing flamenco triplets.

Murphy's Law. You could put off seeing your doctor about a wicked rash . . . fighting it with oatmeal baths and calamine and enough Benadryl to drug a rhino. But the day you give in and show up at the clinic, the rash has evaporated and the doctor squints at your skin with that look of, "I deal with cancer patients, lady. Why are you wasting my time with a few red spots?"

By the time the young doctor entered the room, my pulse was close to normal. His exam was efficient but gentle, and he asked questions in a respectful, quiet tone. Aside from the fact that he only looked a few years older than Bryan, I liked him. I explained what had happened and waited for him to scold me for overreacting.

Instead, he pulled up a stool and folded his stethoscope. "I believe what you experienced was a panic attack."

My smile flattened. Maybe he wasn't so likeable.

"That doesn't minimize what you felt," he said quickly. "It's a real physiological response and can be frightening. But your heart is fine. Your lungs are fine." He pulled out a ballpoint and clicked it open and shut. "That's the good news. Has this happened before?"

I shook my head. "Not really."

He stopped clicking and stared at me, waiting.

"Um. A couple days ago I felt light-headed at the grocery store. I must be fighting off a flu bug. I've been kind of tired."

"Have you been under unusual stress?"

"Mom was in a holdup." Bryan bent down the corner of his magazine but didn't look up. "Is that stress?"

The doctor's eyes widened.

"A few weeks ago I was in a Quick Corner that got robbed. It was . . ." I swallowed, unable to continue.

The Doogie Howser look-alike leaned toward me. "I'm very sorry. Were you injured?"

A nervous laugh twisted in my throat. "No. I'm fine. Not hurt at all."

He waited several seconds in case I had more to say. Then he nodded. "I can refer you to a good counselor. It's normal to need help processing something like that."

Heat bloomed up my neck. He thought I was a nutcase, or some debutante with the vapors (after all, I was in the South now).

I jumped down from the exam table. "I'm fine." My declaration would have been more convincing if I hadn't wobbled.

"Ma'am, I urge you to talk to someone. If not for yourself, then for your son." He lowered his voice. "Seeing a mom suffer can be very frightening for a child."

I glanced over at Bryan. He was squeezing the bulb of a blood pressure cuff, riveted by the hiss of air. He watched the meter and laughed. Yeah, he was a bundle of nerves.

My keys rattled as I pulled them from my purse. "I've got info about a victim support counselor."

The doctor smiled and closed the manila folder, returning pen to pocket. "Good idea. If you have any more problems, follow up with your regular doctor."

Remnants of composure helped me nod and thank him, then dress and hustle Bryan out to the car, trying to outrun the heat of embarrassment that crawled just beneath my skin. All I needed was some chicken soup and time to shake off this flu bug.

They all meant well. First there had been the policewoman at the crime scene, then my mother, and now the doctor, all wanting to convince me to get counseling. I understood the longing to help. Even Tom had suggested I talk to one of the psychologists at the base, or to our pastor. He of all people knew why I couldn't start down that road.

I'd seen what counseling had done to my brother.

Shutting the door on those decades-old memories, I tugged Bryan's seat belt to check it, then hurried around to my side of the car.

"You promised we'd have fun today." My son kicked the back of the seat in front of him. "We didn't even ride the boat. This. Is. Not. Fun." He punctuated each word with another stab of his foot.

"Stop it!" I jammed my key into the ignition. "Do you think it's fun for me? I'm doing the best I can."

Silence like a sudden intake of breath, frozen and held, answered me.

I glanced back at Bryan. He stared at me as if a wicked sorcerer had zapped his mom with an irrationality spell. Suddenly the doctor's comments didn't seem so ridiculous. The moods I'd been battling were hurting my son. Neither of us knew this stranger I'd become.

I swallowed hard and met his hurt gaze. "I'm sorry. I'm not feeling well."

His dark brows drew together under his bangs. "Will the victim person make you feel better?"

So he *had* been listening to my conversation with the doctor. *Drat.*

I started the car and tried to remember how to find the road home. "I doubt it."

For once, he didn't jabber, and with only a few wrong turns, we arrived home a half-hour later. Our house slouched under the trees as if it were a sullen teen saying, "Oh, you again?" Why had we left our weathered old two-story in Wisconsin? That wrap-around front porch had always greeted us like a dimpled grandmother with open arms.

I got out of the car and Bryan joined me on the sidewalk.

Laura-Beth waved from her yard. Didn't she ever go inside? "Hiya, neighbor. Say, I hope you don't mind me saying, but I've noticed your grass is getting long."

Yeah, because I didn't have a pit bull to scratch it all to the ground.

"Sorry, I've been busy. Tom usually does the mowing, and since he's at sea . . ." I was still getting used to saying that phrase. *My husband is at sea.* Conjured visions of lighthouses and whaling ships. My rugged man standing boldly at the prow, salt spray and rays of sunset kissing his face. *Oh, Tom, I miss you.*

"I kin git you some names of boys in the neighborhood who hire out for yard work." She flashed her gap-toothed grin. "Or you could always buy a goat."

I forced an answering laugh and hustled Bryan into the house. Yard work. Goat. Hmm. Could I buy a goat on the Internet? Was there a store called Goats R Us?

When I turned from locking the door, Bryan was standing on the rug watching me. "Mom, what's a panic attack?"

Feigning nonchalance, I shrugged. "I'm not sure. I think it's when someone feels scared for no reason."

Bryan pulled off his shoes, shaking sand onto the floor. He looked up at me with all the earnestness of a seven-year-old. "But you do have a reason, don't you?"

My brilliant son. Tears stung the back of my eyes, and I knelt and opened my arms. He threw his arms around my neck, and I squeezed him hard. His matter-of-fact acceptance eased my shame, but it also kindled my determination.

I had to find a way to shake this off. For Bryan, for Tom, for all the people who counted on me.

After my son wiggled away and ran off to play, I stayed on the floor, huddled on my knees.

"I'm getting worse," I whispered. "Every time I step outside it's an ordeal. I don't like people anymore. I'm snapping at Bryan. And now I'm talking to myself." Sweat prickled along my forehead, and I pushed hair back from my face. "I need a plan."

If you fail to plan, you plan to fail.

I'd said it to Tom often when I organized the youth group famine event and the local fund-raiser for our town library. I'd said it to my boss at the dry cleaners when he struggled with scheduling his part-time help. Now as panic crouched outside my door, I cast around for something—anything. I saw the plastic milk crate full of office supplies discreetly stored under the card table. My tablecloth didn't quite reach the floor. I scrambled across the room and pulled out the crate.

Inside, a chubby file held my notebooks for various past projects—cheap, spiral-bound, and three-by-five size so they would fit in my purse. I unearthed the notebook labeled *Sullivan Relocation Project* and leafed through the pages. I'd broken down each step of getting our house ready to show and on the market, finding a new house in Virginia, planning the move, packing each room.

This file folder of dog-eared notebooks gave evidence that over the years I'd faced plenty of challenges. My notebooks had helped me organize, set goals, and stay on track.

Why couldn't the same process work on solving my current problem? Okay, reclaiming sanity wasn't the same as selling a house. But I had to try something. Time was supposed to heal all wounds, but my brain hadn't gotten that memo. I was finding it harder to function with each passing day. I'd seen what could happen when a mind spiraled out of control. I had to stop this slide before it was too late.

I pulled out a fresh notebook with a sunny yellow cover and grabbed a Sharpie marker. With careful block letters and a firm hand, I printed across the front of the notebook.

*Penny's Project.*

I returned the marker to the holder on the table and chose a sharp pencil. I settled onto the couch with the notebook full of empty pages and was instantly stumped. Where did I begin to find myself again when the dark shadows of trauma refused to let go? When I didn't even understand how they had infiltrated every part of my daily life?

*Focus, Penny. What's your goal?*

I tapped my eraser a few times against the lined paper, then wrote *Penny's Project* across the top of the first page. Beneath it I scrawled, *Don't go insane.*

Okay, that might not be the most positive wording. My eraser rubbed out the words and I flipped the pencil in my fingers. *Move toward healing.*

That was better, but not very specific. What had they told me in that Saturday business class Pilgrim Cleaners sent me to? Make your goals measurable.

I chewed the soft yellow wood of the pencil, then wrote, *Be Penny again, in time for Tom's return.*

The concrete goal helped me turn to the second page.

I'd had plenty of plans for after we settled here in Chesapeake. I'd been sidetracked, but it was time to start moving forward again.

*Join PTA—help out at school.*

*Mow lawn.*

*Take Bryan to the beach.*

*Explore neighborhood.* My writing slowed. These plans should have stirred eagerness in me, but even shaping the letters took unimaginable effort. Maybe I needed more information about the emotions that had sunk their claws into me.

*Research trauma recovery.*

Information would be sure to help. With that added to the list, I had the courage to keep brainstorming. Simple tasks that I used to be able to do without a second thought piled up as daunting as mountains. But these steps would make me normal again before Tom got back.

*Organize kitchen.* I wrote faster.

*Attend mixer for Navy spouses.*

*Back- to-school shopping for Bryan (long past due).*

That one wouldn't be a hit with my restless boy. To make it up to him, I added the next item.

*Get a pet for Bryan.*

I could imagine his whoop of glee when I reached that task.

*Get to know neighbors.*

*Choose a way to volunteer at church.*

My hand hovered over the page. Since I wanted to recover as quickly as possible, I should be able to tackle each of these in the weeks between now and Thanksgiving..

Boldly, I wrote in the crowning goal. *Attend Thanksgiving play at Bryan's school.* Bryan in a Pilgrim costume, with beaming smile, shone in my imagination like a Kodak moment. Warmth curled around my heart, and the eagerness I'd been hoping to stir finally flickered to life.

There. That would do it. Now I had a plan. And failure was not an option.

SUNDAY MORNING I WOKE up feeling achy in all my joints. I was relieved to have a good excuse to stay home from church. A new church could be rich with potential friendships and encouraging fellowship, but it could also be a painful reminder of homesickness and the exhausting process of starting over. Tom and I had chosen a church and gone a few times before he shipped out, but there was no way I could drag myself there today. Instead, Bryan and I watched a service on television. Technology was a marvelous thing. We huddled on the couch and watched a strange congregation relayed to our living room via camera. No shaking hands to share the peace, no shoulders squished beside mine in the pew, no resonance in my throat as I sang a hymn to the heavens made stronger by united voices. Just a distant box. Yet that was a better fit for me than something more real.

What was happening to me?

Several times during the day, I glanced at the waiting notebook. No sense starting a new project when I was feeling sick.

Besides, Bryan needed my attention. From my nest on the couch, I played endless rounds of Battleship, lost at crazy eights, and read *Animalia* with him—taking time to find every possible hidden picture.

Later in the day, Bryan raced toward his room to get a new computer game to show me. His shirt stretched tight across his chest and pulled up from his jeans. Another growth spurt.

"Hey, buddy. Come here."

He skidded to a stop and backtracked, then sprang onto the cushioned arm of the couch and tumbled down to the spot beside me. "Yeah?"

"You need some new school clothes." One of the tasks in my notebook.

He grinned. "So can we go to the mall tomorrow? And can we see a movie and eat at Taco Bell?"

That would entail navigating unfamiliar streets, leading Bryan in and out of busy stores, the beep of cash registers, the crush of strangers. "I have a better idea. Let's look on the computer."

"But Mo-om—"

I gave him The Look, and Bryan cut his whine short and followed me to the monitor. I set my little notebook on the table near the computer and gave it a soft pat of promise. School clothes for Bryan was on my list, and there was nothing wrong with shopping the easiest way possible, was there?

We surfed several Web sites together. He vetoed dozens of my suggestions—shirts too itchy-looking, pants the wrong color or not cool. But we finally settled on a few T-shirts and some new jeans a size bigger. I placed an online order from Sears and released my son to the backyard. That night I drew another red X on the calendar, proud of creating a fairly normal day for my son.

Before I headed to bed, I checked the computer. Another

e-mail waited from Tom. My fingers hovered above the keyboard before I typed my answer.

*Hi honey!*

*Bryan and I went to the Norfolk Botanical Garden yesterday. It's gorgeous. They have an azalea festival every spring. Let's go next year, okay?*

*Yes, I'm keeping busy. Some late back-to-school shopping with Bryan. All the usual.*

*Okay, I know I promised to go talk to someone, but I've been doing great, so it would really be a waste of time. Besides, I have you and mom, and friends. That's all I need. Big kisses (is it okay to send e-kisses to the chaplain? Will it undermine your spiritual image with the troops?)*

*Your favorite wife*

---

The next morning, Bryan fidgeted during our blessing in the doorway. Laura-Beth's son, Jim-Bob, waited on the sidewalk as I rested my hand on my son's head. " . . . and I ask for health and strength for his body and mind, and thank you that he gets to be in the Thanksgiving play. Thank you for loving us so much. Amen."

I stooped down, and Bryan's kiss grazed my cheek. He raced to the sidewalk as if all the energy I'd lost had been siphoned into his small muscles. Jim-Bob gave him a playful shove and their voices rose in laughter. They charged to the corner as the bus pulled up.

When I walked back into the house, the first thing my gaze hit was the yellow notebook.

I couldn't have chosen one with a more subtle cover?

I strolled past on the way to the kitchen for a mug of coffee, pretending I didn't see it. But as I sipped coffee in the kitchen, the thought of a long day alone with my thoughts was pure torture. Time to take charge. One of my self-appointed tasks was to gather information on whatever was wrong with me.

I carried the coffee out to my pseudo-office in the corner of the living room and booted up the computer. When I'd worked at the dry cleaners, I'd been more than a cheery receptionist. I was a wiz at online research. Lipstick smudges, smears of mustard, rare brocade with a chocolate-raspberry stain? Google, link, scroll. I could find the solution.

The crime had rubbed a smear across my psyche. Okay, more than a smear. A stain absorbed deep into the fabric. But a little research should turn up stain-removal steps. I attacked the keyboard and began my search of the Internet, following each promising trail, ferreting facts about crime victims, panic attacks, and emotional health.

Hours later, the back pages of my notebook held a wide array of suggestions and resources. Pencil in hand, I studied my gathered information.

Group therapy was recommended. *Hmm.* Talking to a counselor would be bad enough, but a bunch of strangers? Still, I didn't want to rule out ideas too quickly. I drew a star next to that one.

Talking about the event and even visualizing it to work through emotions was mentioned from many sources. *Ugh.* I drew a line through that idea. Much better to forget.

Medication? I drew a few question marks. Maybe the base doctor could help, if I could get over my embarrassment. Good grief, he dealt with military folk who'd seen much worse. He'd probably laugh me out of his office if I told him my problems with one little traumatic event.

Then there was the spiritual component: prayer, Scripture,

fellowship. I drew an arrow to them, but my hand faltered and the line wobbled.

I swallowed hard.

Those used to be rich and cherished aspects of my life. In the past weeks I'd mouthed the right words and tried not to think about how lost and alone I felt in my battle. But to really involve God in this process, I first had to confront my big question. Where had He been that afternoon? I was afraid to ask Him, because if there was no answer, I wasn't sure I could forgive Him, and losing Him right now was more than I could bear. I'd rather maintain a nodding acquaintanceship than dig too deep and lose it all.

I rubbed my forehead and continued studying my notes. Too much advice. Too many ideas.

A clinking sound near the front door signaled the mail had arrived. Moving with the underwater resistance that had weighted me lately, I closed my notebook and rolled my shoulders. I waited until the mail carrier walked a few houses down the street before cracking open my front door and lifting the lid on the metal box bolted to the brick next to the front door. Reaching in, I grabbed whatever my hand found. After I bolted the door again, I shuffled through the junk mail and saw two red envelopes. My first Netflix movies. Perfect timing. I'd given a few hours to my research and was exhausted. I needed a distraction before I started organizing specific steps to my Penny's Project.

Befriended by a tray of crackers and cheese, and a pot of hot tea—Irish Breakfast, not that weedy stuff Laura-Beth had suggested—I drew the living room curtains closed and opened the DVD tray. An unlabeled disc rested in the compartment, so I set it aside, dropped in the movie, and curled up on the couch with the remote. Images flowed across the television, but even the rollicking adventure movie couldn't hold my attention. After

I'd polished off most of my snack, my eyelids grew heavy, and I drifted to sleep.

My naps had become heavy things, smothering weights that held me under until something intervened to pull me up from the depths. Today a sound woke me: a chubby fist banged the front door about three feet up from the threshold—Bryan height.

"Mom? It's me. I'm home. Mom? Mom!" A worried edge tinted his bellowing call.

I hurried to the door, kicking myself for another lost day and for another day of not meeting Bryan's bus after school. I tried to dredge energy up from my toenails as I yanked open the door and managed a bright smile. "How's my favorite second-grader?"

His relieved laugh burst into our quiet living room. I knelt for a hug and smelled sunshine and dust in the sweet-salty sweat of his neck.

"Know what? Mrs. Pimple said one of the moms could be the head Pilgrim in our play, and I told her you'd be good at it, since you used to be a Pilgrim."

Huh? "Honey, I'm not old enough to be a Pilgrim. And her name is Mrs. Pimblott."

He scratched his head. "But you were a Pilgrim. Back at our old house. Remember, Mom?"

"Our old—?" Light dawned. "You mean Pilgrim Cleaners? That wasn't . . . I mean, I only worked for their office." I'd loved my three-day a week job as office manager. One of the many things I hated to give up when we moved.

He wrinkled his forehead and waited.

I coughed to hide a chuckle. "Those were different Pilgrims."

"Oh. Well, now you can be this kind."

Perform in the Thanksgiving play? Not a chance. But few people can give a direct no to earnest seven-year-old eyes. "We'll see." Every mom's magic phrase when cornered. Sometimes when my son's attention span was particularly short, it was all I needed. Hopefully he'd forget all about volunteering me.

"So can we go to the ocean so I can find a new pet? You said it was a good idea."

"No, *you* said it was a good idea. I said we'd talk about it."

"Know what? Daddy would like us to find a pet. He doesn't want us to be lonely while he's gone."

I tousled his hair and ignored his coy eye-batting. "Sorry, buddy. Not today. I'm still not feeling too good."

"What's for supper? Know what? I think we should have pizza."

"We'll see."

He crossed chunky arms and met my eyes. "I know what that means, Mom." Then with a very adult sigh, he marched off to his room with his backpack.

The long nap must have deadened my brain cells. I couldn't even match wits with a seven-year-old. But I did take a moment to grab my notebook. I penciled in a star by the goal of finding a pet for Bryan. Then by the entry of *Attend Thanksgiving play*, I added, *Be a Pilgrim mom?*

My stomach twisted and the notebook suddenly felt heavy.

*These are just ideas. Gather ideas. Sort them later and make your action steps. Not all of these will work. That's okay.*

After two cups of coffee, I assembled a quick rice and beef casserole and popped it into the oven. No green peppers. Tom hated green peppers—so I left them out on principle. He was thousands of miles away, but I believed he'd somehow feel more loved if I served supper without green peppers. Then I sat on the back steps while Bryan set up a golf course in the backyard.

"Come and try it, Mom." He brandished the broken umbrella he was using as a nine-iron.

"That's okay. I'm having fun watching you." If I came out of the shadow near the door, Laura-Beth would notice me when she watered her tomatoes. She'd flood me with opinions and suggestions. A good neighbor should enjoy chatting over the fence. I used to be the first to strike up a conversation with anyone nearby, but today I wasn't up for it.

The phone rang, and I stepped inside to grab it.

"Penny? Hi! This is Mary Jo Collins, your ombudsman. We met when you first moved here?" Her bright voice held way too much energy.

"Um, sure." We needed to get caller ID. I didn't want to miss a call from Tom, but until I shook off this virus, I really didn't feel like talking to anyone else.

"Whee! Look, Mom!" Bryan's shout brought me back to the steps, phone cord stretched to the limit. "I hit it onto the shed. Don't worry. I can climb up and get it."

"Bryan, no! Don't climb up there. I'll come help you in a minute."

Laughter carried through the phone. "I won't keep you. I know how it is when the kids are little. I just thought we should go out for coffee and get acquainted. After all, with your husband being the chaplain, you and I need to coordinate our support of the wives. And since this is his first deployment, I figured you'd enjoy chatting with someone who's been through it. Nothing else is quite as helpful. So how about tomorrow?" Mary Jo's voice rang strong and competent.

Exactly the qualities I'd lost lately. I coughed a few times. "Let me get back to you. I'm fighting a cold or something."

"Oh, I'm sorry to hear that. Gotta keep yourself in fighting form, so your spouse can focus on his work and not be distracted by worry. That's what I tell all the families. Anyway, the base doctors are good, but if you need any names, let me know."

"Thanks. I'll do that. Bye."

I replaced the phone and wiped my sweating hand on my shorts.

Tom wasn't going to be distracted by my struggles. He was facing enough challenges—even dangers—and it was vital for him to be able to fully focus on his work. As long as he couldn't see me, he'd believe my upbeat e-mails. But what if I still wasn't myself when he got home at Thanksgiving? Would it affect his ability to do his job? This was his dream. Would my problems force him to request shore duty? Or try to resign? I shuddered. I didn't know if he could even do that, but an image suddenly spun into my mind of Tom with hunched shoulders, sitting behind a desk and talking to our old senior pastor. "Yes, it was the work God called me to. But Penny couldn't cope. We had to come back."

"Hey, Mom! I think I can reach it!"

I hurried outside to rescue Bryan from his wobbly perch halfway up a stepladder.

"Yoo-hoo." Laura-Beth strolled toward the fence with one of her twins wedged on her hip. "How ya been?"

I measured the distance to the back door. This compulsion to escape wasn't like me. I mustered a warm smile. "Just getting supper ready."

She nodded. "Never ends, does it? Jim-Bob's havin' another growth spurt, and I don't know where he puts it, but he never stops eating." She squinted at Bryan. "Your boy looks a mite scrawny. Grits for breakfast will fill him out nice. Hope you don't mind a piece of advice."

"Not at all. Thank you." Scrawny? So what if my son looked more like a running back than a tackle? He was healthy and full of energy.

Still, when I went back inside, I added two goals to my notebook. "Coffee with Mary Jo," and, "Try cooking grits."

Somehow, I got through another evening of Bryan's restless demands. After tucking him in and listening to his prayers, I avoided my overwide and lonely bed by camping out on the couch instead. The television could keep me company.

I popped the movie I'd started that morning out of our DVD player. I couldn't muster interest in watching the part I'd slept through. I'd send this one back and watch a new one tomorrow.

The blank disc I tossed aside earlier in the day caught my eye. It didn't look familiar. What had it been doing in the player?

I held it by the edges. Weird. Both sides were bare, with no imprinted title or clue to the contents. Was it a bonus feature included with one of Bryan's VeggieTales movies? Tom and I were careful about what we let our son watch. Had my second-grader been watching something I hadn't pre-approved?

I pushed it into the DVD player and pointed the remote. I'd mastered On and Off but little else. If there were special settings or a menu to navigate, I'd be in trouble.

Static crackled across the screen. Light flickered to life, then disappeared.

I leaned closer.

The sound of a chair scraping and a breath across a microphone came from the speakers. Then the picture appeared in full color.

I blinked. *What on earth?*

It wasn't a movie.

I FUMBLED WITH THE remote to raise the volume and accidentally hit Rewind. The machine hummed as I jabbed the Play button, then held my breath. The squiggly backward motion on the screen halted, and the DVD played again in vibrant clarity.

On the television, Tom grinned from his office on the base. I recognized the location because his Bible commentary filled the shelves behind him. He looked straight into the camera as if he could see me. My heart grabbed, stuttered, and then began the agitated pounding of my washer on spin cycle.

*Oh, Tom.*

He looked past the camera. "Thanks, Jim. I've got it from here."

I heard a door close.

Tom focused on the lens. "Hey, Penny. I ship out tomorrow. I know you're holding it together the only way you can right now. But there's so much more that I wish we could have talked about."

He looked down and twisted a paper clip absently, unbending and reshaping it. When his eyes lifted, raw pain darkened them.

"Penny, it kills me that I couldn't protect you. That I wasn't there. That you went through that alone. And now I'm leaving." He swallowed hard, but kept drilling me with his stare through the screen. "But you're not alone. We're in this together. I had to tell you that.

"I've seen you shaking in the middle of your nightmares. I've heard you cry. I wanted to go back in time and be there to stop it. Instead, all I could do was hold you and try to help you feel safe again. Now I won't even be able to do that for you."

He tossed aside the paper clip and leaned forward, strong forearms on his desk. A half-smile eased the corner of his lips. I edged closer to the screen.

"I know this might seem a little cheesy, but I thought I'd leave you a few messages. Don't listen to them all at once. But next time you miss me, go ahead and play the second one."

*Next time I miss him? Try every minute of every day.*

"And Penny, even though I'm not there to hold you, I'm holding you in my heart. Don't forget." He shifted in his chair and drummed his fingers on the desk. "Okay. That's it for message number one. Turn this off now." A teasing light gave a gold glint to his hazel eyes. "I mean it. Save the rest for when you need them. No cheating." He sat back and crossed his arms, waiting.

Through the wild ache in my chest, and the tears pricking my eyes, I giggled. "You know me too well." Talking to him aloud added to the fantasy that he was in the room with me. "Okay. I'll stick to your rules. But you won't mind me watching this one again, will you?"

I watched Tom's first message five times in a row. Each time I was more tempted to let the DVD keep playing, so I finally pulled the disc out.

This was so like him. On our anniversary last year, he'd hidden little notes for me in all kinds of unlikely places. I was still discovering them weeks later. *I'm glad I married you* on a Post-it under the ice-cube tray. *Penny from heaven* tucked in the toe of my favorite pumps. *I'll always love you* hidden inside a bottle of vitamins.

Curled up on the couch, I imagined Tom's arms around me. His surprise message was better bedtime comfort than hot cocoa. And I had more to look forward to. I smiled and closed my eyes.

But even with the mental image of Tom's strong hold, sleep spun away from me, and the midnight ghosts arrived on schedule. A motor purred past in the street and headlights traced across the curtains like a prowler looking for entrance. Water dripped from the kitchen faucet, and the refrigerator compressor kicked in with a lurch. The sound could mask footsteps. Someone could be hiding around the wall only yards away and I'd never know it. A muffled clatter came from the backyard. Probably just Laura-Beth taking out the trash.

Desperate for distraction, I finally turned on the television. Late-night talk shows were a poor substitute for Tom's voice. I tossed on the couch for hours, finally drifting off to a conversation about the new fashion line designed by a singer I'd never heard of.

---

The next morning, Bryan hit the ground running as usual, and chattered through breakfast, while I longed for toothpicks to prop open my bleary eyes. Dozing with the TV on all night was probably a dumb idea, because now I had a strange compulsion to start juicing everything in the fridge, use a steam nozzle to clean my household surfaces, and order Ginsu knives. Ah the joys of middle-of-the-night infomercials.

"So, Mom, are we going to the beach after school today? Huh? Know what? Dad said I'm the man of the house. Does that mean I'm the boss?" Bryan helped himself to the remnants of my toast.

"Honey, I need to explain the whole women's movement thing to you someday. And no, I'm not up to driving all the way to the shore. I'm still not feeling great."

He glowered into his orange juice.

Guilt propelled me away from the table, and I started scrubbing dishes in the sink.

While Bryan got dressed for school, I tidied the living room and straightened the collection of video games and movies. I needed to choose a safe place for Tom's unmarked DVD. I checked the shelf where I'd set it last night.

The disc was gone.

My throat tightened. My lungs pumped faster but still couldn't seem to get enough oxygen.

I couldn't have lost it. It had to be somewhere. Unless I'd dreamed the whole thing. Could I be that confused? Could weeks of insomnia, flashbacks, and isolation blur the boundary of reality?

I shuffled through some of the movies we owned, opening and shutting cases. Bryan found me shaking an empty Netflix envelope, peering inside as if it were a magician's hat. I struggled to keep my voice calm. "Hey, buddy-boy. I need your help. There's a blank disc around here somewhere, and I need to find it."

He rolled his eyes. "Where did you have it last?" Dead-on impression of me, but I couldn't appreciate the humor.

"Right next to the player."

He joined in the search, poking behind and under the shelves, and finally gleefully pulling all our CDs to the floor in a clatter. "Is this it?"

He held up a disc.

"Careful. Hold it by the edges."

He handed it to me. No label. Silver with a bluish tinge. This was the one. Amazing child. I hugged him until he squeaked.

"Thank you for searching. You're a great helper."

He strutted toward the front door, then jumped up and tried to touch the top of the doorjamb. "I know. My teacher says I'm really smart."

"And humble, too."

"Yep." Again, no grasp of sarcasm.

I shook my head, then held the disc up to the window. Chubby thumbprints marked the surface. I polished it gently with the hem of my T-shirt, then rested it on the top shelf next to a photo of the three of us.

Today, as we paused on the top step for his blessing, Jim-Bob edged a few feet up the path toward our door. "Father, thank you for the gift of life. Fill Bryan's day with the joy of knowing you. And help him with his spelling words this week. Amen." I adjusted the hood of his sweatshirt. He shouldered his pack and leapt down our front steps.

"What was your mom doin'?" Jim-Bob asked as they jostled toward the sidewalk.

"Blessing me. Doesn't your mom bless you?"

Their voices faded as they walked away. Bryan had gotten used to going to and from the bus without me. Fostering independence in a child was a good thing, right? My choice to stay in the house had nothing to do with the way my pulse raced whenever I left my front steps. I watched from the doorway until the bus arrived.

After their pickup, I retreated inside, and the emptiness of the house closed in on me again. I could watch Tom's first message again. Or even the second one. He'd only said to wait until I missed him again. I did. With a bottomless ache I wasn't sure I could survive. But if there were only a few messages, I needed to stretch them out. I'd save the disc as a reward for getting through another week.

Instead of indulging myself, I pulled out my yellow notebook and leafed through my collected notes. Time to continue my project toward normalcy. Talking to a trusted friend had been mentioned by many of the Web sites I'd visited. Sonja had been my best friend back home, and I had vowed to stay in touch when I moved. But she'd been buried in the flurry of back-to-school season with her three kids. And I'd been busy settling into our new place. She knew about The Incident and had sent a card saying she was praying for me, but we hadn't talked about it. I'd wanted to spare her.

I turned to the first page and wrote another small goal. *Call a friend.* With my notebook to give me courage, I grabbed the phone and dialed.

"Hello, you've reached the Johanssen family. Sorry we missed your call."

*Drat.* I'd forgotten about the time difference. She was still at the Tuesday before-school Moms in Touch group. Longing washed over me. What I wouldn't do for a chance to sit on those uncomfortable folding chairs laughing, crying, and praying with other moms.

"Leave a message and we'll call you right back." *Beep.*

What did I want to say? I quietly hung up the phone. There was no way to pour out my heart in a thirty-second message. Besides, she knew Tom had deployed. She was probably thinking of me, probably planning to call me soon. If I left a message I'd sound as if I were needy. I'd let her call when it worked for her.

The phone rested, implacable, on the kitchen counter. I could call my mom, but her worry about me would lead to more prying questions. Besides, she'd doubted my ability to handle Tom's career change all along. I still remembered the conversation vividly.

"Honey, it's wonderful how you and Tom want to serve God. But you're doing that here in Wisconsin. You're such an idealist. You don't realize how difficult it will be leaving everything you know. And the military? Oh, sweetie, can't you get him to see reason? You have a son to think about."

How to explain to her our sense of vivid, clear direction? Tom felt a passionate calling toward this new career path, and I was excited to support him. Sure it would be tough, but I had embraced the beautiful irrationality that demanded faith.

Faith had carried me through the planning and the move, but then conveniently evaporated when I needed it most. My entire universe had shifted off its center that afternoon at the Quick Corner, somewhere between the rows of beef jerky and potato chips. And in the days since then, God had done nothing to restore my equilibrium.

I grabbed the phone. My sister would probably be home. She might not be my first choice, but I wanted to check off a goal from my notebook before I lost momentum.

Cindy answered on the first ring. "Penny, Penny, Penny. I knew you'd be busy settling in for a while, but it's like you disappeared off the face of the planet." She'd never fussed about staying in touch when I'd been in Wisconsin. Sometimes we'd gone for weeks without seeing each other. She probably felt trapped at home with the new baby and was desperate for any conversation.

"How's my little niece treating you?"

"Esther's fine, even though her brother tried to carry her from her basinet and nearly dropped her headfirst. I just wish she'd sleep a little longer. I was up every two hours last night. I don't remember it being this bad last time."

I laughed. "The world's population would shrivel if women remembered everything about childbirth and the months after."

"No kidding. Did I tell you how many stitches I had to get this time? I can barely sit."

Too much information. After seven years, I'd completely blocked any memory of episiotomies, breast infections, and colic.

She was still talking. "Good thing Mom is able to help. Hal's hardly ever here. He's so busy at the dealership." A whine slid into her voice.

I struggled to hold on to sympathy for her. "At least you have him nights and weekends. It's tough having Tom away for three months like this."

"Yeah, but you don't have a new baby to worry about."

When had we started playing this game of one-downsmanship? "Yeah, but you have friends and family around. You don't have to sit alone all day like a hermit."

Long pause. "You never sit around like a hermit. What about your new church? The Navy wives? All your new activities?"

My research about mental health said I should choose a few safe people to confide in. Time to put the advice to the test. "It . . . it hasn't worked out like that. I've had trouble since the shooting." As soon as the words blurted out, I wanted to pull them back.

"You said you were fine."

"It's hard to talk about."

"Is he still on the loose? Does he know who you are?" Her

voice turned fast and breathy, eager. For the first time in our conversation, she sounded interested. "Are you afraid he'll come after you?"

*Not until now, thank you very much.* That was one frightening direction my thoughts hadn't lingered. Vague menacing prowlers maybe, but not the concrete reality of the same boy who— I squeezed the phone. "No, of course not. He'd have no way of knowing who I was, and I wasn't the only witness."

"Then what's the problem? Oh, hold on."

Mewling in the background built to a louder cry, then cut off abruptly.

I moved the phone to my other ear. "Cindy?"

"I'm back. Esther needed to nurse again. Wait a sec." More rustling. "Okay. What were you saying?"

This would be a good time for a graceful exit, but some perverse impulse nudged me forward. Or maybe it was my desperation to find help, any help, even from the unlikely source of my sister. "I've been sort of . . . depressed. It affected me more than I'd realized. I've . . . well, I haven't gone out much."

"What? Oh, wait. Hold on." The phone banged against something and more fumbling sounds filled the pause. "Okay. That's better. So you're saying you've been moping around all this time?"

Why had I forgotten about the part about confiding in a few *safe* people? Cindy was younger than me but had always badgered me with her superior knowledge. The right way to throw a dodge ball. The best things to tell a boy when dating. The only correct way to fold sheets. True to form, she launched into a lecture.

With uncanny accuracy, she rattled off most of the goals in my notebook. Eat better. Get more exercise. Plug in to the community.

I let her rant.

Then she shifted into spiritual finger-shaking. "Don't dwell on one unfortunate moment in time. Shake it off. Have some willpower. And if you really trusted God, you wouldn't be giving in to fear this way. Besides, you're supposed to find the value in every experience so you can give Him glory. A lady who spoke at our church lost everything in Hurricane Katrina and saw a dead body on the street. She didn't get all traumatized. She's speaking about God's power to women's groups all over the place."

Her words blew across the embers of my shame and they flared to life, scorching my sore and tender psyche. I had to make her stop. But how? I was trapped by my lips' inability to move.

"And that's not all. I saw a woman on Oprah who forgave the guy who shot her son. She even visited him in prison. Adopted him. Maybe you could do something like that."

I was choking, drowning. Finally, I drew a gurgling breath. "Well, they haven't caught him."

"Well, I'm sure you'll figure something out. The point is, get over it and make something good out of it."

"Okay. Look, I've gotta run."

More rustling sounds. "Esther, just a little burp. There you go. There's my sweetie girl." She laughed. "Sorry. What were you saying?"

"I really need to go." I got off the phone, drew a shaky checkmark in the notebook, and slammed it shut. Okay, that hadn't helped. So far, this project wasn't a big hit. Maybe I should stop trying so hard and give in to my recent impulses to become a hermit.

Cookie baking filled the hours until early afternoon. As I stacked the last cooled cookies onto a plate, the glint of my wedding ring caught my eye. What would Tom do if he came home to find his wife trapped in the house by fear, talking to herself, unable to handle even simple phone conversations? He'd be distracted.

Worried about me. My weakness could ruin the new vocation he found so fulfilling. What if he ended up resenting me?

I turned to my notebook again and stared at the other action steps.

One of my goals read, *Explore the neighborhood.* Great plan. I could drive around, find the library and nearest parks, maybe stop somewhere and take a walk. In tiny letters, in the palest of gray, I wrote an addendum. *Talk to God about this.*

I grabbed my purse, slipped my feet into sandals, and confronted the front door. I couldn't make myself reach for the knob. Instead, I rested my palm and forehead against the wood, feeling the vibrations of the world of life on the other side: a delivery truck rumbling up the street, a car horn in the distance, the noisy sparrows in the mulberry tree, a dog yipping from down the block. Life. Movement. Energy. So close. So terrifying.

Everything I'd lost in the past weeks rushed through me like the backside of a hurricane, pulling away from me with wicked speed. Tears clogged my throat and burned my eyes. I didn't want this irrational fear, but the longer I pushed against it, the faster my heart raced. Finally I breathed a prayer and yanked the door open.

Our car parked along the curb seemed to be miles away, the space between us vast and threatening.

*Come on, Penny. It's a beautiful, sunny day. Go outside.*

No pep talk could force my legs to move.

*There's nothing dangerous out there. It takes ten seconds to reach your car.*

Logic didn't work, either.

*You're acting crazy. Stupid. What is your problem? Get over it.*

Shame couldn't prod me forward, though it dug talons into my shoulders and cawed raucously into my ear.

*Come on, Penny. Don't give up now. When the bus company you hired for the youth group trip went belly-up, you didn't give up. You found cheap train passes and got the group across country. When the first two offers on the house fell through, you researched ideas on staging a home so the next open house went great. This is just a setback. Remember, you're doing this for Tom and Bryan.*

The air didn't have the crisp chill of a Wisconsin autumn, but at least it was no longer sweltering. Tom's oversized jacket hung in the closet by the entry. It would probably be too warm, but I pulled it on anyway. I needed to bring him along on this adventure. The car keys dug into my hand as I clenched them. Then, with a shaky breath, I stepped through the front door.

Measured steps carried me to the curb. My car lay in wait—a steely-eyed mountain lion watching me. My last outing with Bryan hadn't gone very well. Driving somewhere would take me too far from home and refuge. I stuffed my keys into my pocket and walked past it. Change in plans. A quick walk around the neighborhood was a better first step.

A dark thread of inaudible laughter seemed to mock me, so I walked faster, past the bus stop corner and across another street, desperate to outrun the scornful voice in my head. My attention focused on holding back my tears, so they wouldn't splash to the ground and betray me. I didn't pay attention to where my feet carried me.

*Coward. Baby. Can't even drive. And you dress like a bag lady.*

The snarling voice had shown up a few days after the shooting, and since Tom had left, it spoke with greater frequency. I tried to argue with it or ignore it, but the fight always left me exhausted. I sped up my efforts to outrun the thoughts, nearly jogging past another block of small red-brick houses. A Doberman exploded from behind one of the homes and rushed at the chain-link fence, throwing himself against it with throaty barks of warning.

I grabbed my chest and veered off the curb and into the street until I was well past that house. The sidewalk grew more uneven while broken glass and fast-food wrappers multiplied. A crooked sign in front of one house offered *Hair cuts. Cheep.* I smiled at the spelling error, imagining a row of fluffy yellow chicks chirping as they waited for a styling. Two more houses down, a yard full of plastic play equipment and squabbling toddlers made the *Mabel's Day Care* sign unnecessary.

I reached a small grocery, its windows plastered with *We accept food stamps.* A few more residential homes wedged into spaces next to a Laundromat. Through the glass I saw a United Nations assortment of elderly women stooping under the burden of baskets, smoking, flipping through tattered magazines. Without thinking, I'd headed toward the infamous projects—temporary housing thrown together for soldiers during World War II. Meant to be torn down, it became a refuge of the desperate—a step up from homelessness, but only a baby step.

I stopped short on the cracked sidewalk and turned to go back. The last thing I needed was another experience as a crime victim.

*Jesus Saves!* Sloppy, hand-painted letters shouted at me from across a tinted glass storefront. The corner of the glass was cracked and duct-taped. A dented steel door bore a small cardboard sign, plastered in place with more duct tape. *New Life Mission. You are welcome hear.*

More spelling errors. I smiled, imagining the soft cadence of a Virginia voice telling me, "You're welcome. Hear?"

The door opened, and I jumped back.

A short, thick-necked man with gray whiskers planted himself on the threshold. "Coming in? Don't just hang around on the sidewalk."

Stick a pipe in his mouth and he'd look like an elderly Popeye, complete with out-of-proportion, muscular forearms.

"Oh, that's okay. I . . ."

"Don't need savin'? Every fish in the sea needs savin', child." His smile twinkled, even with the gap of a missing incisor. Sun damage tanned his Caucasian skin and hinted at years of hard living.

A tall woman joined him at the door. In her navy blazer and skirt, she looked like a realtor for high-end properties, not a member of a storefront church. "Barney, stop scaring the window-shoppers. Come along in, baby-girl." A tight Afro framed her creamy dark face, and a chunky wooden necklace broke up the conservative blandness of her outfit. Tired, wise eyes met mine—an anomaly in her strong, unbending body. She might have been in her fifties, but it was hard to tell. Her eyes looked older and her skin younger.

Barney waddled back on bandy legs that seemed more fitted for a ship's deck. "Weren't you looking for a place to talk to Jesus?"

Muscles in my back tightened, and my neck bones tingled. *How did he—?*

"That's generally why folks stand on the sidewalk starin' at our sign."

Two lanky teens strode up the block, shoving each other and cursing loudly. I flinched and stepped through the door.

THE WOMAN BEAMED AT me, then thrust her head outside. "Lamont and Curtis, don't you think I won't be telling your mama that you're cutting school again. And I'll tell her to wash out your mouths, too."

Apparently satisfied, she stepped back in to the strange one-room church and let the door swing shut behind us.

Half a dozen rows of dented folding chairs filled the far end of the room, facing a brown cross painted on the whitewashed wall. A musty smell choked the air, probably from the ancient upholstered couch on the near end of the room or the gaunt man in an overcoat who snored from one of the tattered easy chairs. A coffee table was strewn with garish tracts, and a small bookshelf full of Bibles canted sideways along one wall. Sunlight streaked in through rips in the dark plastic tinting that coated the glass window-front.

"Can I pray with you about something?" The poised middle-aged woman tapped one of her navy blue pumps.

I blinked. At my church, no one would haul a visitor in the door and offer to pray with them without a word of introduction.

She smiled at my confusion. "Sorry. My name's Lydia. You know, like the seller of purple."

Barney snorted. "More like Lydia for her aunt who's full of herself," he muttered.

Lydia lifted an eyebrow at him and turned back to me.

"I'm Penny." I said quietly.

"A Penny saved is a Penny earned." Barney chuckled, then looked at Lydia. "I'll be in back making some calls. Unless the phone's out again. Did you pay the bill this month?"

Lydia's eyebrows climbed further, and Barney laughed as he shuffled his way past the metal chairs and through a door near the cross. Apparently this tiny storefront mission didn't operate with the same efficiency as my church back home.

"So, how can I help you?" Lydia took a few steps toward the folding chairs, and I drifted along with her.

"I was really just out for a walk."

"Mm-hmm." She led me to one of the chairs near the front and we both sat. "I'm sure God won't mind me prayin' for someone who was just out for a walk."

Before I could form further opinions about the two odd people, she took my hand. "Holy Spirit fall on us now. We're needin' your presence. This little lamb is caught in the briars, and we ask you to come for her now. Give her the rescuin' she needs."

This was the most ridiculous, laughable, bizarre experience I'd ever had. A wino snoring in the background, a grizzled sea captain slamming around in the back room, and an elegant Condoleezza Rice look-alike holding my hand.

Yet the loneliness that had frozen into a bundle behind my

sternum began to melt. I had needed to feel God's touch. Now it was as if God held me with a tangible hand. A hand with flesh and blood and skin. Black, bejeweled, with clear nail polish. Who knew His hands could look like this? The fingers that gripped mine offered me support I hadn't sought or deserved.

Tears pricked my eyes as she said a robust, "Amen."

"Thank you." My words came out hoarse but heartfelt. I glanced at my watch. "Whoa, I need to leave. My son gets home from school soon."

She walked with me to the dented metal door and pushed it open. "Come back anytime. That's why we're here."

I squinted into the sunshine, marveling again at how warm it could be on a September afternoon.

Suddenly a teen on a skateboard sailed past, baseball cap backward on his head. A friend ran after him, skidding on hidden wheels inside his tennis shoes. The first boy whooped and spun, heading back up the sidewalk and across the doorway again.

The muscles around my knees stopped working, and my thighs began to tremble, refusing to hold me upright. I stumbled back a step and sucked in a harsh breath.

*No, not now. I have to get home. Bryan needs me to be there.*

Panic crawled up my throat. The harder I fought—reminding myself that I didn't dare allow it—the more it took control of my body. My heart pounded. My lungs felt dry and tight.

Lydia stared at me and poked her head outside. "Take it to the park, boys."

They shouted a good-natured complaint and disappeared down the street.

Still, I wavered a few feet from the open doorway.

*Go! You need to walk home now. Bryan's bus—*

I groaned and reached blindly for the doorjamb. Sweat beaded above my lip, and I licked away the taste of salt.

"Honey, can I call someone for ya?"

Arms guided me away from the doorway and inside to a couch. I let my head sag forward, but the sour staleness of the upholstery churned my stomach.

"I need to . . . my son . . ." A moan vibrated deep in my chest. This dizziness and nausea couldn't be from anxiety. Maybe food poisoning. What had I eaten lately?

A liver-spotted hand thrust a glass of water at me. I looked up and saw Barney frowning at me. "Drink some. It's either that or I throw it in your face."

I choked out a surprised laugh and accepted the glass. A few sips helped the vertigo recede.

"Lamb, you look scared to death." Lydia wrapped an arm around my shoulders.

Barney squared off with her. "You didn't start speaking in tongues or prophesyin' again, did ya?"

"That was only the one time, and—never mind." Lydia turned toward me. "Did I say anything that upset you?"

I drew in a deep, shaky breath. "No. The prayer was wonderful. It's not that. But really, I need to get home." I struggled to my feet and then waited for the room to stop doing a fun-house tilt.

"Cherisse is coming by for the baby clothes anytime now," Lydia said quietly to Barney. "You take care of it, okay? I'll get this lamb safely home."

I shook my head. "Oh, no. Please. I'm fine." But when she took my arm, I let her support me. We stepped out into the sunshine.

"Which way? Despite what Barney says, I'm no prophet. Can't find your house without at least a little clue here."

I gave a breathy laugh and looked around. I'd come past that Laundromat, right? Or was it the other direction?

My throat tightened again. I was trapped. I couldn't find

my way back. And Bryan would get home to an empty house. A shiver spasmed through me.

"Okay. Let's just walk a bit. That'll clear the cobwebs. I'm guessing you aren't from the projects, or am I wrong?" She steered me along the sidewalk.

"No, that's right. It's only a few blocks . . . I think. There's a bus stop."

She gave a throaty chuckle. "That'll help. Not like there're many of those."

Right. I was sounding more like a lunatic by the moment. There were bus stops on every other corner. "This is the right way. I think. There was a barber for chickens. There it is."

"A barber for—? Oh, I gotcha. Cheep. For a minute there I was going to take you back to the mission for a little casting out of evil spirits."

I pulled my arm away from her.

She grinned. "Kidding. So, seriously, are you feeling any better?"

"I'm fine. Sorry. I've been getting over the flu or something. I hate to cause you so much trouble."

"Child, I get up each morning and ask God to give me someone to serve. You aren't trouble. You're my answer to prayer."

The peace in her voice made me ache. Like stretching on tiptoe for a high shelf, I could almost remember what it felt like to ask God for people to serve—instead of spending my day wishing the world would go away. Almost. "The least of these," I murmured.

"Hmm?"

" 'Whatever you did for one of the least of these brothers of mine, you did for me.' "

Lydia beamed. "Exactly. That's what I'm talking about."

When we reached the corner of my block, I was breathing

more evenly. "You must think I'm nuts. I . . . A few weeks ago, I was at a store that got robbed." The restricting band around my lungs relaxed its grip by a centimeter, and I drew in a deep draught of air. Speaking the words hadn't disintegrated me. "I'm still a little . . . I haven't quite gotten over it yet."

"Well, if that don't beat all." Without breaking stride, Lydia reached into her blazer pocket and pulled out a rubber-banded stack of assorted business cards. She pulled one out and handed it to me. "One of the women that comes to our Wednesday night worship is a crime victim. She's been getting some good help at this place."

I pulled to a stop in front of my house and took the card. *Victim Support Services.* I swallowed a laugh. Was God trying to tell me something?

"Yoo-hoo." Laura-Beth shot from her lawn chair and scooted toward us. Her dog gave a halfhearted woof and resettled himself in his patch of dirt. My neighbor leaned on her chain-link fence and gave Lydia an assessing stare. "Howdy."

Lydia crossed her arms, gaze traveling over Laura-Beth's frowzy hair and wrinkled blouse.

"Lydia, this is Laura-Beth, my neighbor. Laura-Beth, Lydia works at the mission a few blocks from here."

Laura-Beth took a step back and held her hands up. "I gave at the office."

Lydia ignored that. "I better get back before Barney makes a mess of things. You come by and visit anytime." She smiled at Laura-Beth. "You too."

"Thanks for your help." I held up the card. "And for this. I'll look into it."

Lydia smiled and marched back up the block, clearly ready to bring order and spiritual life to the neighborhood.

Laura-Beth shook her head. "I hope you don't mind a piece of advice—"

"Oops, I think I hear the phone." I had the ringer turned off, but Laura-Beth didn't know that. I raced into the house and latched the door firmly. My greatest fear was happening. I was going completely insane. I couldn't venture a few blocks from home without a disaster. Terrified by skateboarding teens? Getting lost? I tried to laugh at my misadventure. Tears began to escape, and soon I was laughing and sobbing at the same time. I sank to the floor and leaned against the door, hugging my shins.

*Oh, God. It's getting worse. How am I going to take care of Bryan? I almost didn't get home before his bus. And he's counting on me to help with the school play. And Tom needs to know I'm doing fine, so he can concentrate on his work. He's dreamed of this for years.*

My yellow notebook rested on the coffee table. Penny's Project. This was one project I couldn't fail. The stakes were too high. If I kept slipping away I'd lose everything.

Like Alex had.

*Oh, God. Am I going to turn into my brother?*

Huddled on the floor, I pressed my forehead against my knees, shutting out that thought. How long could I play Hans Brinker and plug leak after leak before the dike came crashing in to drown my sanity?

Outside, the school bus stopped and then roared away. I forced myself to my feet, and when Bryan tapped on the door, I quickly pulled him inside.

"What's wrong now?" His scowl held more irritation than worry as he stared at me. My face always turned blotchy when I cried.

"I'm not feeling good again. I think I need to lie down. Do you want to watch a movie?"

"We don't have any good ones."

"Bryan, please! Just watch something, okay? Stay out of trouble."

His wounded look reproached me, but I fled the guilt and shut myself in the bathroom. I'd never understood alcoholics and addicts and why they would let a momentary pleasure destroy their lives, but today, if I could have swallowed something or shot something into my veins to stop the shaking and the irrational fear—and my shame for not being able to control it—I would have done it in an instant. Was this how my brother, Alex, felt all those years ago? Did I inherit the same gene? Had irrationality been lying in wait for a trigger like the crime? I splashed cold water in my face.

*Don't go there. Hold it together. Just a few hours. Then you can put Bryan to bed.*

While Bryan indulged in afternoon cartoons, I made him a sandwich for supper. My hand shook as I spread the peanut butter, and milk splashed on my hand as I tried to pour it into his favorite cup. At least I had a few homemade cookies to add to the plate. I managed to hold the tray steady as I set it on the coffee table for him.

By bedtime, I was able to slip fully back into the role of a normal mom. I cooed over Bryan, but he held himself stiff in my arms as I read to him.

"Honey, I know this isn't fair to you. It's not your fault. I shouldn't have been crabby to you." I stroked his thick bangs over to one side. "Will you forgive me?"

His eyes were flat as he stared at me. "When is Dad getting home?"

"Soon, sweetie." I hugged him, and my throat tightened. "I'm really sorry."

"Mrs. Pimple sent you another note. It's in my jeans."

"Okay. I'll find it. Let's say our prayers, all right?"

With my help, he dutifully recited an evening prayer that Tom had taught him last summer. I had teased Tom that the prayer was too archaic for a seven-year-old, but Tom insisted that his father had taught him that prayer when he was still in kindergarten.

"I thank Thee, my heavenly Father, through Jesus Christ, Thy dear Son, that Thou hast graciously kept me this day; and I pray Thee that Thou wouldst forgive me all my sins where I have done wrong, and graciously keep me this night. For into Thy hands I commend myself, my body and soul, and all things. Let Thy holy angel be with me, that the wicked Foe may have no power over me. Amen."

Tonight the words battered me. The "wicked Foe" seemed to have a lot of power over me these days, and fear continued to twist my stomach. From one perspective, God had kept me safe in the store that day. I was alive. And today, when I'd had another spell, He'd sent Lydia to guide me home. But in spite of that, I found it difficult to commend myself into His hands anymore.

I pulled the quilt up to Bryan's chin and kissed him one more time. Gathering up scattered clothes, I tiptoed from his room, leaving the door open a perfect six inches. He liked to see the spill of hallway light as he fell asleep.

Our washing machine lurked in an oversized closet off the kitchen. I tossed the clothes into the basket and carefully checked the pockets. Bryan had a habit of forgetting dead beetles or chewed wads of bubble gum for me to discover in the washing machine filter. Today all I found was the note from Mrs. Pimblott.

*Dear Mrs. Sullivan,*

*I had hoped to talk with you about the Thanksgiving play but haven't been able to reach you. If you aren't able to participate, please let me know soon, so I can recruit another parent.*

*I'd also like to arrange an appointment with you. Bryan is a delightful student, but in the past week he's been distracted and irritable. I know you'll agree that we should discuss this before problems escalate. You can stop by my classroom after school any day this week, or call me to arrange a meeting. Thank you.*

*Mrs. Pimblott*

I smoothed the letter, pressing out each wrinkle beneath my fingers. Stark against the top of my dryer, the black ink condemned me. Of course Bryan was distracted. His mother spent half her time avoiding him or snapping at him, and the other half trying to make it up to him.

*God, you've got to fix me faster. For Bryan's sake.*

I groped in the pocket of Tom's jacket looking for a Kleenex. The card Lydia had given me met my fingers. I pulled it out and studied the italicized phone number. Should I call? Could I?

I padded out to the living room and penciled the words into my notebook. *Call the victim center.*

Dark fear threaded through me. If I went to a counselor, wasn't that admitting I was broken? Emotionally disturbed? I'd be starting down the same futile road as Alex.

*Oh, Lord, please no.*

I erased that entry and wrote *Exercise* instead. I drew a checkmark next to *Explore neighborhood.* I'd walked outside, and I'd even talked to God—sort of. At least Lydia had talked to Him on my behalf.

The computer screen beckoned me like a warm companion—the only one available in the middle of a lonely night. With my small yellow notebook at hand, I surfed more sites about panic attacks, the keys clacking beneath my fingers in a desperate tempo. Reading the loops where people wrote about their struggles gave me a glimpse into a wealth of pain. Seeing these stories could *cause* depression and anxiety.

On the other hand, I felt less alone. And here in this jumble of the world's knowledge, there had to be an answer. I scrolled and clicked, skimmed and clicked again. The next page could provide me the key. My eyes burned, but I continued to search.

One blogger linked to a Web site with summaries of recent medical research. I scrolled through indecipherable lingo and began to yawn. Then I stilled the mouse. An obscure site reported a study where people with emotional disorders benefited from small volunteer efforts. Helping others created an emotional upsurge that helped the patients improve. Lydia and Barney at the storefront mission came to mind. Her core strength. His playful enthusiasm. They were busy "doing for the least of the brothers" and they seemed happy.

Inspiration tingled under my skin. I turned to the first page of my notebook.

*Penny's Project,* it read. *Move toward healing. Be Penny again, in time for Tom's return.* I printed an addendum in block letters. *Do one kind thing for someone each day.*

I studied that goal. I'd be able to do nice things for Bryan all day long, but it wouldn't help me conquer my anxiety.

*Okay.* I erased and tried again. *Do a kind thing for someone NEW each day.*

The words sang to me. This could work. But how would I find people? I wasn't even going out for groceries anymore.

Well, I could send my friend Sonja a card without leaving home. And I could call my mom and tell her how much I appreciated her. Or maybe I could make cookies and give some to Jim-Bob next time he played in our backyard. And give a bottled water to the grocery delivery gal. I scribbled headings to new pages. Bryan, Tom, family, neighbors, church, school, the nearby mission.

Then I returned to the first page and added the familiar words, *"Whatever you did for one of the least of these brothers of mine, you did for me."*

I hugged my notebook with a surge of new optimism. I'd dabbled in some baby steps, but this was a breakthrough. Progress. Caring about other people would heal my shaken mind and heart.

I hoped.

# chapter 7

*Twenty-one.* Groan. *Twenty-two.* Grimace.

Fifty crunches and a handful of modified push-ups would revitalize me.

*Argh.* My muscles burned and I flopped back in an nonathletic sprawl. Exercise had seemed like a good next goal from my notebook. The infomercials I'd seen during my recent insomnia-plagued nights had made a convincing argument. "Feeling sluggish? Tired all the time? Not yourself? You need more exercise!" I couldn't afford the oversize beach balls, ropes and pulleys, and other gizmos, but I could certainly do a few basic exercises. If I were to be honest, it also gave me a way to stall before tackling the new "acts of kindness" challenge I'd set for myself—or even worse, confronting the decision to call the victim center.

I had barely been able to pull myself out of bed this morning, but as soon as Bryan left for school, I hit the floor of the living room and started sit-ups.

Bad idea. Nausea roiled through my gut, and I curled on my

side. Was that Bryan's milk money under the couch? I stared at the dust bunnies, feeling as if my body were a piece of lint on the carpet—grubby and lifeless.

A Navy SEAL would push through the pain, ignore the heavy limbs and constant fatigue. I rolled to my stomach and tried a push-up.

My arms wobbled and gave out, and my chin crashed into the floor. Clearly, I was not a Navy SEAL.

*If you fail at these little goals, you're out of options. You'll need to call the victim center and ask for help.*

Adrenaline fed my muscles, and I pressed back up to my hands and knees and did enough modified push-ups to break a sweat. Then I cranked up the stereo and marched in place to a Celtic worship CD. The first song was an energetic reel, and my spirits lifted. I could almost infuse some enthusiasm into my minced steps around the room. The next song opened with a plaintive *a cappella* voice, rich with yearning and passion. The melody was the sort that burrowed past rational layers in my mind and pressed a finger against raw emotions. Buried grief welled up in my spirit. I clamped down on it and quickly switched off the stereo.

I'd heard somewhere that aggressive housework counted as exercise, and I'd let things go in the past few weeks. Maybe folding laundry and dusting would be a smarter idea than calisthenics.

An hour later, the bathroom sparkled, laundry was folded and put away, the mess in Bryan's room was swept into a pile to one side of his bed, and I was steeping a cup of tea in the kitchen. I pulled out my notebook and wrote *Clean house* on my list of goals, and then drew a firm check mark alongside. It might be cheating to write something down *after* I'd done it, just so I could check it off, but I needed the sense of accomplishment. Did cleaning the house count as my daily good deed for someone? No one saw it but Bryan and me. Bryan didn't care that I'd vanquished the dust bunnies. On the other hand, it would make my mom happy. She often recommended housecleaning as a cure-all. This could count as a sort of gift to her.

Carrying my tea in one hand and a dust cloth in the other, I strolled into the living room and buffed the shelves on the wall of our makeshift office. Our CDs were still a mess from my frantic search, stacked haphazardly with Handel's *Messiah* next to a Broadway cast recording of *West Side Story.* We really needed a system for organizing our music. I tossed aside my dust cloth and set my tea on the coffee table. Now was as good a time as any.

I tried to ignore the precious DVD from Tom, still waiting for me on the top shelf. But as I reorganized our movies and CDs, I found myself glancing up every few minutes.

Finally unable to resist, I popped the blank DVD into the player again. With the channels set up for the movie I'd just finished, I pushed the tray in and hit Play.

Snowy static filled the screen.

I tried rewinding, pausing, forwarding. Nothing helped. I poked the DVD rack in and out and examined the unlabeled disc for scratches. I needed Bryan. I'd learned long ago to get his help with electronic equipment. He knew how to program our VCR to tape his favorite cartoon, how to switch to the correct channel to play video games, and what was wrong when I couldn't get sound to play. He could operate three remotes at one time.

I'd probably accidentally hit the wrong button. The disc couldn't be damaged. It just couldn't. Looking forward to the next message had gotten me through several rough patches during the last few days.

I placed the disc carefully back on the shelf. I'd try again later. My housecleaning energy spent, I drained the lukewarm tea and trudged to the kitchen. I'd been letting voice mail collect any phone calls, but I couldn't ignore them forever. When I picked up the phone, nervous beeps warned me that I had several new messages.

There is an art to returning phone calls when you'd rather not. With strategic timing, I was able to leave messages instead of facing live conversations. My mom had library guild on Wednesday mornings, and Mrs. Pimblott was teaching. I even lucked out and got ombudsman Mary Jo's voice mail and assured her, without a quaver in my voice, that I'd be happy to get together sometime. Of course, since we weren't speaking live, she couldn't pin me down.

I muddled through the rest of the week. Each day I struggled to think of a good deed that I could do from my living room. I sent a supportive e-mail to Tom. I'd already thanked him for his surprise DVD recordings the morning after I found the disc. I didn't want to tell him the DVD had stopped working, so I just thanked him again for the first message.

I mailed a donation to World Vision, a nice card to my friend Sonya, and crocheted baby booties for Cindy's new baby. For those minutes, I felt a bit of hopefulness, a slight connection with the woman I used to be. But I continued to battle sleepless nights and dragged through the hours of each day. And the world outside my door continued to be a dark and nebulous monster.

I rationed each ounce of my energy for when Bryan got home from school. I printed out Tom's e-mails for him, and each night after supper I typed my son's responses and helped him send them. I spread out the contents of the craft bin, played endless rounds of Trouble, even designed an in-home obstacle course with couch cushions. But no matter how many activities I planned around the house for him, he remained restless.

"How about the library? Huh, Mom?"

"Daddy said you'd take me to our new park."

"Know what? The beach would be a good idea."

"I have an idea. We can go to the arcade and play games. Right, Mom?"

By suppertime on Saturday, he'd grown tired of my vague, "Mommy doesn't feel good" excuses.

"Well, you should take your vitamins," he shot back in a lofty impression of my mom. Then he stomped from the table and slammed his room door. His unacceptable behavior got him grounded for the rest of the evening. I sulked in the living room, and he sulked in his bedroom.

At bedtime, when he was freshly showered and in flannel, dinosaur pajamas, he nestled into my lap on the couch with three bedtime books. "Know what? This was *not* a good day."

Poor kid. His father was at sea for months—in his mind, practically forever—and his mom a weary stranger. Time to tackle the next specific goal in my notebook. It was a big one, but it might be the breakthrough we both needed. *Take Bryan to the beach.*

"Tell you what. Tomorrow, we'll sleep in—"

"What about Sunday school?"

"We'll skip just this once, and—"

"But we didn't go last week, either."

"And then, after lunch, we'll go to the beach."

He gasped. "Really?"

I smiled. "Really."

Chubby arms flung around my neck. "You're the best mom *ever*. I didn't mean it when I told God you were doing a bad job."

So he had squealed on me, huh? Well, at least he was remembering to pray. Someone in the house needed to.

---

Sunday afternoon, I kept my promise. I summoned superhuman courage for Bryan's sake and forced myself into the car to drive the forty minutes with my son to the Virginia Beach shore. Summer visitors had vacated, and we found a deserted section of dunes. I hugged my knees and stared out at the gray-green waves. The sky hung low and overcast giving a dirty tinge to the water. Seagulls performed aerial dogfights with occasional dive-bombs when they spotted a fish. The breeze tugged hair free from my loose ponytail and wrapped strands across my neck.

Bryan jogged a short distance away and dug into the sand. His shovel scraped pleasantly as he built misshapen mounds.

I drew in a deep breath through my nose and savored the briny scent. The glaring sunlight of the past week had depressed me as it spotlighted the world outside my window, so I welcomed today's clouds and haze. The muted shades of sand, sea, and sky seemed to understand and comfort me. I burrowed my fingers into the sand and lifted a handful. I poured the grains from one palm to another, again and again, letting the wind catch small bits.

A bird glided near and then sailed out over the ocean. *"If I take the wings of the morning, and dwell in the uttermost parts of the sea; Even there shall thy hand lead me, and thy right hand shall hold me."* Words from my old King James book of Psalms floated through my mind.

*Even here? Far from family and friends?*

I stared out toward the horizon. The ocean was bigger than this Wisconsin girl had ever pictured. The hugeness of it stretched something inside the muscles of my heart. The roar of waves rose and fell in a calming rhythm. Maybe Tom was leaning against a ship's rail and watching these same waves. His hazel eyes would catch a hint of sea-green as he squinted toward the horizon, jaw squared in noble determination to support the men he'd pledged to serve, no matter the danger. I was so proud of him. And I longed for him to be proud of me. When he got home, I wanted to be the wife he remembered. Whole. Strong.

Tom had prayed for me. Bryan had prayed for me. Even Lydia at the neighborhood mission had prayed for me. But my throat had constricted each time I'd tried to talk to God about my struggles.

I closed my eyes. "Erase the past. Find me and bring me back to myself," I whispered into the salty breeze. It was my first true prayer about that horrible afternoon.

Peace seeped into me like the moist air that clung to my clothes and pressed against my skin. Bryan romped the shoreline, water murmured in and back, and sand cushioned my limbs. My doubts drifted away, swallowed up in contentment. Laying my needs out before the God who made this vast ocean brought far more comfort than all my to-do lists and self-reliance. My little notebook wasn't a bad idea. Effort mattered. But so did acknowledging my helplessness. I curled up on my Father's lap and heard the beat of His heart, more deep and powerful than the rhythmic waves.

"Look, Mom!" Bryan scampered toward me, hands full of scavenged prizes. Sand scattered over my clothes as he slid in beside me. I laughed, and the wind caught the sound and spun it around us both.

On the drive home, I hummed happily until the fuel gauge light flickered. *Oops. Almost empty.* Tom usually kept the car filled. He'd been gone three weeks, but I'd only driven a few times and hadn't needed to buy gas yet.

"So, Bryan. Which gas station should we try?"

"That one?" He pointed to a Quick Corner on the other side of the intersection.

I drove past. "Let's keep looking." Mile after mile, each gas station glared at me. They all looked too much like the Quick Corner.

*Wait.* That was my old way of thinking. I'd experienced God's peace at the beach. I was going to be fine now. Gas stations didn't need to frighten me.

Dusk deepened the cloud cover to a slate gray, and some of the drivers turned on their headlights. I spotted a CITGO and pulled in to the pump. Overhead fluorescents made the station glow with a halo of humid air.

I took a few deep breaths.

*You can do this. Nothing to be afraid of. Remember the strong God of the ocean washing over you.*

"Mommy? Who are you talking to? Why are you making funny faces? Mom?"

*Turn off the engine. Get out the credit card.*

"Can we go in and get candy? Know what? I used to like Tootsie Rolls, but now I don't. Now I like Laffy Taffy."

A boa constrictor wrapped around my rib cage and squeezed. I couldn't draw a deep breath. Go inside? The credit card pump with the Swipe & Go feature was difficult enough.

*Get out of the car. You can do this.*

Pressure swelled inside my head as a hangman's noose closed around my neck. Maybe I was having a stroke. I gripped the steering wheel and leaned my head back. If I passed out, Bryan would be on his own. I had to push through.

"Mom, can I get Laffy Taffy if I pay you back? It's a good idea. I have millions of quarters at home."

"No." I fumbled for the handle and pushed the door open.

The warm air closed over my face like a wet washcloth. With one hand on the car, I felt my way toward the gas tank. Each breath seemed to strangle me, but I got the nozzle into the tank.

I doubled over, resting my hands on my knees. The dizziness receded for a second. Then gasoline fumes pushed my stomach up to my throat.

*Almost done. Hurry.*

I straightened and fixated on the numbers spinning past on the pump, willing them to click ahead more quickly.

Good enough. Enough gas to last me for a while.

My hand shook as I reached for the automated receipt.

"There. Okay. Now we can head home," I said in my bright, Mom's-in-charge voice, as I slid into my seat and turned to smile at Bryan.

His seat was empty.

"BRYAN? BRYAN!" WAS THAT shrill, hysterical voice really mine?

A quick search confirmed that he'd left the car. The backseat passenger door hung open a few inches. What had he been babbling about when we pulled in? Candy.

I ran for the convenience store. The door's bells jingled and brought a sudden flashback. That same sound—*No! Concentrate.* "My son. Is he—?"

The oily-faced clerk pointed to one of the aisles. My beach shoes slapped the linoleum as I ran.

Bryan squatted midway down the aisle. "Look, Mom. They have Laffy Taffy in four flavors. Can I get some?"

"Bryan Patrick Sullivan, get back in the car now." Clint Eastwood never issued a tougher clench-jawed ultimatum.

Bryan's eyes widened. He threw one more longing look at the candy shelves and then trudged toward the door. I grabbed his arm and marched him to the car.

"Don't *ever* do that again. Do you understand? No! Don't say anything. You listen to me. When I tell you to wait in the car, you wait in the car. What were you thinking?" Angry words continued to spew.

He scampered to keep up. "Ow."

My grip on his arm was tighter than necessary but not as tight as my anger craved. Rage burned through my veins and built into a swirling pressure in my head that made me feel as if my skull would fracture from within.

"Don't say a word. You are grounded." I snapped his seat belt into place and slammed the door.

"That's not fair. All I did was—"

"Shut up!"

I'd never shouted at him like that before. A rational part of my brain knew Bryan didn't deserve such rage. Yet I couldn't push it back.

His chin trembled. "How long am I grounded?"

"Two years." We pulled out of the gas station, and I fought to keep the car steady when my whole body shook with white-hot intensity.

After a long silence Bryan cleared his throat. "I'm sorry, Mom."

I didn't answer.

At home, I sent Bryan to his room. He hurried down the hall with a worried glance over his shoulder, while I followed close on his heels. His door closed safely between us. His bed creaked, and he cried with the same despair and pain he had two years earlier when he'd broken his arm.

Instead of going to him, I ran for my bedroom. I'd tried to control the shakes, but now they grabbed me. The bedroom was too exposed, so I slipped into the closet, pulled the door shut, and sank to the floor. Sobs broke free from deep in my gut, and even with a sweatshirt pressed against my mouth, keening sounds of misery burst from my chest to fill the tiny dark space. I was lost. Memories burst free. A horrible muddle of images, sounds, smells.

I cried until exhaustion lowered me back to the numb place where I'd existed the past weeks.

"What's happening to me?" My whisper met black silence.

I couldn't fight the despair alone any longer. The screaming harridan dragging her child through the gas station, the irresponsible mother who wasn't returning phone calls, the broken woman huddled in her closet—she needed help. The past weeks had changed her.

No, That Day had changed her. The last few weeks had solidified the process like slowly drying concrete. I didn't have the energy to chip at the cement. Besides, even if I could, I wouldn't find my old self inside. That person didn't exist anymore.

*That* Penny was dead and buried beneath a granite slab of fear.

The peaceful interlude at the beach had teased me with a reminder of normality. But the gas station had shaken loose my bundled fears and shown me my healing was far from complete. I huddled into a tight ball, wanting to shrink smaller and smaller until I could disappear.

The closet door swung open. A tiny hand touched my shoulder.

I jerked upright and swiped my face with the back of my hand.

"Mom? I'm sorry I was bad." Bryan shifted from foot to foot.

Remorse crushed my ribs into shards that pierced my heart. "Oh, honey. It's not your fault. I'm just . . . I . . ." More tears stole away my words.

Bryan held out his arms. I rose up to my knees and hugged

him, and let him pat my back. My hiccupping breaths gradually slowed while I soaked in the comfort of his arms. I fought for control I couldn't find, and all the while I knew this was so wrong, so unfair to Bryan. He shouldn't have to parent me while I fell apart.

I needed help.

"I love you, sweetie. I'm okay. Really I am. Could you get my purse?"

He pulled back, his eyes wary and too old as he studied me. A terse nod and he ran from the room.

When he returned I sat on the edge of the bed, trying to remember how a responsible adult should behave. I took the purse and pulled out the card for Victim Support Services. "Honey, I promise I'm going to get help. I'll call them tomorrow."

---

The next morning, as soon as Bryan left for school, I reached for the phone. My fingers fumbled so much it took me three attempts to dial the number. The victim support staffer's voice was reassuring but firm. Within a minute she had me agreeing to attend a support group.

I raised a token resistance. "I always thought of myself as a strong person."

"It takes strength to ask for help," she said calmly. "Tuesday nights at seven. Our offices are just off Princess Anne Road in Norfolk. Do you know where that is?"

Noncommittal murmur.

"How old did you say your son is? Can you find a babysitter?"

I rubbed my forehead, overwhelmed enough by the thought of driving to the center. How could I think through all the steps involved in finding a sitter? "He's seven. Second grade."

"Well, you could bring him and let him play in the lobby. The group meets in the conference room, and you'll be able to keep an eye on him through the glass doors."

Sure. Sounded easy as pie.

A pizza supper went a long way toward securing Bryan's forgiveness for my latest meltdown. After wolfing enough pieces for three grown men, Bryan bounded out the back door to play. With neighbor-boy radar, Jim-Bob's towhead appeared in his backyard a few minutes later. After a brief negotiation, Jim-Bob hopped the fence and the boys began a soccer game in our yard.

Jim-Bob was a year older than Bryan but seemed twice as big and twice as savvy about boyhood lore. I wasn't sure I wanted Bryan playing Tom Sawyer to Jim-Bob's Huck Finn. But Bryan had too much energy to stay caged in the house.

While they romped and shouted outside the window, I turned on the computer.

*How's my favorite husband? We prayed for you tonight at supper. Bryan misses you a lot, but he's doing well. Right now he's playing soccer with Jim-Bob from next door.*

*We went to Virginia Beach yesterday. Not the boardwalk part. A nice empty stretch of beach. It's so beautiful. I could watch those waves for hours. I suppose you're getting sick of seeing nothing but water.*

*Oh, I'm going to the victim center tomorrow night. Just to check it out. I'm really doing fine, but who knows? Maybe I can offer some help to other folks who are struggling. Sorry that my mom keeps e-mailing you. I'll e-mail her tonight. She gets all worried if I'm too busy to return her calls right away. She forgets how busy things can get.*

*Thank you again for the DVD. Hey, why didn't you just give it to me the day you left? What if I hadn't found it?*

*Hugs and kisses, Pen*

I sent chipper e-mails to my friend Sonja, and to my mom, then sat at the dinner table nursing a glass of lemonade. Pizza remnants littered the table, but I couldn't work up the energy to clean up.

"Mommy, can Jim-Bob sleep over?" Bryan charged into the dining area at the same time the screen door slammed shut behind him. Grass and leaves matted his clothes.

"No. You're too young for a sleepover."

He planted grubby fists on his hips. "Mo-om. I wouldn't be sleeping over. *He* would."

I pinched the bridge of my nose. I'd studied philosophy in college, but nothing had prepared me for the logic of a seven-year-old. "Time for your shower. Go tell Jim-Bob you have to come inside."

The longer hours of sunlight here in Virginia were a bit of a curse. Bryan wasn't convinced bedtime was near when he could still see his hand in front of his face outside. He stomped through the kitchen. The screen door slammed, boyish voices hollered, and the screen door slammed again.

Bryan pulled his socks off and dropped them on the kitchen floor. "So, can I have a snack?" He started to open the refrigerator door. "Oh!"

Pulling a crumpled letter from his pocket, he passed it to me and returned to his snack search. "I kind of forgot."

*Dear Mrs. Sullivan,*

*Thanks for your phone message. And yes, your e-mail helped me understand Bryan's situation. I'm sure that part of his distraction comes from missing his father. By the way, Bryan said that you're eager to get involved in the PTA and be a room parent, and that you were very involved at his school in Wisconsin. I'm so delighted to hear this. I always struggle to find parents willing to help. Could you stop in after school tomorrow so we can discuss the Thanksgiving play? He said you offered to fill the role of the Pilgrim mother. Thank you so much, Sarah Pimblott.*

I cleared my throat. "Bryan, you need to talk to me before you volunteer me for things."

His eyes darkened. "But I did tell you. Remember?" His pleading expression begged for more than just my help with the play. He wanted his old mom back again.

"I told you I'd think about it. Honey, she wants to meet with me tomorrow. I . . . I can't. But I'll call her. Okay?"

He met my eyes and waited.

He needed a commitment from me. No more waffling. My withdrawal from life had hurt Bryan too much already. "All right. I'll call and tell her I'll help with the play. It's two months away. I'm sure I'll feel better by then."

A grin split his face. The gaps waiting for his permanent teeth never looked better to me. I even smiled in response.

Tom would get home from his first deployment to find an active, well-adjusted wife appearing with his son in the school play. Two months should give me enough time to recover from this . . . thing . . . that had its fist around my throat. Even if I had to suffer through some group therapy. Even if I had to confront the memories I'd worked hard to forget. Even if I had to fill each page of my notebook with action points and tiny goals. It was a great plan, a great target for me to aim for.

So why did the few bites of pizza I'd managed suddenly congeal in my stomach?

# chapter 9

THE LONG TABLE AND folding chairs barely fit in the cramped conference room at Victim Support Services. A girl with Goth eyeliner slumped in a seat near the door. She shot me a sideways glance and then went back to gouging a pattern into the table using a paper clip. A man with sagging jowls and deep eye pouches sat beside her and tugged on his suit sleeves. He appeared to be about my age, but with the world-weariness of someone much older.

"Hello." A plump woman in her fifties followed me into the room and offered her hand. "I'm Dr. Marci Crown. I'm the psychologist on staff here, and I facilitate this group. I saw your son out there. He's adorable." She pulled out a chair for herself across from Goth girl and Basset-hound man. The seats closest to the door were taken. I squeezed my way to the far end of the table. The others avoided eye contact.

A crowded room with only one door. Couldn't they see this was a fire hazard? A trickle of sweat ran down my rib cage. Panic attacks were bad enough, but this place was going to give me claustrophobia on top of it. I'd have to crawl over the raccoon-eyed teen and the businessman to escape. Why had I agreed to this? The drive to the victim center had drained me, and now I wanted to find an excuse to leave. I half hoped Bryan was upset about being left in the lobby to play on his own—what kind of mother was I to hope my child was upset so I could make a quick exit? But as I expected, my oh-so-resilient child was calmly coloring at the receptionist's desk.

Dr. Marci glanced at her watch, holding it out far from her face and squinting. "I was hoping Daniel would make it, but he asked me to tell you all that he's having a bad day."

"He's agoraphobic." The Basset-hound man tossed the explanation to me.

"Henry, let's not use labels," Dr. Marci interrupted. "Daniel is a lot of things beyond his hesitation to venture out. Let's start with some introductions." She zeroed her gaze onto Goth girl.

The young woman lifted her chin long enough to roll her eyes. "Name's Ashley. Friends call me Ash. Get it? Ash—the debris of destruction." She waggled her fingers and glared at all of us in what I supposed was meant to be a menacing face.

Good grief. Did she really think the nihilistic role was cool? She looked like an adolescent vampire. A vampire who needed a shampoo.

Unable to force a very warm expression on my face, I dug in my purse and pulled out a stick of gum.

"Are you going to keep that?" Henry stared at the foil wrapper in my hand.

My gaze swung from Henry to the gum wrapper.

Ashley smirked. "He's a hoarder."

I almost choked on my gum. This was getting better and

better. I handed the piece of foil to Henry and scrunched lower in my chair.

"Penny, I'm glad you decided to join our group." Dr. Marci poured herself a cup of water from the pitcher in the middle of the table.

*I'm not joining this group. I'm sitting in on one session as penance for freaking out in front of Bryan.* "Thanks. It's nice to meet you all."

Ashley snorted, not faked out by my attempt at sincerity.

"Okay," Dr. Marci raised her eyebrows in Ashley's direction. "Let's get started. Share a little about why you're here and how your week went, and what you need today. Penny, you can go last so you get to know us first."

*Oh, joy.*

The door swung open and another woman scurried into the room. "Sorry. Traffic was awful."

"Glad you made it, Camille. We're just getting started." The others around the table echoed Dr. Marci's greeting.

Finally, someone normal. Camille wore stylish khaki capris with a striped cotton blouse, a silk scarf, and designer sunglasses. Her hair was clean and styled, and she didn't look like the type to collect gum wrappers.

Dr. Marci sat back in a pose of relaxed attentiveness. "Henry, why don't you start us out?"

Henry cleared his throat. "Could I have some water, please?"

Dr. Marci passed him a stack of Styrofoam cups. He pulled off two, palmed one to slip into his jacket, and poured water in the other. No one else at the table even blinked.

I shivered. Bunch of weirdoes. How was this supposed to help me shake off my anxiety? Well, at least it would reassure Tom that I was getting help. If I could endure the rest of the hour, I'd be able to e-mail him all about how much better I was.

Henry was talking about his week. "Well, I'm still having trouble sleeping. I'm . . . well, I hate to say it, but I'm scared to sleep. The nightmares get so bad."

I leaned forward. Maybe someone here did know what I was going through.

"Can you review why that's been a problem . . . since we have a new member in our group?"

Henry smoothed his tie and looked at me. "Awhile back I was on the floor of the stock exchange. Hundred-hour workweeks." His chest expanded. "Top of my game. Then came the dot-com bust. I had a lot of clients deep into high-tech stock." He seemed to shrink before my eyes, a soggy balloon the day after a party. "Lost my job. Moved back to Virginia to live with my parents for a while. Had some health problems. Then I got mugged one night. Beat up pretty bad. Something in me just . . . broke. I haven't gotten back on my feet since." He shrugged. "I lost my temp job and haven't been able to go out on interviews."

*Wow.* What would it feel like to know you were responsible for people losing their life savings, their retirement funds? And to have invested your life in a career that chewed you up and spit you out? And then to be mugged. Talk about getting kicked when you're down. No wonder he was struggling.

Henry's words had grown more and more quiet until he stopped, shoulders caving forward.

Ashley did something odd. She rested a hand on his arm. Long black nails, silver rings on every finger—a strange picture against the sleeve of Henry's business suit. She turned her dark eyes from Henry and glared at my end of the table. "Yeah, well, I'm so over telling my story. Stepfather couldn't keep his hands off me. Mom didn't believe me. When I was old enough I hit the streets. Same old, same old. Did what I could to get by." She flexed her hand, admiring the metal armor of her jewelry. "A year ago,

I decided to get out of the life, but that didn't go so well. My . . . ex-employer didn't like that idea. He broke a few bones to make an example of me. Doc Marci helped me find a shelter to stay at. I'm sort of a long-term project."

I'd helped Tom work with some troubled youth back at our church in Wisconsin, but none had been treated this harshly by life. Suddenly I saw Ashley's fragile bones and haunted eyes instead of her don't-mess-with-me disguise. *Lord, bring some loving people into her life. Bring her some of the happy childhood she never had.*

Dr. Marci looked at me. "We help people who've been in long-term abuse situations as well as single traumatic events." She directed a fond smile toward Ashley. "It takes a lot of courage to rebuild a life."

Ashley's lips flickered in a half-smile. "Clean for a year now."

Henry nodded. "How's the job?"

She used a few colorful words to describe it. "I ain't gonna spend my whole life saying, 'You want fries with that?' but it's a start."

Camille fingered the scarf at her neck. "So how are you dealing with . . . you know . . . depression and stuff?"

Ashley glanced over at Dr. Marci who gave a nod.

"Still cutting. But only once this week."

My stomach tightened. There'd been a girl in the youth group back home who found comfort in slicing her own skin. Her inner misery was so intense that physical pain actually brought a sort of relief. Ashley talked for a few more minutes while I struggled to imagine her life. I'd dress in black, too, if I'd lived through what she had. I was glad she'd found this support group.

"This is getting too heavy. Your turn." Ashley turned toward Camille.

The classy woman pulled off her sunglasses. Yellow and green bruises framed one eye. “I called him today.”

A collective groan rose from the group.

She pursed her lips. “You don’t understand.” She seemed to remember I was there and turned toward me. “My husband.”

Tom’s gentle eyes flashed in my mind. I trusted him like no one else. How could a woman pick up the pieces from that kind of betrayal? I was here because I’d seen violence, but at least it wasn’t at the hands of someone I loved.

“A large percentage of violent crime is perpetrated by family members,” Dr. Marci said quietly in my direction. “It complicates the recovery from trauma.”

I’d expected a support group of people like Henry—victims of a one-time violent crime, trying to get past the way the shock had changed them. I’d never anticipated meeting people whose day-to-day life provided recurring trauma.

Camille played with a strand of her hair. “It’s not fair for me to walk away without giving him another chance.”

“It’s not fair for him to use you as a punching bag,” Henry said.

Dr. Marci took a sip of water. “Did you tell your counselor at the shelter that you called him?”

Camille dropped her chin and shook her head.

Ashley groaned. “Are you completely stupid? It took you months to work up the courage to get away.”

“Let’s stay constructive.” Dr. Marci remained calm and nonjudgmental. One of those counseling tricks. Did she ever want to shake one of the victims she counseled? “Camille, what feelings triggered a need to contact him?”

“I felt sorry for him.”

“And?”

“And . . . maybe I decided some of this was my fault.”

Henry and Ashley both started talking. Dr. Marci helped Camille unravel some of her feelings, with animated input from the others around the table. I sat back and played with my wedding ring. A quick glance at Bryan assured me that my child was doing just fine, so I turned my attention back to the group. As out-of-place as I'd felt when I walked in, there was no doubt these crime victims cared about each other. I'd just met them, and I already ached for what they'd gone through and wanted to see them recover.

"Okay, Penny. Your turn."

Heads swiveled my direction.

My skin prickled, and heat rushed to my face. I shook my head. "Wow. Um. My problems seem so insignificant. I'm not sure I belong here."

"So why are ya?" Ashley demanded.

"I . . . I've been having trouble sleeping and just don't want to go out anymore since . . . it happened."

"Tell us about when this started," Dr. Marci said.

I stared at the table. "I was in a Quick Corner. A guy . . . Well, there was a crime." I couldn't go any further. If I pulled out one more fact the dam would break. The images would flood me again. "I'm not doing too bad, really. I just need some time to shake it off. I feel bad taking up your time." I shot an apologetic glance at Ashley. "I had an easy childhood. I've got a loving husband, no career stresses. Just that one scary event. And I wasn't even hurt. You've all faced things I can't even imagine. I'm embarrassed to be here with my little issues."

Ashley picked at a cuticle, drawing a bead of blood. "Cut yourself some slack. When you aren't used to people being evil, it's gotta shake you up to see somethin' like that."

Her compassion made me catch my breath. "Thanks," I said hoarsely.

The discussion moved on, but I tuned out. I'd hit my limit for openness with a group of strangers. Voices rose and fell, laughter erupted a surprising amount of times, and the water pitcher was passed around the table.

"All right, that's all for tonight." Dr. Marci managed to sound regretful as if she'd like nothing better than to spend more hours with our table full of misfits. Maybe she would. Behind her Dr. Phil jargon, she seemed sincerely caring. "You're doing good work. We'll see you next week."

Camille pulled some postcards from her purse. "I'm still going to Wednesday night services at the New Life Mission in Chesapeake. It's a great place. You're all invited if you ever want to come."

Henry grabbed one, but probably only to add to his collection of gum wrappers, pens, and other garbage in his jacket pockets. Ashley shook her head and sketched a wave as she strode out the door.

I accepted a postcard from Camille. "I live near the mission." And if I hadn't embarrassed myself so much when I dropped in on my walk, I might have considered going to the weeknight service.

Camille gave me a smile. "Maybe I'll see you tomorrow."

The room was emptying and I sprang to my feet.

"Penny, can I speak to you a minute?" Dr. Marci stayed in her chair.

Feeling like a student kept after school, I froze while the others left.

Dr. Marci pushed out the chair next to her and patted it. "I'm glad you came. Did you find it helpful?"

I stepped closer to her but didn't sit. "I . . . I don't know."

"Does the idea of counseling make you uncomfortable?" She tilted her head.

"No. Not at all. I need to get Bryan home." I dug in my purse for the car keys.

"You waited a long time before asking for help."

The keys cut into my palm as I squeezed them. Dr. Marci's legs were blocking my escape, and it didn't look as if she planned to move anytime soon. "Let's just say it doesn't work for everyone."

"But you haven't really tried yet," she said quietly.

Muscles in my chest tightened, and I sucked in a tight breath. "I wasn't talking about me."

She nodded slowly, digested that. "I see. Well, I'd like to schedule an appointment with you."

"Instead of this group?"

"In addition."

Great. She must think I was a real mess, to need private tutoring. I shook my head. "I really don't—"

"Mom? Are you ready?" Bryan held the doorframe and leaned into the conference room. "Did it work? Are you better now?"

All my reasons for getting help crashed back into my mind. "Almost ready, buddy." I turned back to Dr. Marci and sighed. "When can you see me?"

"Let's go check my appointment book. I think I have a free hour Thursday morning."

On the drive home, my thoughts circled around the troubled souls I'd met at the group session.

"Mom, what was wrong with that one girl's eyes? And did you see the metal in her head?"

"She was just wearing too much makeup. And the metal is like earrings. . . but just other places—like her lip and eyebrow."

He was silent for a moment. "Cool. Can I get one?"

"I've got an idea. Why don't you ask Dad about that when he gets home?" Tom's face would be something to behold, but he had it coming. He was the one that had prodded me to go to Victim Support Services.

"So when are you going to meet with my teacher? I told her you helped with all the plays at church."

"Soon. I promise."

"So you feel better?"

"I guess."

"Then we should celebrate and have ice cream." My little con man grinned at me through the rearview mirror.

"It's already past your bedtime."

He sighed, but without much genuine frustration. He seemed content to engage in the typical boundary testing of our relationship and let me win a round or two.

After he was tucked in for the night, I tiptoed out to the living room. A murmured prayer tumbled from my lips as I pushed Tom's DVD into the player. Maybe I'd put it in upside down last time. With no labels, it was hard to know. *Let it work. Let the DVD play tonight.*

I crouched on the floor in front of the television and waited.

Tom's beautiful face filled the screen and I stifled my joyous whoop so I wouldn't wake Bryan. This time I didn't even consider stopping after the first message. I closed my eyes and savored Tom's voice, pretending he was in the room, inches away. Then I leaned forward, ready for the next part of the recording.

# chapter 10

"MESSAGE NUMBER TWO." TOM gave the camera the shy half-grin that I remembered from the first time he asked me out, or when he used to look up from playing his guitar for the youth group and catch my gaze across a room full of teens, or when he waited to see my reaction as I opened a birthday gift from him.

I touched the screen. What I wouldn't give to feel the softness of his blond hair, or the sandpaper of the invisible stubble that he tickled me with at the end of the day. "This feels weirder than I thought it would." He frowned. "Hey, you aren't listening to this right after the first one, are you? I only have time to make a few of these, so spread them out. If you kept going, turn it off and wait at least a week or so."

After a pause, he sat back and continued. "Okay. Penny. I hope this doesn't sound like an empty platitude, but I have to tell you. I'm praying for you every morning. I say your name. I ask God to protect you and to be the arms around you when I can't be. I pray for every part of you. I pray for the health of your body. For your mind and your emotions. For how tired you must feel at the end of a day of chasing Bryan around when I'm not there to play soccer with him and wear him out. I pray you're eating well and staying healthy. I pray for your heart, that you're making friends, that you're feeling the support of the community there at the Navy base or at church. I'm praying that God brings some surprises into your life while I'm gone."

He looked down and cleared this throat. "You didn't want to talk about it, and I get that, but let me go there for a minute. If I'd gone through what you did, I'd be wondering why God let it happen. If you are"—he lifted his head and his gaze searched me—"it's okay to have those questions. I'm confused, too.

"Be brave a little longer, okay?. There are so many things wrong on this planet, but it won't always be this way. And in the meantime, I'm asking God to make himself real to you."

Why couldn't he talk about something else? He'd always been a great sweet-talker, telling me how soft my skin was, how much he loved my long, thick hair, how when he watched me change clothes it drove him to distraction. He enjoyed making me blush. I didn't want him being Chaplain Tom right now. I wanted romance, or dreams for our family, or even small talk. Anything but this spiritual depth that left me exposed.

"Hey." His eyes lit. "How about if I bless you right now?"

He clearly wasn't feeling my reluctance as he spoke to me through the television, so I gave a resigned nod. I couldn't turn away from anything he wanted to say.

He held up his hands the way I'd seen him do so many Sunday nights when he led the contemporary service at our old church. The power of his faith was potent, especially in the face of my crippling doubt. His skin held a glow that wasn't caused by the florescent lights in his office. His chest expanded with a deep breath, and he smiled right into my heart. "The Lord bless you and keep you. The Lord make His face shine upon you and be gracious unto you. The Lord lift up His countenance upon you"—his hand slowly traced the sign of the cross—"and give you peace. End of message two."

The words of his blessing fell over me like a warm ray of sun, and I clung to that benediction when I crawled into bed an hour later. My body curled into a tight ball under the quilt as the dark memories began their nightly invasion.

*Block it out. Think about something else. Penny, you did a brave thing today by going to the victim center. Tom would be so proud of you. Dr. Marci will be able to help you. The Lord bless you and keep you—*

*The Lord bless—*

*The Lord—*

An image played across my mind, of lonely, broken Henry clutching my gum wrapper. The victim center hadn't cured him so far. Or the others. Would I end up like them? Would neighbor kids one day point when they saw me and whisper about the crazy lady with a hundred cats?

Or worse, would I continue this journey into depression like my brother? Would I—

*Don't go there.*

But bleak scenarios continued to skip across my imagination, building on each other, escalating, crowding out my ability to remember any bright corner that life could hold. Stealing my hope.

How could one tragic event change everything inside me? I'd seen crime reports on the news all my life, but I'd never wanted to shut out the world and hide like this before. I'd attended my share of funerals and seen bodies empty of life, but the grief had never triggered week after week of nightmares. People all over the world faced worse than what I'd experienced and they didn't crumble.

*I should be stronger than this.*

Was God as disappointed with me as I was with myself?

It was well after three in the morning before I managed to sleep.

---

Thursday morning I poured out my troubles to Dr. Marci. Flashbacks, insomnia, panic attacks, I shed my pride and talked about the battles where I was losing ground, and told her about Penny's Project and the small kind acts that I hoped would restore my ability to focus on others. Although I'd dreaded this appointment, Dr. Marci was easy to talk to, and the forty-five minutes passed quickly.

"Other people experience worse things than one violent crime, and they get over it." Self-loathing tasted sour in my throat after my brutally honest summary. "Why is it affecting me this way?"

She stopped writing in her steno pad and offered me a gentle smile. "The perfect storm."

When had we started talking about the weather?

She leaned forward, her eyes bright behind her matronly glasses. "You recently moved away from everyone you know. That's a major stressor. Your husband began a new career. Now he's deployed. You have anxiety about his safety. All very understandable. And in your family history you mentioned your brother. You may have a genetic predisposition to—"

I held my hands up, blocking her words as if they were a volleyball spike. "I get it. Okay, there's a good reason for me being such a mess. But I've still got to hurry and get past it. Tom is counting on me. Bryan is counting on me."

"Have you told anyone the details of your experience yet?"

I wished I could read upside down and catch what she had been writing. "Sure. I told the police everything when they showed up."

She waited.

"Oh, you mean other people? No, not really. I want to put it behind me."

"And have you gone back to the Quick Corner?"

I shifted on the lumpy couch and shook my head.

"Okay."

Although she wiped any trace of judgment from her tone, I still heard it. "You think I need to do those things to get better?"

"As long as you can't look at it, that moment in time is holding power over you."

I winced. Look at it? The memory forced itself into random moments of the day, blazed through my nightmares, triggered emotions that terrified and drained me. I wanted help to *stop* being forced to look at it. She was going to make things worse.

Dr. Marci glanced at her watch. "In the meantime, your project is a very positive step. I look forward to hearing how it goes when you come to group next Tuesday."

I left her office and hurried through the lobby of gray-green walls and the people with gray-green spirits. Could they tell by looking at me that I was . . .

What was I? Depressed, anxious, traumatized, and nutty as a Rocky Road sundae?

Like Alex.

Pressure built behind my eyeballs as I crossed the parking lot. My hands fumbled with my car keys. My foot hit the gas pedal with too much force, and the engine raced as I cranked the starter.

Dr. Marci's words pierced me again. *"Genetic predisposition."*

Why wasn't I bouncing back like others who had seen evil, sudden and up close? I had my answer. Because my mind was flawed.

I aimed the car for home, chased by dread that had coiled in a dark corner of my heart for ten years. All it had taken was the perfect storm to trigger my own descent from sanity. I had become my brother.

I drove past a convenience store on the corner, and it leered at me, mocking my efforts to hold back the irrational terror it conjured.

The restraint that had held me together all morning fractured. My arms shook, and my heart raced for no reason. Anger rose up to pulse at the back of my neck. I'd sat through the group session. I'd talked with Dr. Marci. I'd even come up with a proactive project to get my life back on track. Yet I was still a mess. What if nothing worked? What if I continued down this road unchecked? I'd seen the chain reaction. Witnessed it up close in Alex.

*Admit it, Penny. You're crazy. You can't keep pretending to be normal. You're going to lose Bryan. And Tom. You'll lose everything.*

Once the thoughts took hold, fear spiraled out of control. A sob grabbed me, but I fought back tears. I'd never cried this often before. Even when I was pregnant. Even when hormones raged after Bryan was born. The weepiness of recent weeks humiliated me each time it struck. And it was further proof I was broken. If my mind never healed, my life would be a series of gray-green institutions where nightmare images contorted my thoughts.

That terrifying future set loose more sobs, and the tears sprang loose. I could barely keep my car on the road.

A sudden whoop behind me made my stomach drop to my toes. A glance in the rearview mirror revealed the flashing lights of a police car. I pulled over, and more tears erupted—tiny prisoners breaking through the walls and rushing to freedom. I couldn't hold them back.

A hefty policeman swaggered to my car, and I rolled down the window.

"Ma'am, you were driving mighty slow and weaving. What's going on?"

I turned my puffy eyes and tear-swollen face toward him. "I . . . I don't know. I'm sorry. I was at the victim center for counseling, and I guess it got to me, and . . ." To my complete humiliation, I burst into another round of tears and couldn't speak. At least I was able to hand him my license. The car's registration was harder to find, but I finally pulled it from the glove compartment and passed it to him, noticing too late that a half-eaten sucker was stuck to the back. The thought of Bryan set off another round of tears. Poor kid, having a crazy mom like me.

The man sighed and rubbed the back of his neck. "Ma'am, would you get out of the car, please?"

He thought I was drunk? At eleven in the morning? I choked out a laugh through my tears—probably not helping my case.

Cars slowed as they drove by, and I shivered at the sensation of being gawked at as I walked a straight line, balanced on one foot, and touched my nose. He handed me a Breathalyzer instrument.

"This doesn't react to Listerine, does it? I used mouthwash this morning."

He tugged the brim of his hat down, but it didn't completely hide his eye roll. "No, ma'am."

The policeman's face gave nothing away as he studied the results, but I knew he was revising his opinion. I turned to him with an apologetic smile and the flashing cherry on the top of his squad car hit me full in the face.

The tingling exploded without warning this time. My blood

seemed to flash freeze in my veins. I sucked in a couple tight, rapid breaths, but it didn't help.

I tried to form words. "I d-d-don't feel so . . ." Then I reached for the support of the pavement. Arms caught me and eased me toward the ground. When I was able to breathe again, I looked up at a grim face that waited for explanation.

"It's *your* car," I said. "The police cars. It brought it all back. Last month? The Quick Corner in Chesapeake? I was there."

His square-edged frown softened. He gave a soft whistle. "I'm sorry. I heard about that one. So you've been getting help?"

I sighed, my muscles suddenly limp, as if I'd finished an hour-long spin class. "That's what I tried to tell you. I was at the victim center to talk to someone."

He nodded. "Okay, ma'am. But next time maybe you should bring a friend along to drive you. You don't want to be driving when you're that upset."

"Okay." How was I supposed to find someone to drive me when I didn't know anyone in the area? But I'd agree with anything just to get away from him.

He studied my license. "You're almost home. Tell you what. I'll follow you to be sure you get there safe. Okay?"

In his mind, this probably passed as kindness. But did he have any idea how embarrassing it would be to drive home with a police car on my tail? "Will you at least turn off your lights?"

When we pulled in front of my house, Laura-Beth left her lawn chair and hurried to the sidewalk. "Why, Penny, what on earth happened? You didn't see another crime, didja? What are the odds?" She fluffed her brittle hair and smiled at the policeman who had stepped from his car. Apparently he wouldn't trust the community's safety until he'd escorted me to my door.

I studied the anthills along the sidewalk cracks. "He stopped me for driving too slow."

She snorted. "Well, if that don't beat all. I didn't know they gave tickets for that."

"I didn't give her a ticket, ma'am." The policeman tugged on his belt, trying to pull it up over his paunch. "I offered to escort her home to be sure she got here all right."

Laura-Beth put an arm around my shoulders. "Well, I can take care of her now. You run along. Thank ya kindly." She guided me toward her house. "Someone needs to look out for ya. Can't leave my house or the twins would tear the place apart."

I tried to resist. To aim for my own home. But everything took too much effort.

She threw open her screen door and guided me inside, through a cluttered living room with the same floor plan as ours. Her twins sat on beanbags a few feet from a television, identical thumbs in matching mouths. They didn't pull their gaze away.

Laura-Beth led me to the kitchen in the back of the house. Even though her windows were open to the backyard, the room reeked of cigarettes and kitty litter that needed changing. The windows had a thin amber coat from years of tobacco, giving them a stained-glass effect.

I sank into a chair and pushed away the overflowing ashtray.

"Oh, sorry 'bout that. I'm always after Ray to quit, but he's gotta have some little pleasures. Poor man works so hard." She grabbed a glass from the dish drain, rubbed it on her sleeve, poured some lemonade and handed it to me in a fluid movement.

I sipped, letting the tart drink pucker my lips and swish warmly against the insides of my cheeks.

"Sorry. Our ice maker broke, and I can't get the kids to remember to fill the trays, so there's no ice right now."

"Mmm. This is fine. Thanks." Somewhere in the past weeks I'd lost my ability to carry on easy conversations. I tried to remember how it worked. "What does Ray do?"

Her teeth flashed, and she sank into the chair across from me. "Factory work. Die-cutting metal. Well, that's his main job, but he's also been helping a friend with some construction after hours, 'cause they cut health benefits at the factory, and Ruthie's got asthma, so we gotta keep up on her medicine and all."

"Ruthie?" My mind used to sprint joyously, but today it was limping, barely able to maintain my end of the conversation.

"Yeah. The oldest. You remember. Ruthie-Mae?"

I nodded and took another drink. Two high chairs cut into floor space, toys were scattered underfoot, and the counters were cluttered with boxes and cans that didn't fit in the cupboards. Along the top edge of the wall, patchy remnants of an old border stood out against the yellow paint.

Laura-Beth followed my gaze. "I bought a new border and keep meanin' to put it up, but it's a two-person job, and poor Ray is so tired come nighttime, I don't have the heart to make him help."

Unbidden, the youth room at our church in Wisconsin sprang to mind. With the help of several teens, I'd painted, hung paper, and made new curtains. I'd also put up a new border in the women's rest room at the church.

In my purse, the notebook with Penny's Project pulsed like radium, throbbing in time to the headache pinching behind my eyes.

"I can help." I blurted the words and then wanted to pull them back.

Laura-Beth beamed. "Ya' don't say. I was hopin' when you moved in that we'd become best of friends. Ya' just never know about people. But I had a feeling."

She tore open a package of generic wafer cookies and tossed

them toward me. "Let's git started, and you kin tell me all about yourself. And maybe another day you can help me gussie up the bathroom, too."

I took another gulp of lemonade and shuddered.

In spite of my qualms, I had a surprisingly good time helping Laura-Beth. As we scrubbed the wall, she told me her life story. As we lined up the border, she gave me her opinion on every current affair she could think of. As we wiped off the excess glue, she told me about her hope of opening her own beauty salon one day. The twang of her voice and swoosh of my sponge against the wall created music that soothed me. The simple, normal activity helped me avoid my demons for a few hours.

When I left, I was exhausted and eager to retreat to the safety of my own walls. But I took pride in adding this good deed to my Penny's Project notebook. *"Whatever you did for one of the least of these brothers of mine, you did for me."* Did Jesus need help with wallpapering? A smile teased my lips. Hard to say. But this was tangible progress by any standard. Who would be my target tomorrow?

# chapter 11

THE NEXT MORNING, JIM-BOB didn't wait for Bryan on the sidewalk. While I said my brief prayer for Bryan, Jim-Bob came right up to our steps. His gaze roamed the gutters, the tree, his shoes—everywhere but me. Something prompted me, and before my amen, I added a quick petition. "And bless Jim-Bob today, and thank you that he's our neighbor."

Jim-Bob's freckles pressed together in a face-squashing grin, while Bryan blinked at me in surprise. I watched the boys walk to the corner. Then I ducked back inside, locked the door, and trudged to the kitchen, where my notebook waited and Folgers brewed.

I poured a mug of coffee and settled at the table, paging through my notebook. I'd been ducking conversations with my mom, hiding behind voice messages and e-mails. She'd love for me to call—just to let her know I was thinking of her. After a deep breath, I punched in the number.

She answered on the second ring with a harried, "Hello."

I held my cup near my face fortifying myself with the smell of the steam. "Hi, Mom."

"Penny? Is it really you? I thought you never had time for the phone anymore."

I clenched my teeth and took a slow breath through my nose. "How's it going? How's Cindy doing?"

"Esther has colic. Cindy's worn out. I'm on my way over there now. And then I have a dentist appointment. You know, I thought things would slow down when I retired, but I'm always running. Oh, and the chamber of commerce meeting is tonight, and I promised to bring refreshments. They love my chocolate oatmeal bars. So you've been too busy to call all week?"

"I'm sorry about that."

Her tone softened. "Are you managing okay without Tom? I have a hard time when your dad takes a fishing trip for a week. I honestly don't know how you're going to last three whole months."

I felt a glimmer of warmth, a connection. How far could I build on this hint of understanding? Intimacy was a gift, and I wanted to offer my mom a gift today, the way the support group on Tuesday had given their honesty to me. "It's hard. I've been kind of . . . down."

Awkward pause. "What do you mean?"

"I've been tired all the time. I thought it was a flu bug, but it's more than that. I'm having trouble doing things. . . . I'm just . . . kind of not myself." The words slipped out like minnows and darted away.

She scooped them up. "You know what I always say. If you're down in the dumps, give the house a good cleaning. That'll cheer you right up."

"Yep. That's what you always say."

"My friend Janice was feeling blue last month and I told her all she needed was to get busy. Listen to happy music. Open the curtains. Try a little harder."

On the page with my mother's name, I doodled into my notebook. *Happy music, curtains, try harder*. My shoulders sagged. "You're probably right."

"You know it." The compassion I'd imagined disappeared behind the crisp commands of a drill sergeant. "Nobody likes a whiner. Besides, you have Bryan to keep you company and cheer you up. How is my darling grandson, anyway?"

I took my cue and brightly filled her in on Bryan's progress in school, his friends, and his upcoming play. After a little more chatting, I hung up and rested my head in my arms. This good deed had been more exhausting than helping Laura-Beth.

A month ago I might have spouted the same pep talk. I'd never had much patience with people moping through life and giving in to their moods. But that was before I'd felt the fierce power of a turbulent mind—the power to disrupt everything. Eating, sleeping, talking.

Alex had tried to tell me once. I hadn't understood. Hadn't tried to understand. Had my brother felt this? These fractures through the landscape of the brain? Had I tossed him the same thoughtless Band-Aids in the face of aching wounds?

A warm, grassy breeze slipped through the open kitchen window and lured me back to another summer day twenty years earlier.

"Don't tell me you understand!" Alex shouted the words with such force that spittle flew through the air. The tranquil wooden porch in front of our house couldn't offer him comfort. He didn't seem to see the towering oak tree with our old tire swing, or the broad lawn bright with clover and Creeping Charlie. He clutched his hair, shaking his head like a horse fighting a curb bit. "It's like ants crawling in my head, faster and faster."

Alex's depression of the past months had annoyed me. I was fourteen and clawing for some measure of popularity at the high school—I didn't need my seventeen-year-old brother moping around. His new descent into desperation terrified me. "Let me get Mom. She can call your doctor."

"It's not helping. Mom keeps telling me to try harder. And the doctors just talk and talk."

He sprang to his feet and ran into the house. The screen door slapped shut behind him.

Funny that after all these years, that sound remained a vivid memory.

*Oh, Alex, I didn't understand. I thought you were demanding more than your fair share of attention. I thought that since it left no physical marks on you, the depression couldn't be all that bad.*

Of course, the physical marks on my brother came later. Sunken, haunted eyes, weight gain from yet another medication that didn't work, pale skin as he withdrew from life. Immersed in my own adolescent selfishness, I'd resented all the trouble he was causing our family. Cindy had been young and oblivious, but I'd chafed against the way his mental illness disrupted my life.

At school, whispers stopped suddenly when I walked to my locker. I couldn't bring friends over. I missed pep band performances when my dad picked me up from school early because they had to take Alex to the hospital again.

Alone at my kitchen table so many years later, grief poured over me, and I begged the memories to carry me further back to happier times.

Alex had been the one to teach me to ride my bike. Dad was busy at the store the summer I was seven, and Mom couldn't push a bike in her low-heeled pumps and tailored shirtdress. Appearance had always been vital to her, and jogging down the street of our small town with her scrape-kneed daughter shrieking from the bike seat was not on her priority list. Alex didn't care who was watching. He owned the street. He owned the world. "Come on, Pen. Work those pedals!" I wobbled and tilted and flew. I could still hear his whoop of triumph as he let me go. I got all the way past the Olsons' porch before tipping over.

---

Saturday morning I sat at the kitchen table again with my notebook, and stared out the screen door. The Penny's Project idea had merit, but I needed some creative ideas before I ran out of the people I knew and had easy access to. Bryan was out back, swinging on a rope Tom had hung from a gnarled tree branch. His feet skimmed the tall grass as he experimented with different ways to dangle. Maybe I shouldn't have resisted Tom's repeated attempts to teach me to start the mower before he left. The grass had definitely gotten too long.

Since I didn't have a goat, I really needed to tackle the problem. My budget was stretched thin because of all the ordering in I'd been doing, and the thought of interviewing neighbor kids to hire exhausted me.

I could figure out how to start a mower. How hard could it be? I pulled on my tennis shoes and pushed a gardening hat over my unruly hair. Mowing the lawn could be my good deed for the whole neighborhood and fill another day's slot in my notebook.

The metal shed door shrieked in protest as I slid it open. A coiled hose snarled my ankle. When I kicked it free, I bumped a pile of tomato cages that tipped over and scraped my shins. I finally wrestled the small mower out to the lawn.

I'd seen Tom do this a hundred times. I studied the machine and found the string that he always yanked on. I gripped it and pulled. It refused to move. *Wait.* The grip bar at the handle must play a role. I squeezed and held it and pulled the string again.

Success. This time the string pulled out and curled back in.

But the engine didn't start.

I rolled my shoulder a few times, got a firm hold on the string, and jerked hard.

A halfhearted sputter answered me from the mower. I let go and walked around the mower, studying it from every angle.

Bryan leapt from his swing with a thud and ran over to me. "Dad always pushes that button." He pointed to a small black button on the body of the machine.

"Okay, buddy. Thanks." I pushed it a few times, then gripped the handle, squeezed, and yanked the string. It took the coordination of a circus magician, but this time I achieved a throaty growl. I grinned at Bryan.

The growl died.

"Maybe it's out of gas." My son kicked the rusty red body of the machine.

"How can you tell?"

Bryan pointed to a cap on the side of the body. After a few minutes of wrestling I got it loose and peered into the dark innards of the tank. "I see something sloshing. I think. I can't tell."

"Here." Bryan handed me a twig.

I dipped it into the tank and pulled it free, trying to look intelligent as I studied it. "Yep. I think it's low. Well, so much for that idea."

"Can I come with you to buy gas?"

I pushed the mower back to the shed. "I changed my mind. I'm not going to mow today." I hunted through the shed and found some clippers. "But I can do some trimming."

So I set to work along the edge of the fence between our yard and Laura-Beth's. Then I hand-trimmed another six inches of the yard out from the fence. Our yard wasn't too big. If I kept clipping, I wouldn't need to go to the gas station to fill the gas can.

An hour later, I sank to the ground rubbing my aching back. Was I actually so desperate to avoid going to the gas station that I would try to cut my whole lawn with a pair of clippers? I wasn't sure what the medical definition of crazy was these days, but I suspected this qualified.

"Is that how folks cut grass in Wisconsin?" Laura-Beth leaned on the chain-link fence. One of the twins held her frowzy skirt and sucked his thumb. The other toddled a short path back and forth like a caged tiger.

I dropped the clippers and pushed my sweaty hair off my forehead. "The lawn mower ran out of gas."

She opened her mouth, and I knew what was coming. The obvious question. *What idiot doesn't know how to go buy some gasoline?*

"Hey, I think we've got some in our shed. Let me check."

Minutes later Laura-Beth and her twins gathered to watch while I carefully poured gas into the mower. After a few tries, the motor started. Everyone cheered, including me.

"Can Bryan come over and play with Jim-Bob?" Laura-Beth yelled over the engine.

I nodded and they all cleared out and left me to my yard work.

That night I made a simple stir-fry for supper. Bryan waved his arms as he talked, even with his fork in his hand. By the time the meal was finished, rice littered the whole room, as if we'd hosted a wild wedding reception.

"Tomorrow is Sunday school, right?" Bryan looked up from hiding a broccoli spear under the edge of his plate.

Sunday already? I began picking up stray pieces of rice from the table, one by one. I couldn't avoid it forever. Getting involved at the church was one of the goals in my notebook that I'd put off for too long. "Yep, I guess so."

"Can I invite Jim-Bob?"

"Not this time. Okay, sport? Maybe some other time. It's time for your bath."

He gave me an arch look. "Know what? If I had a pet, it could take a bath with me. Wouldn't that be cool?"

"We'll talk about it when your father gets home."

I collapsed on the couch a few hours later. Bryan was asleep, the kitchen was picked up, and the quiet began to oppress me. I flicked on the television. Infomercial. News. Crass comedy show. Infomercial. Sports highlights.

I hauled myself off the couch and pawed through our small collection of movies on the shelf. The glint of the unlabeled DVD caught my eye.

*No. Not yet.* There were still so many weeks before his return.

Instead I booted up the computer and typed an answer to Tom's last e-mail.

*Hey there, favorite husband.*

*Okay, I guess it makes sense that you planned to tell me about the DVD if I didn't mention finding it. But your plan was still risky. We could have stuck it in a Netflix envelope and mailed it off by mistake. Crazy man.*

*Guess what? I mowed the lawn today. Okay, stop laughing. With this crazy warm weather, it was turning into a pasture, and I figured if you could do it all these years, so could I. Yes, I should have let you train me in, but it didn't take me long to figure it out (with Bryan's help). But don't worry about your job security around here. I'll be happy to relinquish the chore when you're back.*

*I'm glad to hear you've finished your initial visits to each of the crew at their stations. I know it must be hard to know if you're making a difference, but you are. How do I know? Because you make everyone around you stronger.*

*Thanks for the blessing in your second message. And for telling me you're praying. Don't worry. It didn't sound like a platitude. It helped.*

*I guess I can admit it has been a little hard to figure out where God fits in all this. And not just the crime. The war, your deployment, the other people who have had to deal with trauma. Raises a lot of questions. But tomorrow Bryan and I will be going back to church. Maybe God will whisper some answers to me.*

*Hurry back before you forget how to mow the lawn.*

*Inappropriate kisses, your favorite copper-top.*

# chapter 12

HOPE COMMUNITY CHURCH SAT demurely in the center of a wide lawn. The simple, modern building held only a few hundred members. Yet to me it loomed huge; the number of people hurrying in from the parking lot seemed overwhelming.

"Come on, Mom." Bryan bounced from foot to foot. "There's my teacher."

"I'm coming." I forced myself to follow my son to his Sunday school room. Bryan's teacher, a young woman with stubby pigtails, was rushing to set out craft supplies around the table.

Fighting my instinct to flee, I stepped into the room. "Can I help?"

Bryan's teacher looked up and smiled. "Thanks. You're a lifesaver. I'm running late again, and if I don't have everything in place before a dozen second-graders descend, the whole hour is chaos."

"Tell me about it. I only have one, but he keeps me hopping."

I tweaked Bryan's nose and reached for a coffee can of crayons and distributed them around the table.

Bryan went to a chart on the wall and studied the gold stars. "See, Mom. I missed three." He turned to his teacher. "It wasn't my fault."

"I'm sure God understands." Her pigtails stood at attention as she grinned. She thrust a pile of construction paper into my arms.

By the time I had dealt out a generous variety, more seven-year-olds scampered into the room, and I ducked away.

I made my way toward the sanctuary, careful to avoid eye contact with other parents delivering their children to classrooms. The narthex was crowded, and everyone seemed to know each other. The happy chatter grated on my nerves, and I dodged around a few clumps of people and slipped into the back of the church.

Usually, a deep sense of homecoming descended on me every time I went to a Sunday service. Even when we had first moved here and visited, I felt embraced by the worship time and welcomed into the fold like a long-lost cousin, part of the body—the mysterious interconnection of roles. But in the past weeks, I'd stopped being a useful part of this organic community.

Now I was a gangrened limb that deserved to be cut off.

My stomach burned. To comfort myself I opened my shoulder bag and pulled out my notebook and pen. *Sunday—helped Bryan's teacher set up for class.*

The sourness in my throat retreated. Sitting here was beyond uncomfortable, but I was doing it. And my project gave me at least a glimmer of hope. I was beginning a slow climb out of my lonely pit.

Music swelled for the opening hymn, and I stood with everyone else. This morning, Tom was on a destroyer leading a small group of sailors in worship just like this. Back home, my parents, sister, and friends were all turning their thoughts to our Creator and Savior. A sense of community routed my loneliness, even though I knew no one around me. Maybe instead of amputation, the infusion of grace from worship would bring healing to the wounded limb that I'd become.

The pastor stood and welcomed the congregation. Then, as he had the other times we'd visited, he asked everyone to greet one another. I shook hands with a bearded old man sitting in front of me. Then I turned to greet the person who had slid in from the other side of my pew.

Stringy bangs, dark hair, red-rimmed eyes. The young man gripped my hand.

My smile froze, and liquid nitrogen surged through my veins. *It's not him, Penny. It's not.*

But he looked like him. That was enough. Too much. I backed out of the pew and made it the few steps to the door. Good thing I'd sat in the back of the church.

Casting aside the last of my control, I raced across the narthex and out into the morning sunshine. Over a landscaped berm, a city park stretched toward a pond. The play equipment was blissfully empty. I kept running until I reached a small picnic shelter. I dropped onto a metal bench and buried my face in my hands. My body spasmed as if I'd touched a high-voltage wire.

*Oh, God, oh, God, oh, God. Make it stop.*

Horrible minutes passed while my body responded to a panic so deep I had no hope of controlling it. I feared I'd pass out. Then I hoped I'd pass out. Anything to make this crawling terror vacate my body. For a long time the physical sensations dominated my mind, blocking out rational thought. When those burned away and I could think again, my first thought was black despair. I couldn't even sit through a church service. How on earth was I going to receive the spiritual help that was part of my "healing checklist"?

My blouse was damp from the cold sweat that tried to purge the fear from my pores. All my muscles felt heavy and limp. My head ached.

Dr. Marci had warned me to expect setbacks. But now that I'd identified the post-traumatic stress, I'd expected to have power over it. I'd also thought that my project would help me leap forward into well-adjusted normalcy.

Normal? I didn't even know what that looked like anymore. When the hour was up, I slipped into the church, grabbed Bryan, and hurried home.

---

Tuesday night I actually looked forward to the victim support meeting. I needed to know that I wasn't the only person who was having trouble functioning on planet Earth. I'd sent a card to another of my Wisconsin Moms In Touch friends for my Monday random kindness, and was running out of people to help. So Tuesday I decided to reach out to Henry.

When he entered the conference room, I handed him a small bag.

He looked inside and gave me a crooked smile. "Wow. Thanks. This is really nice of you."

"What is it?" Ashley drawled. Skin flushed with a combination of sheepishness and appreciation, he showed her what Bryan and I had collected all week: gum wrappers.

"So, Penny. How was your week?" Dr. Marci's questions caused all eyes to turn to me.

I slumped lower in my chair. This still wasn't comfortable, but I felt a little more prepared to open up. "Not great. Thursday I helped my neighbor put up wallpaper, but the next day I had a rough phone call and got pretty depressed. Saturday I managed to cut the lawn, but Sunday I freaked out at church and couldn't stay."

"One day at a time. They said it at drug rehab until I wanted to scream, but it's true." Ashley pushed up one of her sleeves and turned her forearm toward me. Fine scars tracked across her skin, but none were fresh.

I understood. "You had a good week."

She sniffed and tried to hide her grin, but we all saw it. Camille applauded lightly. "Way to go."

"And how was your week?" Dr. Marci turned to Camille.

The door nudged open before Camille could answer. We all watched as it eased another few inches. A man's caramel-brown face peeked into the room and then withdrew. Dr. Marci stood and gestured toward Camille. "Go ahead. I'll be right back."

This group had the gift of not finding anything strange. That alone made this a safer place for me than the "real world." Our discussion continued, and I was genuinely excited to hear about Henry's job interview and Camille's progress at finding a new place to live.

Ten minutes later the door swung open and Dr. Marci coaxed the slight, elderly man into the room. "Daniel, this is Penny. She just joined us last week." He dropped his chin and gripped the back of a chair as if trying to anchor himself. I could see the quiet tension of his muscles, the yearning to run.

The others greeted him warmly but gently, as if he would bolt at any sudden noise.

"So what were you discussing?" Dr. Marci sat down and expertly drew focus away from Daniel. As Camille talked about the apartment she'd found, Daniel gradually eased into the room and took a seat.

A week ago these people had seemed a troubling mirror of

what I was becoming. Victims, yes, but also misfits who hadn't been able to bounce back. But now I saw a courageous woman finally deciding she wouldn't let the man she loved hit her anymore, and a girl with a horrific past who had depths of compassion hidden behind her piercings and vampire makeup, a lonely man who had climbed and fallen and was trying to find his footing. And now, Daniel.

"Daniel, tell us about your week." Dr. Marci pitched her voice low and calm.

"I . . . I didn't go out much," he whispered. Then he brightened. "Sammy's doing better, though."

*His imaginary friend?*

"His dog," Henry explained.

Daniel nodded. "Samson. Sammy for short. He had an ear infection. But it's better now."

Dr. Marci leaned forward. "Dan, you and Penny have some things in common."

He stared at the floor.

"So when are you going to really tell us about what happened?" Ashley braced her chin on her fists and raised an eyebrow stud at me.

I felt the challenge. Could I go there? Was I ready?

Dr. Marci nodded.

I sucked in a deep breath. "It was the dumbest thing."

Henry barked a laugh. "That's always how it starts."

I smiled wryly. "I suppose so. It's just that I keep thinking about how different things would be if I hadn't been craving a Coke."

"Coke?" Ashley straightened up.

"A Coke. A soda."

"Oh." She sat back, her flare of interest dampened.

"That's what I mean. It was so silly. We'd been unpacking

boxes." I turned toward Daniel. "We're new to the area. It was so hot, so I told Tom I'd run down to the Quick Corner and get a Coke Slurpee for us to share. It was the middle of the afternoon."

My stomach clenched. "Somehow that made it worse. The bright sunshine. Violence is supposed to happen in the dark, you know."

The understanding murmurs around the table gave me courage. "So I grabbed my purse, hopped in the car, and drove about a mile. I was in the store. You know, looking at the candy bars and telling myself I was trying to eat healthier."

I closed my eyes as I talked, and traveled back to the display of junk food. Snickers? Milky Way Dark? Or some healthy trail mix with sunflower seeds and raisins? An elderly couple came through the aisle, and I edged away to give them room. The woman had tight white curls and gave me a bright smile. She carried a store basket over one arm. Her other hand was tucked in the elbow of the man who walked slowly, planting his cane with each careful step.

"Florence, just make up your mind." Affectionate teasing filled his raspy voice. "If you pick a Ding Dong today, you can still get a Snowball tomorrow."

She giggled and slanted a look toward him like an eighty-year-old Scarlett O'Hara. "Let's be really wild and get Twinkies."

He laughed and grabbed a two-pack of Twinkies, a Ding Dong, and a Snowball and put them all in her basket.

"Why, Stanley, you're spoilin' me."

"Hmph." A dimple appeared on his weathered cheek as he fought back a smile.

They headed to the front of the store, as I imagined Tom and me in fifty years, arm in arm, making our daily trek to the corner store for a treat, comfortable in a lifetime of bickering, teasing, living, and loving. I smiled and crouched down to grab some red licorice for Tom.

The bells jingled at the door. The old-fashioned sound transported me to the general store of Mayberry. *I could get used to this friendly Virginia neighborhood.*

"The money. Now." The harsh order near the front of the store was so incongruous that I froze, kneeling behind the candy aisle.

The young African-American woman at the cash register gasped. "Okay, okay. Take it easy. Here."

My sluggish brain began to make sense of the conversation. Still crouched, I crept to the end of the row. On the other side of a display of Slim Jims, a teen brandished a gun. His stringy hair hung limp beneath his baseball cap. My heart battered my chest and breath choked in my throat.

*A gun? This can't be happening. Someone do something.*

The old couple stood near the counter. Stiff. Trembling as if Parkinson's had captured their bodies. The woman gripped her husband's arm with both hands now, the red plastic basket still slung over her arm.

*Oh, God, oh, God, oh, God. Help us.*

The cashier pulled out bills and stacked them neatly as if she were helping a customer. "Here. That's all there is."

He swore and waved the gun wildly. "Come on. You've gotta have more. What about your purse?"

I caught a glimpse of his face as he threw a wild glance around the store. Drug-crazed, angry, barely touching reality.

*Get help. Get help.*

If I could back out and call the police—

My arm bumped a shelf, and a few peppermint sticks slipped from an overstocked box and hit the floor with a clatter.

The boy swung around. Time fragmented in a series of freeze-frames. At the counter, the clerk covered her mouth with both hands, capturing her silent scream. The gun fired before the boy completed his pivot. Once. Twice. The blast hurt my ears. Not the light pops of television-drama gunfire.

The elderly woman lurched. Her arm flinched inward as if protecting the Twinkies in the red plastic basket. Then she fell back against the shelves. The row of magazines wavered.

Cordite—the scent that rises from the corner of the park where fireworks are set off on the Fourth of July—filled the air. More sharp cracks.

*No, no, no! This isn't real. Someone help us!*

The husband collapsed downward, one hand reaching toward his wife. His cane clattered to the linoleum. She continued to fall, sliding down the row of magazines and to the floor. Issues of *Redbook* cascaded down around her.

The gun swung in my direction. "Look what you made me do! I'm gonna kill you!" His red-rimmed eyes didn't seem human. He was a caricature. Wild, slavering, twitching. The face burned into my memory. Hatred, contempt, and a level of desperation I couldn't understand. Even in my shock and terror, a tiny corner of my mind pitied him.

Then he squeezed the trigger and I closed my eyes to die.

# chapter 13

"IT JAMMED." I TWISTED a tissue in my hands. When had tears begun to slide down my face? "The elderly couple died because of me. I should have died, too." My breath hitched in my lungs. "I should have died *instead*. Not them."

I finally dared to look up. Ashley's mascara traced smudges down her face. Camille's eyes were full. Henry shook his head sadly. Daniel watched me with deep brown eyes that matched his skin. He didn't pull his gaze away. "We're . . . glad . . . you didn't die."

He said the quiet words with effort, which made them an even greater gift.

My nose started to run, and I blotted it with the tissue. "Sorry. I didn't mean to fall apart."

"That's why we're here." Dr. Marci passed me another tissue, then looked at the others. "Penny's come up with a creative project." Her gaze returned to me. "Would you share it with the group?"

Did they really want ideas from a frazzled mom with puffy eyes and a red nose?

"Let's hear it," Ashley demanded.

I couldn't back away from her challenge. Briefly, I explained my Internet research, and my goal to do something kind for a new person each day, and how it forced me to make a few connections with others.

"Smart," Henry declared, the bags under his eyes shrinking as he smiled. "Every time I try to get motivated to get a new job or meet new people, I think of a million reasons not to. But this could help me get out there."

"I like it." Camille crossed her hands elegantly on the table. She still wore her wedding ring, but she had held strong to her resolve not to run back to her husband this week. "At the shelter, it's easy to get all wrapped up in my own issues. But there're a lot of other people who could use some encouragement."

"Let's all do it. Okay?" Ashley tilted her chair back on two legs. "Worth a try."

Henry shifted in his chair. "Oh, I don't know about that—"

"Come on," Ashley growled. "You gonna let Pollyanna here show you up?"

He adjusted his tie. "No. I'll do it if you will."

Whoa. I hadn't meant to start something here. "But I didn't . . . I mean . . ." I tried to explain that my little project wasn't a universal cure for trauma. They ignored me and jabbered about people they planned to target during the coming week. The project had taken on a life of its own. I glanced at Dr. Marci.

"Thank you," she mouthed over the chatter.

Great. Now I was stuck with the idea. And I had no clue how to find someone to help tomorrow.

Daniel had remained fairly quiet. "Is it . . . all right . . . if it's a stranger?" His gentle voice startled everyone. Heads did a Wimbledon swing to Daniel and then to me.

I returned the serve with an easy lob. "Of course."

Now I'd just need to figure out how to cross paths with strangers while staying safely on my living room couch.

---

Wednesday night, Bryan and I walked to the New Life Mission. I wasn't sure what motivated me to overcome my powerful impulse to stay in the house and instead venture to their evening service. Maybe it was easier than coming up with any other diversion for Bryan's seven-year-old restlessness. Maybe I longed for the fellowship I'd missed on Sunday. Maybe I needed to connect with some new people for my project.

Mild October air carried the scent of stale french fries from a local fast-food store and the heavy sweetness of dryer sheets as we passed the huge vents of the Laundromat. My son was delighted for any outing and buzzed around me happily. Even with that distraction, my muscles tightened as a man passed us across the street and later when a group of preteens galloped by with a basketball.

"Is the park near here?" Bryan stared after them and rubbed his hands.

"I haven't found it yet." I hurried toward the dented door of the mission, which was propped open.

He scowled. "You haven't looked."

Instead of following the course of that argument, I pressed my hand against his back and steered him inside. There was no way for me to slip in unobtrusively, since Lydia and Barney hovered near the door greeting people as they arrived.

"Penny! Good to see you again." Lydia leaned forward and offered her hand to Bryan.

I nudged Bryan and he shook her hand. "This church smells funny."

Barney rubbed a hand over his mouth and sent a wink my direction. "Well, lookie what the wind blew in. Glad you're back. In for a Penny, in for a pound, eh?" Glee creased his whiskered face, then he turned to call a greeting to a passerby.

Bryan plopped onto one of the folding chairs in the back row, behind a scattering of about twenty people. I scanned the room, relieved to see old women, a few younger women with children, and only a couple of elderly men. No young men. No baseball caps. I settled into the aisle chair beside Bryan.

"You came." Camille squeezed past us and sat beside my son. "It's good to see you."

Bryan quickly launched into a description of his recess soccer game that day, and Camille's smile grew broader.

Barney walked up the aisle in his rolling gait and leafed through a tattered hymnal. Lydia followed him, stopping to pat my shoulder and smile. My face heated as I thought of how unstable I must have seemed last time I'd been here. I suddenly realized she'd never asked for explanations. She hadn't demanded information about who I was or why I was struggling. She had simply prayed for me and helped me home. Even after I told her about the crime, she didn't pry. It was as if she understood that each person she met would have wounds—some hidden, some on the surface—and the name of the wound wasn't a high concern for her. During the past weeks, I'd hated bearing the label of victim, or post-traumatic-stress sufferer, or lonely Navy wife. Here I wasn't labeled. I was simply Penny from the neighborhood.

"Let's sing." Barney led out in a gravelly rendition of "What a Friend We Have in Jesus" that brought an unexpected clog to my throat. Wobbly, elderly voices rose in approximate pitches, and warmth rubbed my skin. After a few more unsteady hymns, Lydia stood in front of the painted cross, opened her pocket Bible, and preached with a ferocity that pulled me to the forward edge of my chair. For a while, her words soothed my soul like aloe on a sunburn. I wanted to soak in the comfort, but was distracted by Bryan's squirms, and the equally squirmy unease that twisted my nerve endings whenever I was out in public. Part of me screamed to run home and bolt the door. But at least a small part of me was able to savor these minutes of touching the real world.

Barney followed Lydia with a time of prayer and an invitation to come up and talk to him about any needs or other "God stuff." Camille and I stood by the back row of chairs and talked briefly while Bryan explored and the room slowly emptied. The dark sky outside the propped-open door worried me. We needed to get home.

But I was slowed again because Lydia hovered in the lounge area between the rows of chairs and the front door.

"Thank you." I edged around her and beckoned for Bryan. "This was . . . amazing. How long have you been working here?" I asked.

She patted the shoulder of an old woman who shuffled past. "About two years. We're sponsored by the Presbyterian district office. We hold services on Sunday and Wednesday nights, distribute clothes, and fill in the gaps when the local food shelf runs low. But mostly, we're here to listen. Listen to what the Lord wants us to do. Listen to what people need."

I nodded and shifted a half-step closer to the door. "Oh, thanks for recommending the victim center."

She smiled. "I saw you chatting with Camille. Is the group helping?"

"A little. And I also figured out a project to help me get past this. I'm trying to find someone to help each day."

Her smile grew. Her eyes reminded me of the poster of Jesus' face hanging over my teacher's head in third-grade Sunday school. Same soft kindness and burning intensity mixed together.

I braced my shoulders. "I figure if I fill the next two months with good deeds, I'll be back to normal by the time Tom is home from his deployment."

Her eyes narrowed as she studied me. "Can I offer you a thought?"

"Sure." *Everybody else does.*

"Let the Lord show you who He's wantin' your help with. You don't have to be doin' this in your own power, you know."

My project was the one thing I'd been getting right. Was she implying I wasn't letting God lead me? Who was she to criticize the way I was working out my healing? "I guess I didn't look at it that way. I've sort of—"

"Sermon time is over, Lydia. Time to give it a rest." Barney lumbered up from the center aisle.

Lydia rounded on him. "Why did you make us sing 'Jesus, Savior, Pilot Me' again? I've been tellin' you no one knows that song."

"Anyone with an ounce of salt water in their veins understands that hymn." Barney lifted his bristly chin to confront Lydia's regal height. She was only an inch taller than him, but her posture made her seem even taller.

I glanced at my watch. "I'd better be going. It's almost Bryan's bedtime."

Lydia and Barney paused in their squabbling to stare at me. "Do you need help finding your house again?" Lydia asked.

Heat crawled up from my neck. "No, thanks. I've got it figured out."

Barney looked at me closely, and behind the Popeye roughness, his eyes held concern. He ran a hand over his head and tugged his ear. “Lydia, you been bossing people again? She looks a little put out.”

“No,” I said quickly. “Your wife was just giving me some suggestions for a project I’m doing.”

He stared at me blankly for a beat. Then he hooted. “*Wife*? Lord, spare me.”

Lydia’s eyes grew round, white flaring around her brown irises. Then she started to laugh, too.

Barney sank onto the edge of the coffee table and grabbed it for support as his whole body shook with chuckles. “I probably deserve to suffer in a lot of ways, but thank heaven that’s not one of them. It’s bad enough working with her.” But affection flecked his eyes as he glanced at her.

The fire in my face threatened to scorch the roots of my hair. “I’m sorry. I thought . . . and the way you argue . . . and . . .”

“Barney is a volunteer from our church.” Lydia fumbled with a large cross pin on her blazer lapel. She tried to look affronted, but a mahogany blush darkened her cheeks. “When you do this kind of work, you take what you can get.”

“Gal, anyone who can put Miss Saint in her place is welcome here. You’ll come back, right?”

I looked at the two odd missionaries: the scruffy, short, white man with a gift for grousing, and the polished, erect, African-American woman with a penchant for bossing. “I will.”

---

Thursday morning, two Pennys were back in Dr. Marci’s office for my appointment. One Penny crossed her legs and balanced an open notebook on her knee, desperate to take any road that would help me heal. The other Penny sat fence-post stiff, willing to move forward but only if it didn’t involve looking back.

Dr. Marci sipped coffee at her desk and jumped right to the

topic I wanted to avoid. "So have the police updated you? Have they caught him?"

How was hashing everything through with her going to help me forget it? This whole thing was backward. "No, and no."

"Does that frustrate you?"

Answers weren't easy in a counseling session. Any comment could lead to deeper revelations. How did I feel? Such a complex question. "Honestly?"

"Of course."

"I'm relieved. I want it to go away. If they catch him, I might have to identify him. Maybe testify." I wasn't a brave crusader. I wanted to pretend the whole thing never happened. Shame soured in my stomach—the way it had that day.

"Ma'am, can you describe him?" the policewoman had tapped the end of her ballpoint pen against a small notepad. I was sitting on the curb next to a stack of bottled water and a pallet of motor oil. Most of the activity was inside the store, behind us. Police voices murmured, and someone was setting up cones and waving cars away from the pumps.

I had strained to remember, but my brain couldn't lock on to anything important. Instead I saw vivid images of tennis shoes, without laces, their tongues flapping open. "It all happened so fast. Baseball cap—black, maybe dark blue. Long hair, stringy. He was white, pale. His hair was really dark. Young. So young."

"How tall was he?"

"I . . . I don't know. I was on my knees looking up, so it's hard to say. How are they?" I knew the answer. I'd knelt by their bodies, tried to stop the blood, and gripped the dear woman's cold hand while we waited for the police. But I held on to hope that they would be revived. I turned and tried to see past the policewoman into the store where paramedics crouched beside the old couple.

Her professional mask stayed firmly in place. "Did you know them?"

I shook my head. How could I explain? I didn't know them, but I knew them. Knew that they smiled at strangers. Knew that they teased each other. Knew that she had a breathy laugh, and he had a dimple. Knew that they were what I hoped Tom and I would be one day. Knew that it was my fault they'd been shot.

A few yards away, the young cashier answered the same questions, her voice shrill and animated. "He was whacked out, man. I'm tellin' you. The guy was flyin'. I handed him the cash, but he was yelling, and then he started shooting. Don't know what set him off." She cursed and tossed her beaded braids back.

"It was me." My throat was hoarse as if I'd actually released all the screams this scene deserved. "It was my fault. I made a noise and he panicked."

The policewoman jotted more notes. "Ma'am, sounds like the guy was already twitchy. Now I know you're shook up, but did you see if he had a car? When he ran out, did you hear an engine?"

"Call the morgue." One of the paramedics straightened and shook his head. Blood stained his gloves.

A mewling sound rose from my throat. "No. No, no, no."

"Is there someone you can call?"

Red lights circled in remorseless rhythm. Voices rose and fell. Summer heat bent the air as it rose from the blacktop near the pumps, thick with the odor of gasoline and stale hot dogs. After a few tries, I remembered our new phone number, and the police contacted Tom. By the time he arrived, my limbs had begun to tremble. The crime had sent an earthquake through my view of the world, and the aftershocks traveled right into my body.

"Before Tom got there, the policewoman gave me the card for this place." I lifted a hand to encompass Dr. Marci's office, and the whole dreary building. "I remember thinking it was so weird that the sun was still shining. You know how if you go to a movie theatre during the day, when you walk outside afterward, it seems weird? Like it should really be nighttime? Like so much time has gone by. Or maybe because you usually see movies at night and you're used to walking out to dark skies? It was like that. Everything had changed, but it was still bright. People kept driving past as if nothing had happened. That seemed so wrong."

I shifted restlessly in my chair. "Look, do you really think rehashing all of this will get rid of my panic attacks? That's my real problem."

"We'll talk about that next week. For now, you're doing great. Be gentle with yourself. Let your project help coax you forward, but don't push yourself too hard. Give yourself permission to take time to heal from this trauma."

"Yeah, yeah. Sleep, eat, exercise, reduce stress, blah, blah, blah."

Dr. Marci laughed at my sullenness. Apparently she took it as a good sign. Where did sarcasm fit in the stages of healing?

When I got home, I pulled out my notebook and wrote down anything helpful from my appointment that I could remember. The page with my list of good deeds held a large blank line for Thursday. I hadn't fulfilled my project for today. I should have brought Dr. Marci a muffin and counted her as my good deed. *Drat.*

Bryan wouldn't be home for three hours. I ought to be able to come up with something by then. I made a peanut butter sandwich and slouched at my kitchen table. I'd had little appetite these days, but with my limited activities I wasn't burning many calories anyway. The thought of soft drinks especially turned my stomach. If I hadn't been craving a Coke that night . . .

I pushed away from the table and grabbed my purse. I needed to get out and do something nice for someone. Then I could curl up on my safe couch and watch TV until Bryan got home. I'd had my fill of driving today and had nowhere to go anyway. So I walked down to the corner where Bryan's bus came each day. Unless I planned to do a good deed for a mangy squirrel or a couple of robins, I'd need to keep walking.

After another block, I reached a sign for the city bus. A young man was already sprawled on one end of the bench. He wore a baseball cap, which stalled me for a moment. But he was black, not the pasty Caucasian of the teen from the shooting. That was a plus. His Ruben Studdard–size shorts hung low on his skinny frame, showing a few inches of boxers. Dreadlocks dangled beneath the cap, covering his ears and reaching his shoulders.

I sat next to him, barely able to glance his direction. I felt as clumsy as I had at my first high-school dance, trying to start a conversation. "Sure is another nice day," I offered softly.

He nodded.

"I'm not used to the weather staying this warm into October. I'm from the Midwest. We get a few days of Indian summer, but nothing like this."

He bounced his chin a few more times. A man of few words—but he seemed friendly. Now, what kind thing could I do for him?

I gave another sideways peek. "I like your shirt." At least I liked the orange shirt with the turned-up collar better than his sagging shorts.

He didn't look at me, but he pursed his lips and nodded again. Then he leaned forward and looked down the street.

Okay, so the compliment hadn't made his day. What else could I do? I fished in my purse. "Here. I have an extra bus pass. I'm not going to use it."

Hampton Roads Transit had seemed like a great way to get around while I learned to navigate the unfamiliar streets. One of the routes through Chesapeake went straight to the Norfolk Navy base. But being trapped on a bus was even more terrifying than driving somewhere. At least in my own car, I could pull over if I started to hyperventilate or cry.

The young man ignored me.

"I said, you're welcome to use my Farecard. Honest. I don't need it anymore, and it's still got ten rides on it."

He wiped sweat from his forehead with the back of his hand and adjusted his cap. His head tilted away from his hunched-up collar, revealing a wire. An earbud flashed behind the dreadlocks.

The head bouncing suddenly made sense. He hadn't heard a word I'd said.

I sagged back against the bench. Another failure. Now what? I barely had the strength to drag myself back home, much less hunt for someone new.

Mustering a determination that was more desperation than courage, I tapped the man's arm.

He jumped and turned to look at me, pulling out his earbuds. Tinny music thrummed loudly enough for me to hear the beat. He glowered at me.

"I have an extra Farecard." I forced a weary smile and held out the pass. "Could you use it?"

"Why?" He glanced around as if this were *Candid Camera*, or maybe *America's Most Wanted.*

I shrugged. "Didn't want it to go to waste."

He still hesitated. How hard did I have to work to give something away? Good grief, people were suspicious these days.

"You're sure?" He reached out and touched the ticket gingerly, as if he feared a slap on his hand.

There was fun in baffling someone . . . surprising him with a random act of kindness. I grinned. "It's like that movie. *Pay It Forward*."

His laugh was low and rich, a James Earl Jones sound that resonated in his chest. He finally accepted the card from my hand. "I liked that movie. Thanks, ma'am." The bus pulled up, and he shouted his thanks again as he mounted the steps. The delight in his smile made me giggle.

Accomplishment flooded me. I stood and walked toward home with a lighter step. I'd won a triathlon. I'd gotten Bryan fed, clothed, and off to school. I'd endured a grueling counseling session and didn't play too much verbal dodge ball with Dr. Marci. Then I'd reached out to a stranger and brought him a smile. I deserved another message from Tom's DVD.

I hurried into the house and loaded the disc. Curtains drawn, pillows plumped, air-conditioner set on low, huge mug of chai tea, I made a ritual of my preparation. But when I hit Play, nothing happened.

Maybe I'd put the disc in upside down again. I popped it out and flipped it, hoping the messages from Tom would cooperate and appear. I couldn't soothe a wild stallion, but I'd become a DVD whisperer, coaxing the recording to play. Gnawing my lip, I waited for the visit with Tom that I so desperately needed.

MY COAXING WORKED, AND Tom's face grinned out at me. During our busy days of unpacking and settling in, I hadn't spent enough time just staring into his eyes, tracing the lines of his jaw, watching the earnest furrow deepen on his forehead, and enjoying the dimple full of mischief flicker across the right side of his lips.

I watched the first two messages, reciting some of the words with him. Once again, the blessing he spoke sent a tingle down my spine, as if gleams of God's countenance really could shine on me.

"Message three," Tom said. "This one—"

He paused, mouth partially open. The pause stretched beyond a moment of gathering thoughts. I held my breath, then let it out in a *whoosh* as I realized the recording had frozen. Our rented movies did the same sometimes, when a scratch or smudge interrupted the play. Bryan would forward past the bad section.

I tried Fast Forward but nothing moved. I hit Play again and again. Rewind did nothing. Then the screen went blank.

Not fair. So not fair. I pulled out the disc and babied it with glass cleaner and a soft cloth, removing any signs of fingerprints on either side. Still nothing. Even after I fiddled with the disc for several minutes, the finicky recording wouldn't give me any more. I growled and threw a pillow at the DVD player.

Stomping to the kitchen to start supper, I checked my voice mail. I'd decided to keep the ringer off, since the sudden sound of the phone still threw my anxiety into high gear.

My mom's voice held a querulous tone. "Are you so busy you can't even call within a week?"

Mary Jo, the ombudsman, remained determinedly cheerful. "You're not still fighting that virus, are you? We really need to connect. Call me."

My friend Sonja had talked fast and left a long, detailed summary of their dog's surgery, her kids' soccer games, and her frustration with one of the women on the committee for the church nursery. Her energy and wit used to make my day. Now listening to her felt exhausting.

Mrs. Pimblott left a friendly message wondering when I could meet with her about the Thanksgiving play.

I saved all the messages. Maybe I'd make a few calls tomorrow. Or not.

The last message opened with a crackle and a soft hiss. "Pen? It's Tom. I was hoping you'd be there."

I squeezed the receiver, wanting to wring each precious sound from it.

"I'm great. I've lost a little weight. No, I'm not seasick. Stop laughing. I was made for this. Look, I know we decided phone calls just made it harder, back when I was at basic. But I'm on the carrier today and had access. I couldn't resist. Your e-mails are great, but I sure would love to hear your voice. I'm riding the Holy Helo tomorrow—I'll be out visiting the destroyers."

Tom's energy and confidence resonated through the phone, and I could picture him with the rotors of the helicopter churning the air as he crouched and ran to board, ready to be carried to the next ship that needed a visit.

"How have you been?" His tone lowered to the gentle concern I'd grown to dread. I didn't want him to tiptoe around me. He was treating me the way everyone had always treated my brother. Did he think—?

"I'll e-mail soon. I probably won't try calling again unless I e-mail you first. Glad you like the DVD. Be sure to listen to message three. Give Bryan a big hug from me, and tell him I'm proud of him." I could almost feel the muscles of his arms flexing as they circled around me. "Still on target to get home for Thanksgiving. Love you."

And he was gone.

I replayed the message five times. Then I gave in to my heavy loneliness and crawled in bed for a nap. I'd been beating myself up for being tired all the time, but Dr. Marci said it was part of the healing process. Well, valid or not, I couldn't fight it anymore. My mind and body demanded to shut down.

At least I set the alarm clock this time. That woke me soon enough to shake off my woolly-headedness so I could greet Bryan like a normal mom when he came home from school.

He joined me in the kitchen to tell me about his day.

While we talked, I moved ahead on another tip from my notebook. "Okay, kiddo. Laura-Beth said that she makes grits all the time, and that's why her kids are so healthy. Hand me the kettle."

"Sounds weird. Grit? Like the stuff Dad used on our old driveway."

I punched an opening in the box and poured some into a measuring cup. "That was dry concrete mix, not grits."

"That *looks* weird, too. Are you sure we're supposed to eat it?"

"I'm sure it'll be great once we cook it."

He made a face. "Why don't we go to McDonald's?"

"Because we want to learn about living in the South."

"But Mom, they have McDonald's in the South. The bus goes past two of them on the way to school."

Bryan could engage me in a debate worthy of a top district attorney . . . on almost any topic. Like any good defense lawyer, I used one of my sharp legal skills: diversion. "Why don't you go out back and see if Jim-Bob wants to play soccer?"

He bounded away in a flash, relieved to escape further kitchen duty.

I studied the back of the box of grits. The basic recipe sounded awfully bland, but one for Cheddar Grits with Bacon caught my eye. I didn't have any bacon, but I had a jar of Bacos. That would work as a substitute. Instead of grated cheddar, I substituted a jar of Cheez Whiz. Close enough. I squinted at the print. A can of artichoke hearts? Good grief. I wasn't Rachael Ray.

Instead, I pulled a bag of broccoli from the freezer. Following the instructions, I brought some chicken broth to a boil and stirred in the grits. Then I mixed in all the other ingredients, poured it into a baking dish, and popped it in the oven. It smelled pretty good. However, the texture was runny, so I upped the temperature on the oven a little, and instead of an hour, I set the timer for ninety minutes to be sure the concoction thoroughly cooked.

Then I ventured out to the back steps to watch Bryan. Laura-Beth was in her yard, hanging up white T-shirts and Ray's immense boxers. Not the scenic view I longed for.

Her eyes were sharper than I'd realized, because when she turned from clipping some tube socks to the line, she spotted me.

"Howdy, neighbor!" Clothespins spewed from her mouth and she beelined for our fence.

I hoisted myself up and walked over to meet her. "Is your dryer broken?"

She laughed. "Why run the *eee*-lectricity when the sun can do the work? I noticed you don't hang out your laundry."

I looked at our yard. "I guess we don't have a clothes pole."

She squinted. "Well, if that don't beat all. Never noticed before. Too bad you didn't catch that before you bought the house. Well, I guess you can string something between the house and your tree. That'd do ya."

Sure. I'd get right on that. I'd love to give the neighbors a show of my unmentionables.

"So, I saw you down to the corner when I was driving back from the Kmart with the twins. At the bus stop. Is your car broke?"

I didn't want to explain my project to Laura-Beth. "No, I was just . . . sitting there for a while."

She twisted her mound of frowzy hair into a knot and clipped it with a clothespin. "Well now, I hope you don't mind some advice . . ."

I'd lost count of how many of her conversations opened with that line.

"You wanna be careful. We have a lot of crime around here. You know what I mean?"

Laura-Beth waved and headed back to her laundry basket. The words she'd said swirled around my head—an incantation to conjure memories. Bloodshot eyes. A voice snarling and spitting curses. Tense angles on a frenzied face under a baseball cap.

I raced into the house to splash cold water on my face. My hands paused under the flow of liquid, and I studied them. My fingers didn't look very different from those that had clenched the gun: slender, with pale skin and chewed nails. I couldn't dismiss him as an aberration. Whatever he'd done, he had been a human. As much as I tried to define his actions as animalistic, the fact remained he was once a little boy like Bryan. He'd drawn pictures of dragons and knights and built castles of Legos. He'd kicked a soccer ball around a backyard. One day he'd shot two people, tried to kill me, and then run into the sunny afternoon.

Sadness poured over me. I let myself feel the despair. Dr. Marci had encouraged me to stop shutting down my thoughts. She said that as emotions were stirred up, I should feel them, process them, and come to terms with them.

But they were as unwelcome as my meddlesome neighbor. Still, I opened the door and invited them to stay for tea. I agreed with them that the crime was a horrible, tragic example of what people were capable of. And slowly, the feelings thanked me for the sandwiches and took their leave.

The timer on the stove beeped loudly.

Maybe Laura-Beth's culinary suggestions were more helpful than her warnings about the dangers of our neighborhood.

Bryan, ears always tuned for the sound of imminent food, barreled into the house. While he washed up, I lifted the casserole from the oven and set it on the kitchen table.

The orange-tinted lump didn't look at all like the picture on the box. I poked it with a fork, and the tines couldn't pierce it. Bryan had been right. Apparently grits were the same thing used to make concrete driveways.

*Hi, Tom-o-my-heart,*

*It was wonderful hearing your voice today. I played the message again and again. Sorry I wasn't home. I was out for a walk. I've been experimenting with southern cooking, so I'll have some new recipes for you to try when you get home. But tonight Bryan and I decided to keep it simple and have bologna sandwiches. I'm glad you got your sea legs right away. I was wondering how well you'd be able to preach the Gospel while doubled over the rail. LOL! Are you ever . . . scared? Yes, yes. I know we are always in God's hands. But I just wondered. Do you ever worry when the ship heads into hostile waters?*

*Come home soon. I need you to take your turn at tucking in Bryan. Tonight he begged for* Hop on Pop, *and my tongue still hasn't untangled. We finished up with some of the* Rootabaga Stories, *since those are your favorite.*

*I watched the first two messages again today. They helped a lot. But then the disc locked up. Don't roll your eyes at me. I pushed all the right buttons, and even cleaned the thing. If I don't get it to play, you'll have to call again and tell me what you said, okay?*

*Remember your promise. You ARE coming home safe, aren't you?*

*Two million hugs, Pen*

IN SPITE OF MY failure with the grits, I woke on Friday with a distant star of optimism flickering in my heart. During the past week I'd begun to join the human race again—the support group, the worship service at the mission, my small good deeds that forced interaction with people. And nightmares had only woken me twice last night. A huge improvement.

I pulled on a crisp blouse and my best jeans, fastened my hair back with a shiny barrette, and even touched some mascara to my lashes.

"How come you're all dressed up?" Bryan asked, digging into his instant oatmeal.

"I thought I'd drive you in to school today and chat with your teacher a little."

His eyebrows disappeared under his mop of bangs. "Am I in trouble?"

"Should you be?" I hid a smile.

He reached for the jam. "The gum in Chelsea's hair was Aidan's fault, not mine."

I glanced at my watch. Too bad I didn't have time to pull a few more interesting tidbits from my son. "I've been exchanging messages with your teacher, and I thought it would be a good idea to touch base. And I feel up to it today."

An inner debate played across his face. Hooray, Mom was acting like a mom again. On the other hand, it was safer when moms and teachers didn't collude. He decided on a grin. "Then she can give you the stuff about the play."

Some of my confidence fled. I swallowed the last of my coffee and stood. "Let's go, buddy. And tell me more about the gum in Chelsea's hair."

The squat grade school right-angled a generous playground full of sand and climbing equipment, while green wedges of landscaping marked off the parking lot and softened the line of the chain-link fence behind the property. Children in sweatshirts and jackets rocketed skyward on swings, whooped along a sliding bar, and raced around the curly slide and suspension bridge.

"Here, Mom. I'll meet you inside." Bryan tossed me his backpack and raced to a geodesic jungle gym.

I locked the car and hitched his bag onto my shoulders. What did they put into these heavy textbooks for second graders anyway? I'd have to ask Mrs. Pimblott.

I stared at the red doors. Another mom with a pigtailed daughter edged past me and hurried inside. Smoke billowed from a stack on the roof, as if the building were a tiny factory, pumping out educated children. I took a few deep breaths and smelled the ravioli on the menu for the day's school lunch.

I'd felt the tug of anxiety when I left the house. Using tips from Dr. Marci, I had acknowledged the fear and moved forward anyway. Getting into the car had been another battle, but I'd pushed through. Now I stared at the noisy, chaotic building full of people. Could I walk inside? I took two more steps.

"Look, Mom!" Bryan's voice carried over the other shouts and giggles from the playground.

I turned to find him. He hung upside down, his knees barely hooking him over the rail at the top of the dome. Inside the metal form, he dangled far too high above the packed sand. His hair swung down toward the hard ground beneath him. My throat constricted.

"Bryan! Get down!"

Too late. His stubby legs slipped. The heel of one tennis shoe grabbed at the bar for a second but then gave up. He hit the ground headfirst with a dull thump, his body splayed in a broken shape.

"No!" I dropped his backpack and sprinted to the jungle gym. I dodged around a boy in my path.

Bryan sat up and rubbed his forehead. "Did ya see that?"

I plunged through the tangle of metal bars. My rational eyes saw him stand up and laugh. My irrational mind only saw my past nightmare. The boy in a green shirt falling and not moving. The pool of blood.

"Bryan!" The only word that I could choke out. I grabbed for him.

A bell rang, and he wriggled away. "Where's my pack?"

I pointed toward the red door, but my hand trembled. I tried to snatch him back, but he ran off, oblivious to the creature descending on me. The other children disappeared as well, funneled into the door. My whole body shook on the sifting sand beneath me.

*He could have been killed. People die every day. The world isn't safe.*

The threat pierced my skull like talons and screamed into my brain.

*Need to get home. Get away. Run.*

I stumbled through the sand and toward the parking lot, my hands groping for the car as if I were blind. I yanked the driver's side door open and leapt inside. The click of the lock gave me a couple seconds of security. I panted a few desperate breaths and started the car.

Somehow I found my way home, raced inside, and bolted the door. As I leaned against the front door, my rasping breaths quieted. I was home now. Safe. But the silence was heavy with menace.

Floorboards creaked from the direction of the kitchen. The house settling.

A chill blew across the back of my neck. What if he'd found me? The boy with the gun?

*Hide. Hide.*

I ran to the bedroom and locked the door behind me.

A branch scraped the siding beneath the window. Just the wind. Or was someone out there? The furnace kicked in with a wheeze. The ductwork rattled with the footsteps of dozens of nightmares advancing. Every sound held a threat.

I cast my gaze around. The open closet offered refuge. I wedged myself inside and closed the door behind me. I curled tight, shrank, pressed my back against the corner.

Oh, God, oh, God, oh; God.

*Wait it out. You've been here before. It'll pass.*

Some remnant of sanity coached me like a gentle doula, helping me through this brutal contraction. If only I could believe these panic attacks would eventually end.

Heat and cold played tag through my body. My stomach roiled. I curled tighter to try to contain the shakes.

The world tilted in strange directions. I rode out the dizziness minute by minute, a miserable carnival ride that wouldn't end. How many minutes were passing? Or was it hours? Days? Slowly the floor leveled out. I leaned against the closet wall and drew slow, trembling breaths. Rational thought crept back gradually, along with the devastating knowledge that I'd failed again.

"All these years I thought I had strong faith, but a test comes and I crumble. I never knew I was so weak. What's wrong with me?" The nearby terry-cloth bathrobe muffled my raspy whisper.

My self-loathing gave way to a stab of anger. After all, God made the universe spin. Now He was letting it swirl out of control. Didn't He see what was happening to me? Didn't He care? Hugging my knees, in the dark, I found my voice.

"Sure," I croaked through my dry throat. "You spared my life. I'm supposed to be grateful. But you could have saved their lives, too. You didn't.

"Why, God?" A levee in my heart burst apart. I was shouting now. "Why? Why couldn't the gun have jammed the first time he squeezed the trigger? Why couldn't he have picked a different Quick Corner? Why couldn't you have let me slip away and call for help? None of this had to happen!"

My fury opened the spigot on all my pain. Sobs poured as I spat the words. "And why isn't my mind strong enough to sail past this? Aren't you supposed to protect the minds and hearts of your children?

"What about Alex? How can you issue commands about how we're supposed to live, but then take away someone's mind so they can't? Is that fair? Is it?"

My chest heaved. "Which is it? Are you that cruel? Or are you loving but helpless? You wish the bad things didn't happen, but you can't do anything about them? I don't know which I'd rather believe."

As my anger surged outward in waves, the bedrock fear in my soul finally emerged like a beach at low tide. "If you're cruel or if you're weak," I whispered, "then I have no guarantee. My mind could completely fracture. Like his."

That was it. The fear that had lurked in my heart for twenty years. I hugged my knees more tightly. How would God respond? A crack of angry thunder? A bolt of inspired wisdom that would explain everything? An angel to touch the jagged stone in my chest and melt it away?

Nothing happened.

I cried until the last of the churning emotions flowed out to sea, and exhaustion brought quiet to my heart.

In the stillness, a warm thickness gathered in the air. Cynics would say the closet simply grew stuffy. But it was more. God drew near. Unimaginable tenderness gathered me, cradled me, murmured that I wasn't alone. And into my thoughts came the memory of a story I'd heard on the radio years earlier.

A researcher had studied Alzheimer's in various groups. He was especially interested in a Minnesota convent—a closed population that could be interviewed over time. During the course of his work, he interviewed a nun who had been diagnosed with early Alzheimer's. He asked her about her fears . . . since she knew what was ahead. "My greatest fear is that I will forget my Jesus." She had smiled through tears. "But even if that happens, I know my Jesus will never forget me."

Today her words flowed gently over my soul. The incoming tide was soft and clean, not like the churning waves that had poured out of me. I'd never raised my deepest questions with God back when Alex's mind fragmented all those years ago.

Now they all lay at His feet, along with my hurt, shame, and fear about the shooting. I crawled from the closet and eased upright. My bones felt lighter.

Suddenly hungry for more words from God, I opened the drawer of my nightstand and took out my Bible, turning to the Psalms I had been reading weeks earlier. My bookmark rested at Psalm 62, and I settled on the edge of the bed as I read the first verse. *"My soul finds rest in God alone; my salvation comes from him."*

Well, I certainly hadn't found rest anywhere else. Then my eyes caught verse eleven. *"One thing God has spoken, two things have I heard: that you, O God, are strong, and that you, O Lord, are loving."*

I read it again and again. How could I wrap my mind around this riddle? Was God too weak to stop evil? No. He was strong. Was He too cruel to care about protecting me? No. He was loving. Even if He never explained the way this played out in my life, maybe, just maybe, I could learn to live with that mystery.

Later in the afternoon I tackled a different mystery. I cleaned Tom's DVD again, then tried to sneak up on the new message by fast forwarding, and eventually the third message played. I breathed a word of thanks to God for this precious bonus after all the other work He'd done in my heart today.

"Message three." Tom glanced down, and for the first time I noticed some three-by-five cards on his desktop. There was something irresistibly sweet about him preparing note cards for these brief broadcasts. I scooted close to the television and hugged my knees.

"Promise not to gloat with this next one, Pen. I'm gonna admit something tough." He cleared his throat then charged ahead. "From the first day I told you I felt called to the chaplain program, you've been so great about not worrying. You said you would choose to trust. That if this is the calling God has given me, you won't let your mind circle on the fears of things that could happen."

He ducked his chin, but I still saw the rueful smile. "I never realized what I was expecting from you. It was easy to tell you, 'Don't worry, God will take care of me.'

"Until I was on the other side of the equation.

"I've gotta be honest. After the shooting, I had a hard time fighting back fear. For me to head into danger is part of the job. We deal with it. But when I pulled up at the gas station and saw you sitting at the curb with all those police cars, the ambulances . . ." His voice grew thick, and he swallowed. "I could have lost you. It tore me apart. And I've had to wrestle with the picture in my head every day since.

"I didn't want to tell you before I left. I was busy being strong for you, and figured that my fears were the last thing you needed. But I just want you to know, I finally realize what a huge gift you've given me . . . how much courage it has taken for you to be my wife and trust me into God's care when I'm on deployment. And I'll be telling the men and women on the ship, too. Reminding them that their families back home deserve respect and gratitude for their courage." His eyes met mine. "I'm proud of you, Penny."

My heart expanded, throbbing with strength. Over his words, my Father whispered an echo of confirmation. So undeserved after my failure at the school this morning—but so welcome as a glimpse of the person I could become.

Tom ran a hand over his face. "Whew. Okay. Enough of that." He laughed. "I wish I could tell you this tape will self-destruct in five seconds. This is a little too mushy. The next one will be lighter. I promise. Now turn off the DVD." He sketched a wave, and reluctantly I hit the Stop button.

AFTER I EJECTED THE disc, I cradled it in my hands. "Thank you, Tom," I murmured. "How did you know what I needed to hear?"

So much for regaining my fragile grasp on sanity. I was sitting in my living room talking to a shiny polycarbonate disc. I put the DVD on the top shelf. I needed to get back to work trying to be worthy of the respect he had for me.

I pushed to my feet and fought against the familiar wave of fatigue. A cup of tea might help. I headed for the kitchen, pulled the fridge door open, and stared. Lunchtime had snuck up on me, but I wasn't very hungry. It was too much work: making a choice, assembling a meal, chewing, swallowing. I'd missed a lot of meals lately. The good news was that I'd lost my extra ten pounds of padding. Even my spandex workout pants hung loosely around my hips. Maybe I should write a book. *The Post-Traumatic Stress Diet.*

While I dunked the tea bag, I noticed the phone's message

light. I'd finally caught up on answering all the tormenting messages, and now another one had come in? With a sigh, I hit Play.

"Penny! Call me!" Cindy's voice held breathless intensity. "You're never going to believe it. How—"

Her voice was cut off by a baby squeal with an operatic vibrato. My niece had some powerful lungs.

"Shhh. Hold on a minute, sweet pea. Let me put the phone down. Mommy's coming."

The screaming rose in pitch and Cindy blew out a breath in frustration. "Call me right away. I mean it."

I shuddered. Whatever it was that had Cindy's knickers in a twist, I didn't need any more drama. If it were that important, she could have told me. I hated when people left messages of urgency without bothering to give the information they claimed was so life and death. Besides, I'd had a rough morning, and still needed to come up with my kind deed for the day. Then I had to plan weekend activities for Bryan. A new DVD and popcorn would keep him happy tonight, but he wouldn't put up with a hermit mom for two solid days. Cindy would have to wait.

Carrying a second cup of tea to the living room, I went online and placed the week's grocery order. The Internet was an amazing place. I searched out fun things I could do with Bryan, working hard to ignore the fear that crept up my throat at the thought of venturing out again. There was a park with a great climbing structure only a few miles away. The image of my son tumbling from the school's playground equipment flashed in my mind. I clicked away from that page. A zoo in downtown Norfolk, some museums, lots of historic sites, and a nearby arcade. I printed out info on several options so Bryan and I could look at them together.

Next, I popped in to the official Web site for Navy chaplains and skimmed through the news, trying to feel some sense of connection to Tom. Instead of getting insights into his new role, I was reminded of the full width of the ocean between us.

It was my own fault for not getting involved at the Navy base. Mary Jo had tried to draw me in, but I'd avoided her. When Tom had made plans to enter the chaplaincy program, I imagined myself working by his side, comforting Navy personnel and spouses. My intentions had been torpedoed, but it wasn't too late. With a few keystrokes, I did a search for Weblogs of military wives.

Heartfelt stories on various blogs stirred my compassion. I wasn't the only Navy wife who sometimes felt lonely, deserted, and confused. The comments sections were the most revealing. Women shared words of encouragement, advice, and comfort. This was something I could be part of from my own living room.

I pulled out my yellow notebook and wrote today's goal. *Offer words of support to strangers on computer discussions.*

Lost in cyberspace, clicking from one post to another, I missed my cue of the lumbering bus engine. Once again, Bryan's small fist pounded against our door and sent me scurrying to unlatch it.

"Hi, sweetie. How was school today?"

He shrugged and dropped his backpack in the middle of the entryway. "Fine. I'm going over to Jim-Bob's."

I knelt and squeezed him. "Bryan, 'May I please go play with Jim-Bob?' "

He wriggled free. "If you want, but we're making a skateboard ramp, and I didn't think you liked skateboarding." He darted back out the door.

I straightened and squeezed the bridge of my nose. His jacket sleeves were knotted to his backpack straps. I untangled them and held the jacket for a moment, breathing in his little-boy scent of chalk and gummi worms. Parents are supposed to celebrate a child's steps toward independence and self-reliance. Bryan had his own friends and interests, and didn't want to linger on the threshold with his mom. That was a good thing.

Still, I felt a touch of desperation. Bryan wasn't only learning independence. He was being forced to parent himself—to detach from the tangled, incapable mess his mother had become. I couldn't will away the panic attacks, nightmares, and agoraphobia—or the effect those things had on Bryan. But I could try to make it up to him.

I placed an online order for pizza, prepared a new kid's Netflix movie, and arranged my printouts of fun weekend activities.

Later that night I wiped tomato sauce off Bryan's chin and settled back against the couch. "So should we go to the zoo? Or how about this park?" On the television, Nemo struggled to find a way out of the fish tank.

Bryan hitched one shoulder in disinterest. The whole evening I'd identified with Nemo's dad, trying to find my son again.

"You don't want to go to the zoo? You loved it when we took you to the one in Milwaukee."

He shifted away and pulled his feet up onto the couch. "Whatever."

The word stung. I grabbed the remote and hit Pause. "Bryan, what's going on? Don't you want to do anything fun this weekend?"

He picked at a hole in the big toe of his sock and didn't look at me. "Sure." His lack of enthusiasm was so out of character, I touched his forehead with the back of my hand.

"No fever. Are you feeling okay?"

He pulled off both socks and shoved one into the toe of the other, then began using the sock club to whack the arm of the couch with casual thumps. "Can we just watch the movie?"

I pulled him onto my lap. "In a minute. What's wrong?"

He flung his head back and narrowly missed clocking me in the mouth with his hard skull. "You said you were going to talk to my teacher about the play. You never even came in to see my room. You keep saying we're going to do stuff, but we never do."

Guilt hit me with more force than a head butt to the jaw. "I know. I'm sorry. But I'm getting help, and I really think I can handle a little fun this weekend."

He leaned away and slanted a look up at me. "How about if we go to the pet store? Know what? Dad thinks we should get a pet. It would cheer you up."

I laughed. "Okay. We'll visit the pet store. But maybe we should wait for Dad to get home so he can help choose a pet."

Bryan shook his mop of hair, sending flecks of dust airborne. "Nah. I know what kind he likes. He doesn't like snakes."

*Thank heavens.*

"Or cats. But he loves horses and great big dogs."

I tickled Bryan's ribs. "Sorry, hon. I was thinking of something smaller that you could keep in your room."

"A rat?"

I cleared my throat and nodded toward the screen. "Maybe a goldfish? Your own little Nemo?"

"We'll see." He shifted toward the couch cushion beside me and nestled against me as we finished the movie.

After I tucked Bryan in bed, I settled at the computer and found the closest pet store. If we went early, before it got busy, I should be able to manage. I had to. Bryan needed this.

Night shadows coated the living room, and headlights occasionally flickered across the windows as cars drove down our street. I wrapped Tom's big jacket around me like a bathrobe and opened my e-mail program.

Tom's messages had arrived faithfully, but did little to broach the distance I felt. Tonight he dug deeper.

*Hey, shiny Penny,*

*Just a quick moment to check in. I miss you and Bryan every minute. I'm glad you've enjoyed exploring the new neighborhood and that Bryan has made new friends. The work is a challenge, but I knew it would be. Some days I know I've said just the right thing to a kid who needed encouragement. Other times I feel useless and wonder why I'm here.*

*How have you been feeling? Really. Don't get me wrong. I love your e-mails. But I can't tell how you are. I really want to know.*

*Play some John Denver and think of your Rocky Mountain boy, okay? Miss you. Tom.*

A few thin tears glossed my eyes as I smiled, surprised to still have any tears left in me. I took a moment to cue up a CD of John Denver music before composing my answer. Somehow the music helped me resist my usual chipper message. Words poured from my heart.

*Hi, Tommy-boy.*

*You said you wondered how I've been feeling. I've been numb. I can't seem to remember how it feels to be happy, interested, hopeful. I'm sick to my stomach half the time. Strange sensations like electric shocks crawl through my intestines at odd moments.*

*No matter how hard I try not to think about the shooting, no matter how I block it out with music, a television show, or even humming to myself—my body remembers. It shudders with memories that I don't want, but can't seem to erase.*

*You know what it is? It's that I can't trust people anymore. I took it for granted. Sure I know the church teaches we're all sinners, but that was theoretical. The people in my life have been basically nice. Maybe nice to the point of phony at times, but safe.*

*Now I've seen a vulgar truth that I didn't look for, like stumbling over a porn magazine on a park bench. The image sears the mind no matter how fast you turn away.*

*The bullet didn't enter my head, but the image did. The image of evil. Of callous disregard for life. The terrifying truth of my own helplessness and the world's unpredictability.*

*Can I ever go back? Can I ever walk through a grocery store without my shoulders crawling up toward my ears in fear?*

*Maybe I'm not numb, after all. It hurts. Isn't that weird? I came through without a scratch, and yet the pain of a bullet would be better than this. That man—that boy—wanted to kill me. No one's ever wanted to kill me. Well, except for Cindy back in fourth grade when I painted her Barbie Dream House green.*

*I guess you're facing that, too, aren't you? There are people over there who want you dead. Do you feel as lost as I do?*

I scrolled back and read through my letter. He didn't need this from me. His job held enough stress. If he thought I was struggling, he wouldn't be able to focus on his work. And I'd be to blame for the people he couldn't help.

The mouse targeted the Delete icon, and clicked away my moment of raw honesty.

# chapter 17

THE SMELL OF CEDAR shavings and pet droppings blended with the chaotic sounds of yipping and chirping. The pet store was a carnival of sensations, and so noisy that even if I had a panic attack, no one would notice. I found comfort in that fact and relaxed while Bryan ran up and down the aisles, pointing out the tarantulas (Not in your lifetime, buddy), the St. Bernard puppy (Yes, he's adorable, but do you know how big they get?), and the skink (What's that? A cross between a skunk and a mink?).

"These goldfish look nice. We could get a little bowl and some pebbles and you'll be all set."

Bryan shook his head. "You can't play with a fish."

This from the boy who played all afternoon with a dead crab.

"How about one of those?" Bryan's eyes lit as he reached over a wire pen to let a ferret sniff his hand.

"Buddy, our house is small. We need a little pet that can live in your room." I glanced around for a sales clerk and another adult voice of reason.

A young woman with thick glasses and uneven bangs who had been restocking a shelf of chew toys came to my rescue. "Ferrets are fun and playful, but they have a very distinct . . . scent. So if you're planning to keep the pet in your room they might not be the best choice. And they get into everything."

Bryan's face fell. The woman, whose name badge read *Sandra,* knelt beside him. "Let's see. You're a big guy. Do you go to school?"

He puffed out his chest. "Yeah."

She nodded seriously. "That's what I thought. The ferret would get lonely."

"I could bring it to school."

"I'm sure the ferret would love that, but for some reason, schools around here won't let you bring a ferret with you. Isn't that the pits?"

They nodded together in mutual sadness about the lack of pet-friendly policies in the public schools. But Bryan wasn't ready to surrender. "Mom could play with him while I'm at school. Then neither of them would be lonesome."

Sandra glanced up at me and smiled. "But this is supposed to be your pet, right? You don't want to have to share with your mom." She made it sound very uncool.

Bryan turned from the pen with a sigh. "I guess not. But I want a pet I can play with."

"Well, if you like furry critters that like to play, maybe a—"

"Rat?" Bryan jumped up and down a few times.

I chewed the inside of my cheek and gave another subtle shake of my head to Sandra.

"How about a gerbil? They're lots of fun to play with." She led Bryan to a display of small rodents. He dismissed the gerbils as not furry enough and the guinea pigs as boring. He finally narrowed the choice to hamsters. The Habitrail playland was so entrancing that my son abandoned his earlier longings for horses, dogs, and ferrets.

The hamsters were a bargain at only five dollars, but the cage, bedding, wheel, space-age connecting tubes and observation deck added up to a staggering bill.

"I should have gone ahead with the goat idea," I muttered as I pulled out my checkbook.

Sandra laughed. "I think you'll enjoy this more. It's a good choice for a boy his age."

An older Asian man with a spindly mustache hurried in behind the counter. "Sandra, I need you to clean the cages in the back and restock the kitty litter shelves." He clapped his hands a few times. "Lots to do today. Hurry up."

His name tag read *Manager.* I breathed a quick prayer of gratitude that I didn't have to work for someone so gruff and demanding. Sandra didn't lose her smile. She handed me my receipt with genuine warmth.

Inspiration hit me. "Excuse me, sir. You're the manager?"

He turned from rummaging in a box behind the counter. "What? You have a complaint?"

"No. I just wanted to tell you that Sandra is the most helpful sales clerk I've ever met. She made this experience a pleasure, and I wanted you to know that."

He did a comic double take, and his mustache wiggled as he pursed his lips in confusion. Sandra pushed up her glasses higher on her nose and blinked. "Thank you, ma'am." A small blush spread across her cheeks.

"She does all right," the manager conceded gruffly.

"Mom, come *on.*" Bryan tugged on my purse. "Gimli wants to get out of his box. We have to go home."

I smiled a last good-bye to Sandra and let Bryan propel me out of the store. "Gimli?"

"You know. Like the dwarf?"

Ah, yes. *Lord of the Rings*. We settled into the car, and I pulled my notebook out of my purse.

"Mom, whatcha doing? Gimli's gonna surf-ocate."

"That's suffocate. They don't make surfboards for hamsters. And he has holes in the box." The cardboard conveyance to get Gimli home looked disturbingly like a Happy Meal container. If Laura-Beth's dog got a hold of him, Gimli *would* be fast food.

A blue paper clip marked the page of my last entry and I quickly scribbled, *Saturday, October 9. Praised pet store clerk, Sandra, to her manager.* Another good deed. A flush of pleasure filled me. A kind act toward someone new each day. So far, I hadn't missed a day. I wondered what stories the victim support group would have to share on Tuesday.

---

"Why did you talk us into this lame idea?" Ashley narrowed her raccoon eyes at me and propped one thick-soled boot on the table.

Dr. Marci walked past to take her seat and gently pushed Ashley's foot off the table. "You sound angry."

The unwashed girl growled and crossed her arms.

Ashley's personality was as prickly as the metal piercings sticking out of various places on her face, but her instant attack when I walked into the conference room wasn't fair. I sat down and scooted my chair in to the table. "It was *your* suggestion that the whole group try this. I never asked you to."

Her lip curled. "Whatever. It's still a mistake."

Dr. Marci's calm expression never wavered. "Okay, Ashley. Let's start with you. What experiences did you have this week?"

Our strange clan was all present and accounted for. Camille wore an elegant blazer, and hadn't bothered with sunglasses. Makeup was enough to mask the last faded bruises on her face. Henry sat stiffly at the far end of the table, drumming his fingers and picking at his watchband. Daniel sat closest to the door, his chair angled for a strategic getaway in case his agoraphobia got the best of him. I'd had to edge around him to get to an empty seat.

Ashley glared at me. "So, I told a guy at work that he was good with people. He thought I was coming on to him, and the rest of the day he found a dozen excuses to rub up against me on his way past the register to the kitchen."

Henry's lips twitched, but Dr. Marci leaned forward and met Ashley's eyes with compassion. "And how did you handle that?"

Ashley bared her teeth and cracked her knuckles. "Let's just say I set some boundaries."

Daniel and Henry gave each other worried looks. Dr. Marci cleared her throat. "All right. But what about the other people you did something nice for?"

"I don't know. I helped some old bat in my building carry her groceries up the stairs. But she didn't even say thank you. She looked at me like I was a bug." She swung an accusing look at me again. "I suppose you had fun sprinkling sunshine everywhere, huh?"

I opened my notebook and stared at the pages. "Not really. I called my sister and she gave me an earful about how I need to snap out of it." Sympathetic murmurs hummed around the table. "And I gave a Farecard to a guy at a bus stop, but I had to talk him into it."

I looked at Dr. Marci. "I went to the pet store with Bryan this weekend and got him a hamster."

"Hey," Camille interrupted. "That doesn't count. Bryan's not someone new."

"No, that wasn't the good deed."

"How was it?" Dr. Marci asked.

"I didn't freak out or lose it in the store—which was a huge success. Bryan was thrilled to get a pet. And I told the store manager that his clerk had been really great. I think that was my favorite good deed of the week. She was so surprised."

Henry reached down to grab a pen that someone had dropped under the table and pocketed it. "What'd you do for the other days?"

I looked at my notebook. "I posted encouraging comments on a few blogs and sent an e-mail card to a friend back home."

"E-mails?" Camille looked at Dr. Marci. "Does that count?"

Dr. Marci drew a slow breath, probably feeling weary of herding cats. Counseling our group of quibbling misfits clearly required vast reserves of patience. "Penny designed the project to help her growth. I'm sure you can adapt it to—"

"So e-mails count?" Camille looked at me.

"Well, after we got home from the pet store, Bryan couldn't stop chattering. Then we had an hour of panic when Gimli escaped through a loose connector tube in his Habitrail and disappeared. He finally showed up under the couch, and Bryan had to coax him out with sunflower seeds since I was scared to touch the little fur ball. It squeaked its exercise wheel all night and scratched in its cage, so I didn't sleep well. Sunday I was too wiped out to go to church, and Bryan threw a tantrum about missing Sunday school. So my good deeds for Sunday and Monday had to be something easy."

The faces around the table stared at me in silence, apparently taken aback by my burst of words. Then Ashley gave a slow grin. "Soundin' a little defensive there, Supermom."

Henry nodded. "You gotta be careful about spending all your time on the Internet." Dull color rose up his neck as he glanced at Dr. Marci. "It's not healthy. Some people can get, you know, addicted to stuff."

Ashley snorted. "Hey, don't talk to me about addictions. My problem with this whole scheme is that people don't really care. It doesn't make a difference. Let someone ahead of you in line, and they don't even thank you—you just lose your own place. People need to stick up for themselves. *We* need to stick up for ourselves. That's why we're here, right?"

Daniel shifted in his chair. "L-l-l-little things. Well. Th-th-they can matter." He leaned his bald brown head forward like a shy turtle extending his neck, but he didn't raise his eyes. "One time Sammy got out of the yard and ran down the block, and a lady brought him back. She didn't yell at me. Sh-sh-she said, 'You have a beautiful dog.' " He suddenly looked up and beamed at us. "It still makes me happy when I remember it."

My heart throbbed with tenderness for the timid man. One tiny act of kindness had meant the world to him. How little we realize the secret wounds and longings in the people we see each day.

Dr. Marci nodded. "I think the challenge of Penny's Project is that you aren't guaranteed to see results. You offer a kind act and move on, without knowing the rest of the story."

"Until heaven," I blurted.

Again, startled faces turned toward me.

"I mean, my mom used to say that when we get to heaven, we'll find out the rest of the story. She thinks God will open up some sort of scrapbook and show us the things we did for other people, and the behind-the-scenes ways it made a difference that we never knew."

Ashley slouched lower in her chair. "If God's keeping a scrapbook on me, I'm in big trouble."

"Let's get back to the updates on our week," Dr. Marci said. "Camille?"

The discussion continued, sometimes encouraging, sometimes cranky, and sometimes weird. In spite of, or maybe because of, the diverse personalities of our group, I again drew comfort from the evening.

When I got home and settled Bryan down with a tape of *Adventures in Odyssey*, I even felt strong enough to listen to the phone messages. The light had continued its angry beeping since Cindy's message on Friday, but I hadn't worked up the strength to listen to them over the weekend.

"Penny, why haven't you called me back yet?" Cindy sounded more like her irritable self in the second message she'd left. "Fine. Be that way. But you better call Mom and Dad if you won't call me."

Predictably, the next message, which had been left on Sunday, was from my mom. "Penny, this is your mother. I asked Cindy to call you, but she said she didn't get a hold of you. You know I don't like talking to these machines. Would you call me?" There was a pause, and I heard my dad's voice mumble in the background. "Penny?" she continued. "Your dad wanted me to tell you. It's about Alex."

Alex?

Shock froze my breath in my lungs. What possible news could there be about Alex? Had the police identified a body?

The room seemed to tilt. I slid to the floor in the kitchen while the rest of the collected messages played out, but I couldn't hear them over the roaring in my ears.

I HAD BEEN A single girl spreading my wings at college when I got the phone call from my dad. His voice was hushed, and I had to ask him several times to speak up.

"Sorry," he growled. Dad was comfortable chatting about fishing lures, woodworking equipment, or the Green Bay Packers. He became gruff and awkward when he tried to express affection—although to give him credit, he kept making the effort. But today the strain in his voice hinted at something beyond shyness. "Your mom is finally sleeping. I didn't want to wake her."

"Dad? What's wrong?"

"It's Alex."

I braced myself. Part of me had expected this call one day. All throughout my high school years, Alex had wavered in a dark melancholy with occasional frantic suicidal plunges that threw our family into months of chaos. Doctors tried on different diagnoses like fashion styles. Depression, schizophrenia, bipolar disorder, borderline personality disorder. Each time we'd ride a current of hope toward shore for a short distance before a riptide pulled us back out to the deep, treacherous waves of uncertainty.

When life became an unending series of crises, I learned to numb my reaction. So when Dad said my brother's name, perhaps I can be forgiven for sighing and thinking, *Oh, this again.*

"I thought insurance was going to let him stay long term at the hospital this time?"

"Penelope, it's not . . ." He coughed. At least it sounded like a cough, or maybe a stifled sob.

I sank onto the edge of my dorm-room bed, my stomach going hollow. Dad never used my full name. I'd always been his little Penny-pie.

"Did he . . . ?" I couldn't finish the question.

"No. At least we hope not. But he left."

"Left?" Where could he go? Alex barely functioned with the diligent care of his parents and a team of doctors. "What do you mean?"

"Gone. He wasn't in a locked ward. He walked away. Left a note."

"Did he say where he was going? When he was coming back?"

"He . . . he only said he couldn't stand psych units anymore and not to worry."

Not worry? What was Alex thinking? Ever since his first suicide attempt, worry dictated every action, every word, every decision our family made. For five years I watched it gnaw away my parents' strength, destroy our home, tear apart our family. How many meals had ended with Alex sulking away, Dad turning stony, and Mom and Cindy on the verge of tears?

Sure, Alex's inner pain left him no reserves, nothing from which to offer basic thoughtfulness to others. A part of me understood that. But to disappear and tell us not to worry? Didn't he realize his flight would once again throw our family into chaos?

Outside on the commons, a few co-eds shrieked in the middle of a game of Frisbee. Dust motes glided down a ray of afternoon sunlight toward my education textbooks on the desk. My fingers tightened around the phone and my other fist clenched in my lap. "I'll take the bus home. I should be able to get there by tomorrow—"

"No." Dad cleared away the gravel in his voice, his voice firmer. "Absolutely not. Your classes are important. You have to keep living your life. I'll call you as soon as we find him."

We argued for several minutes, but Dad won out. I had three major papers due the next week and a test coming up, and besides, I was tired. Tired of my life hitting freeze-frame each time Alex was worse.

"Promise you'll call me as soon as you hear from him?"

"Yes, of course. He'll be all right. I'm sure he'll show up here at home anytime now."

But he didn't. Not that week, not the next month, not the following year. He had completely disappeared.

The social worker who had managed his case for years met with our family that spring. "It's more common than you might think. Men and women with mental illness don't want to be a burden on their families. Or they don't like pressure to take medication that has side effects. Or paranoia drives them to escape."

"But what can we do?" My mom twisted her charm bracelet, the one with three little silver figures—a boy and two girls. Alex, me, Cindy. "What will happen to him?"

The social worker closed the file. "Some live on the streets. Some find a place to stay with friends. Sometimes they find their way home when they're ready for help."

Impotent rage burned in my chest in the face of her matter-of-fact pronouncement, even though I knew my anger was unfair. She was being honest and trying to help us understand that there were limits to what love could solve—even love as zealous as ours.

My parents spent their fund for a twenty-fifth anniversary trip to hire a private detective, but he came up empty. We didn't grieve, because we refused to believe Alex was dead. Mom bought him a Christmas present each year and tucked it away in the attic after the New Year came and the holidays passed without word from him.

Friends at church finally stopped asking if we'd heard anything, which was a relief. At a class reunion some old friends asked what my brother was doing. I stammered that he'd disappeared while I was in college, and we'd never heard from him. The shock on their faces sealed my feeling of shame. My own brother had disappeared into the mists of mental illness, and I hadn't been able to stop him. He'd never called, never mailed a birthday greeting, never sent a postcard. Even if he had wearied of Dad and Mom's efforts to help him heal, he could have reached out to me.

The joy of my wedding day was tempered by the knowledge that Alex didn't even know I was getting married. Alex might not even know who we were anymore, or who he was. He might not be alive. What were his chances of surviving? If he'd stayed in our small farming community, we would have heard. Had he hitchhiked from the regional hospital to Milwaukee or Chicago or St. Louis? Was he sleeping under a bridge somewhere?

A few years later when Bryan was born, enough time had slipped past to soften some of the shadows. Alex's absence had become a family trait like pointy chins or big ears. It was part of our identity. The pain never left us, but it dulled into something manageable. Sometimes I'd meet someone new and they'd ask if I had siblings. "A brother and a sister," was easy to answer. If pressed for more information about where they lived or what they did, my tone would flatten slightly when I'd explain, "We don't know where my brother is right now," as if he were backpacking through Europe for a few months rather than missing for more than a decade.

Now I was safe on the east coast. Miles and years from all that pain and confusion. And my mother's voice brought it all back through the crackling recorded message. Still huddled on the kitchen floor, I hugged my knees as waves of fear raced through me. Every atom in my being wished I hadn't heard her message, but it was too late. Now I had to know. No matter how bad the news might be, I had to know.

I pulled the phone down to my lap and dialed my parents' number. My mother answered, the sound of clattering dishes in the background.

"Mom, I got your message. What happened?"

"Well, it's about time you got around to calling. You'd think in this day and age a body could get a hold of their child when something important comes up. With all those cell phones and instant messages and gizmos, does it do any good? No. I'd be better off sending the Pony Express—"

"Mom!" I took a deep breath. "You said you needed to talk to me about Alex?"

She sniffled and let out a strangled sound.

I braced myself, pressing my back against the kitchen cabinet for support.

"It's a miracle!" she cried. "He's here. He's back."

Whatever I thought I'd prepared myself to hear, that wasn't it. "What? How? Are you sure?" Ridiculous words broke from my choked throat while the emotional center of my brain waved a hand to say, "Excuse me. I'm confused. What exactly am I supposed to feel now?"

My mom giggled, sounding as young as my sister. "Of course I'm sure. He's sitting at our table. Here. I'll give him the phone so you can talk to him yourself."

"No, wait. Mom—"

"Penny?" The man's voice was strained, quiet. A stranger. "How've you been?"

Every muscle in my body tightened. "Fine." *I'm married. I have a son. I'm living in Virginia, and Tom's at sea. All of which you'd know if you'd bothered to pick up a phone once in all this time.*

He drew a slow breath, seeming to reach for something to fill the years between us. "Mom showed me some pictures. I can't believe you're an old married lady and a mom. Good for you."

My jaw clenched in an effort not to scream. "Where. Have. You. Been? Why did you . . . Why?" The last word came out as a whimper.

He sighed, the bravado out of his tone. "I'm sorry, Penny. I didn't mean to shock you."

The sorrow in his tone finally gave a hint of the familiar. I could almost believe it was melancholy Alex . . . or his ghost. "Why didn't you . . ? Do you have any idea how . . ?" I pressed my head back against the kitchen cupboard. "What am I supposed to say?"

"Sis, you don't have to say anything. You don't have to do anything. I just wanted you to know I'm here. In case . . . well, if you decide you want to . . . you know. Talk sometime?"

"Talk?" A stupid, tiny word that could never hope to explain away a dozen years of silence. I tried to muster some warmth, some joy, but my shock was too overwhelming. Everyone knew the prodigal son's brother was a stick-in-the-mud. I didn't want to be painted with that brush. Yet, I didn't know what to say to him after all this time. "Are you . . . well?"

He laughed. "You mean, am I still nuts? Only enough to keep

life interesting." More clatter sounded in the background, and a baby squawked. Cindy and her kids must be having supper at my parents' house. One big happy family. I felt more alone than ever.

Alex cleared his throat. "I've missed you."

Hurt speared through my veins. "Then why didn't you—" I cut myself off as tears threatened. I would not go there. I couldn't afford more emotional chaos in my life right now.

"It's a long story. Look, I've been catching up with Cindy and the folks, but what would you think if I drove out to visit you sometime next week? I'd rather see you in person."

"I . . . I don't know." The background noises changed, and I heard a dull click. Alex must have stepped into the pantry and closed the door behind him, the same way we all did when we were kids trying to snatch a private conversation with a friend. In spite of my emotional vertigo, I smiled.

"Sis, you know how everyone can be here. It's hard to talk right now. But I'd really like to see you. You were the one person who . . . I thought about you a lot . . ." His voice trailed off.

"It's not really a good time. I just . . . things have been . . ."

"They told me. The holdup. I'm sorry." Genuine compassion breathed through the words. More than I'd heard from anyone else in my family in the past few weeks.

Suddenly the ambient sound shifted, and I heard the pantry door crash open. "Honey, the food's getting cold." Mom warbled querulously in the background.

"I'm coming," he said. Then he apparently turned back to the receiver. "It was great hearing your voice, Pen."

"Alex, I—"

"Mom's giving me the look. I better go."

"I made your favorite tuna casserole." Mom's voice carried from the kitchen.

Alex sighed. "I never liked tuna."

In spite of the tension, I snickered.

He chuckled in response. "Let me know if you change your mind. I'd love to visit, but only when you're ready."

Past my confusion and shock, a ribbon of warmth curled around my heart. Alex had always been troubled, but he'd been real. When a boyfriend had dumped me in high school, my mom had told me to pretend I didn't care. Alex had let me bleed the pain all over him until my obsession cleared out of my system like a bad virus. Trapped in his own realm of potent emotions, he never belittled another's feelings.

"I guess you could come out here. I'm not promising anything." Emotion clogged my words.

"I understand. Thanks. I'll call you in a few days." His volume dropped to a whisper. "Take care of yourself, sis."

I hung up the phone and shook my head. Alex. After all this time. What had he been doing? Where had he lived? Did he find help for the depression?

And why had I agreed to his coming out here? I was already on overload trying to function. Trying to cope so I wouldn't become like Alex. Seeing him was such a bad idea. I couldn't handle more upheaval, could I?

*Lord, calm my heart. Thank you that Alex is alive. Give me strength.*

Sleep wasn't planning to meet me anytime soon, so I made cocoa and settled in front of the computer screen.

*Dear Tom,*

*Something unbelievable happened.*

*Alex showed up. He's at my parents'. I know this is supposed to be good news, and it is. Of course it is. I should be thrilled. My brother's alive, and he seems to be doing okay.*

*But instead of feeling happy, I'm scared. It hurt so much—all his struggles back when I was in high school and his disappearance when I was in college.*

*I don't know what to say to him, and I'm not sure he can make up for all the years he abandoned us. I've gotta figure out how to handle this because he's driving out to Virginia next week.*

*Yeah, yeah. I know. Penny the pushover. He asked and I didn't know how to say no.*

*Pray for me, okay? And for our whole family.*

*I've been listening to our John Denver collection and dreaming of you, Rocky-Mountain Boy. I have to skip over "Sunshine on my Shoulder." Ugh! That one's a little too sweet, even for me.*

*I admit "For Baby (for Bobby)" still makes me cry, like when we sang that to Bryan when he was little.*

*I miss you. I can't imagine what this separation would be like if we didn't have e-mail.*

*Your DVD messages have helped, too. I listened to the third one, and it meant a lot to me. Made me feel stronger. How did you know what I needed to hear? How did God know exactly what I would need at that moment? To be honest, I haven't been bouncing back from the shooting very well. The victim center group is helping, but I guess I've got some post-traumatic stress going on. I know you've studied all about it, but whatever your books said, trust me, it's worse. But I had a good talk with God about it the other day, and I think it's getting better.*

*No matter how well a day goes, we have a huge gaping hole in our family without you here. Bryan and I can't wait for your return.*

*A million hugs, and a few too-passionate-for-a-chaplain kisses.*
*Your Penny*

This time I didn't delete the e-mail. I read it a few times and decided it didn't sound too weak or needy, so I hit Send. I'd finally had the courage to share some of the struggle with Tom.

Still wide awake, I began my search of Navy-spouse blogs, hopscotching from one to another via recommended links. I also found several sites about post-traumatic stress and nodded in identification as I read about experiences that the bloggers shared. When I paused to stretch out a kink in my back, I was surprised to see that it was two in the morning.

I took a moment to check for new e-mails, not that there was much chance Tom could have replied already.

But he had! My fingers flew to click it open. *Auto response. Communications will be unavailable until further notice. I'll respond to your message when they are restored.*

DESPAIR CAME OUT OF my throat as a low moan. Tom had warned me that there would be times during his deployment when communications would be locked out. They might be doing maneuvers. They might be headed for a hot zone. I understood the need for security. But this couldn't have hit at a worse time. My body slumped with exhaustion, but my neurons fired off fragments of loud, chaotic thoughts. A cold, empty bed held no appeal, and sleep would probably evade me again. Instead, I opened my browser. Yahoo! Games sprang open to the bookmarked Spider Solitaire. I sighed with the pleasure of the familiar and rested my chin in my left hand while the right guided the mouse. The cards flipped and moved, and the patterns created a mental Novocain. I played the game over and over, enjoying the way my nerve endings deadened more and more with each repetition.

*Just one more try. Almost won that one. Let's try it again.* Seven onto eight. A full row of hearts. Again. Again. I slipped into a gambler's trance.

After winning a long round, I rubbed my eyes and looked at the clock. Three thirty? That couldn't be right. I stretched and turned off the computer. Some folks might criticize all that wasted time, but it was either that or tossing in bed for hours. Solitaire was healthier than sleeping pills, wasn't it?

When I leaned back in my chair and closed my eyes, black and red cards flashed across my mind's screen. Maybe I *had* played too long. I pushed out of the chair, stumbled to the bedroom, and collapsed on the bed without bothering to change into pajamas. Alex used to struggle to sleep at night, too. For the first time, I realized how much that must have added to his loneliness. Since the shooting, my body rebelled against the same schedule as the rest of the human race. Tired all day, restless all night.

I began the drift down toward unconsciousness. Suddenly, my muscles gave a reflexive jerk and startled me awake. With a deep breath, I coaxed my limbs to relax again, and thought about a verse from Psalms, letting it chant soothingly to my brain cells.

Hovering on the edge of sleep, I might have dozed for a few minutes. Then my heart suddenly lurched against my ribs, stuttering into a frantic race that jarred me awake. Adrenaline surged through me in pulsing waves with nowhere to go. No nightmares had triggered the sensation. The terror was just suddenly *there*. I hugged my pillow and prepared to ride out the feelings. Cold sweat and shakes shut out all logical thought. I wanted to pray, but all I managed to say was, "Jesus. Help. Please. Jesus, help."

Again and again I said the words, grabbing the hem of His robe, ignoring all the scornful disciples who stood in my way on a dusty Palestine road.

*This isn't fair. There wasn't even a trigger this time. No sound of a gun, no sight of a teenage thug. Just a panic that jumped from zero to sixty in a millisecond.*

When I thought the horror couldn't grow worse, my mind added a torment along with the physical sensations. The orange peel texture on the bedroom ceiling created shapes in the darkness. Distorted memories flickered through my mind. Bryan's disappointed eyes. The old woman in the lavender blouse falling backward. The swirling red police lights. Camille's bruised face at the support group. Blood spreading across the glossy linoleum like a child's finger painting.

I was strobing into madness. More images battered me as I squeezed my eyes shut and worked to take slow, deep breaths. It seemed like hours before the adrenaline stopped sending "fight or flight" messages through my nerves and let me sink back into sleep. But even there, tortuous images chased me. Ships exploding. Tom sinking beneath waves. Bryan tumbling and tumbling . . . the thud of his body hitting the ground beneath the jungle gym. The man with the gun. Blood coloring the sand. "No. Please, no!"

"Mom?" Bryan cried in fear, tugging on my arm from his crumpled place in the wet sand.

"Mommy? Wake up! Please."

My eyes flew open. Bryan stood beside the bed, his hand clutching my arm. His tears caught the mottled gleam from the night-light.

"Oh, sweetie. You're okay." I reached for him.

He hesitated. That moment of uncertainty broke my heart.

Then he stepped into my arms. I held him, patted him, and made shushing sounds to comfort us both.

"You were screaming." His words sounded grumpy, spoken with his mouth pressed against my shoulder. But the tremble in his small bones held more fear than anger.

"I'm sorry. It was just a bad dream. I didn't mean to wake you."

"You were screaming," he said again. Plaintive. Declaring the injustice of it. A mother was supposed to reassure and comfort, not jar her child out of bed with hysterical screams.

I carried him back to his bed and sang his favorite Sunday school songs until my voice went hoarse. Long after he fell asleep, I continued to stroke his hair and whisper promises to him.

---

The next morning was a crazy scramble to make Bryan's lunch and find his library books that were due. How did one of them end up under the bathroom rug? If I hadn't stubbed my toe against it, I never would have thought to look there. Throughout the morning rush I kept kicking myself. *Why didn't you lay out his clothes last night? Why didn't you check to make sure his bag was ready? You should start making lunches ahead and freezing them so it's easier to pack them each day. You're failing as a mom. Maybe you should send Bryan to stay with your parents.*

We only had time for a quick prayer on the front steps. Jim-Bob now pressed close to Bryan every morning and expected to be blessed as well. I placed one hand on each boy's head, bemused by Jim-Bob's insinuation into our family tradition. "Dear God, thank you for giving us the gift of life. Keep these two fine young men in your care today and bless their time at school."

"Amen." They chimed in. Jim-Bob gave a freckle-stretching smile. Then they both raced to the corner where the bus was pulling up.

I closed the door and sagged onto the couch. With closed eyes, I visualized a plan of attack. Taking a shower and putting on fresh clothes was a good idea but too much effort. Maybe I should use my tiny bit of energy to do supper preparations, so there'd be a good meal to pop in the oven tonight. And of course, I also needed to help someone today for my Penny's Project notebook.

The weight of options pressed me down into the cushions. Finally I forced my body up. Maybe Tom had been able to send an e-mail.

I booted up the computer and tapped my fingers while my ISP collected new e-mails. Nothing from Tom, but an early-morning note from Mrs. Pimblott popped onto the screen. Tempted to shut down the program, I bit my lip and clicked it open instead.

> *Mrs. Sullivan, I appreciated your past e-mail about Bryan and the reasons for his distraction. I have seen some improvements, but yesterday we had another incident. He has been having some temper problems, and I'd really like to meet with you in person. Let me know a time that is convenient for you. Thank you. Mrs. Pimblott.*

I groaned and rubbed my face. I was such a bad mom that now my intelligent, amiable son was having more trouble in school.

He'd never had trouble back in Wisconsin. Even when Tom was at chaplain school in Rhode Island for eight weeks, Bryan bounded through each day cheerful and secure—full of stories for his grandparents, eager for visits to Aunt Cindy's house, delighted with first grade and all his friends at church and school.

My mom had warned me that life as a chaplain's wife wouldn't always feel manageable. "Wait until you're stationed somewhere alone, where you don't know anyone, and Tom is gone for months at a time. What will you do then? Who will baby-sit when you need it? What will you do if you break an ankle? Or if one of those hurricanes hits?"

I'd laughed at her anxiety. "Mom, God's called us to this road, so He'll provide what we need. I'd rather take risks for God than stay safe and miss opportunities to serve Him. Just think of how much Tom and I will grow through the experiences we'll have. And more important, think of all the people he'll be able to serve."

"He's serving people here. Our church needs him."

With the arrogance of ignorance, I patted her arm. "Don't worry. He'll provide. It's all in His hands."

I still believed that. God was all-powerful. But apparently, I was pretty powerful, too, because I had the ability to ruin His plans and His work with my weakness and failures. Look at Bryan. His problems in school were clearly caused by the instability I'd brought into our home.

Mrs. Pimblott's note was gently worded, but I could read behind the polite code. She was really saying, "You're a terrible mother. Your child can't do well in school, because you're creating such a bad home environment. And why have you ignored my messages about setting up rehearsal times for the Thanksgiving play? You're inconsiderate."

I bolted away from the computer and grabbed Tom's jacket from the closet by the front door. A short walk. That's what I needed. Something to help me escape this prison of dark thoughts. Tom's jacket covered my rumpled, slept-in clothes. I coaxed my hair into a loose ponytail and pushed myself out the door.

Laura-Beth was kneeling on the sidewalk in front of her double stroller, readjusting a strap on one of her twins. I tiptoed backward, retreating into my entryway.

Too late. She spotted me. "Yoo-hoo! Well ain't this a great coinkydink? Going for a walk?"

I jammed my hands into the jacket pockets and trudged toward the sidewalk. "Just wanted some fresh air."

"Know just what you mean. Some days I feel like if I don't get a change of scenery I'm gonna scream." Laura-Beth pushed her double stroller up the sidewalk, giving an extra jolt against the handle when we reached a particularly uneven seam in the concrete. "Old Mr. Simpson lived in the house on this corner up until a few years back when his wife died—rest her soul. The guy who bought it is rentin' to some college boys. Bad for the neighborhood with their carryin' on."

The toddlers rattled happily along while Laura-Beth kept up a running commentary. We reached the Laundromat and she sniffed. "Don't bring your laundry here at night by your own self. Ain't safe." Without taking a breath she continued a dissertation on where I should shop, what time of day to water my lawn, and which soap opera had the best actors.

When we reached the street before the mission, she stopped and turned the stroller. "Well, this is far's I go."

I stooped to tickle the chin of Mary-Lou, whose tuft of hair made her look like someone from Whoville. "I think I'll walk a little longer."

Laura-Beth shrugged but didn't seem to take offense. I watched her head for home and thanked God for the sudden silence, then crossed the street.

Once again, I'd wandered the blocks from relatively tidy homes to more troubled and broken streets. Not so different from my life in the past weeks. My world had been a safe neighborhood with neatly trimmed grass. Now it was unkempt with cracked and uneven sidewalks, populated by poverty and despair.

Maybe Laura-Beth's chatter hadn't been such a bad thing. Her presence had muted my anxiety. The worries clamored back now. I was doing a terrible job of parenting. Maybe I should send Bryan to live with my parents until I got my life under control. Maybe I wasn't fit.

My shoe hit a half-crushed lighter on the sidewalk and sent it skittering into the gutter.

Too many things were hitting me at once. Alex was back. Coming for a visit. What could I say to him? Was I about to be pulled back into cycles of hope and fear while his mental health played hide-and-seek?

And Tom. He had done all he could to reassure me, but every Navy ship was in harm's way by nature of its role. He was a non-combatant, but that didn't mean enemy fire would detour around him. And even if he survived his deployment, could I handle future stretches of separation? Maybe I'd never learn to cope with long-distance marriage.

I approached the door of New Life Mission. Should I drop in? Offer to help with something?

Before I could decide, Lydia raced out. "I'll be at Norfolk General until the baby comes," she called over her shoulder. She turned and her face lit. "Penny! Great to see you. Wish I could chat. One of the young gals in the projects is having her baby." With a grin, she jumped into a battered Mustang at the curb. The car pulled out with a grinding of gears.

Barney leaned against the doorway and shook his head, raw admiration in his face. "She'll make sure the labor goes right on schedule. Even babies don't mess with her. And she'll beg, borrow, or steal all kinds of baby clothes and fixin's for them, too."

"She is . . . forceful. Have you worked together long?"

His eyes turned wistful. "Been helpin' down here a year now."

I thought of the way Lydia threw her shoulders back and tossed her head when she scolded him, and the way he blustered and groused while hiding his grin. I had a sudden inspiration for my day's good deed.

"Lydia sure depends on you. Respects you. The way she looks at you, it's no wonder I thought you two were married."

He rubbed his stubbly chin. "Don't know 'bout that. She wouldn't want nothin' to do with an old salt like me." But he squinted down the street where her car had disappeared. "You comin' in?"

"No thanks. But I'll stop by again. And I think I have a box of some old baby clothes and blankets I could bring by."

He gave me a nod and strode back into the mission, whistling a sea chantey.

My seeds of matchmaking carried me most of the way home. For a few minutes, I'd been Normal Penny again. Would she stay around this time?

---

The next morning I had my answer. Nightmares had harassed me again, and I met the morning with a frantic impulse to pull away from the overwhelming tasks of normal life. I couldn't even venture out onto the doorstep. I whispered a brief blessing for Bryan in the living room and sent him out the door to the bus.

Was this how it had been for Alex? More and more fractures in the delicate balsa wood structure of the mind, until one morning he woke up and could no longer muster the effort to be sane?

I needed to crawl into a cave and pull the entrance in behind me.

Today's appointment with Dr. Marci loomed as a Herculean task. Expose more raw feelings? That idea bordered on the insane—and I should know. I'd been making a few border crossings lately into the land south of sanity. Dr. Marci was making things worse, anyway. Talking about The Incident had been a huge mistake. I called the office and canceled.

Then I turned to the computer. Mrs. Pimblott's e-mail requesting a meeting still waited for an answer. Right. Showing up shaky and sweaty with the harrowing effort to drive to the school . . . she'd know something was wrong with me. An e-mail was safer.

*Mrs. Pimple,*

*Thank you for your note. I'm sorry I haven't talked to you sooner, but I've had some health problems. I'm guessing that's why Bryan has seemed distracted. About the Thanksgiving play, I'm honored you asked me, and I'd hoped to be feeling better in time to participate.*

I paused. The play was so important to Bryan. And my participation had been my benchmark—a symbol I was whole and sane and able to function as a mom again.

*I can't. I can't. I can't.* The compulsion overpowered every other intention. The pressure to face a public event was crushing me. She needed someone she could rely on. I owed her a straight answer.

*But I think you'd better go ahead and find a new Pilgrim mom. Thanks for your understanding. I'll talk to Bryan about his need to stay focused during class, and I promise to come in and meet with you when I'm able to.*

*Sincerely, Penny Sullivan*

I hit Send. Shame washed through my body, but it was coupled with relief that was as potent as a gasp of air to a drowning swimmer. I'd figure out how to break the news to Bryan later. I pulled the note from the Sent folder to read again. Had I explained myself well enough?

The salutation jumped out at me.

"No, no, no." I dropped my forehead to rest against the computer screen. She was going to hate me. What parent calls the teacher Mrs. Pimple?

With cheeks hot, I wrote a quick follow-up.

*Mrs. Pimblott,*

*Please excuse the spelling mistakes in the last e-mail. I mentioned health issues. I haven't been sleeping well, and really shouldn't be allowed access to a keyboard when I'm this foggy. So sorry. Anyway, thanks for being such a great teacher. You've eased Bryan's transition to a new state and a new school a lot.*

Self-deprecating humor and groveling had gotten me out of scrapes in the past. Maybe she wouldn't even notice the mistake in the first e-mail.

Overwhelmed by the effort it had taken to untangle myself from commitments, I crawled back into bed.

I woke up sometime after noon feeling muffled—as if a wet towel covered my face and my limbs were sandbags. Had I actually e-mailed my final answer that I couldn't help with the play? My failure made even my lungs feel heavy. I made a cup of tea and sat at the computer. A few rounds of solitaire distracted me from the dull ache behind my eyes until the tea could do its job and clear my head.

No one wanted to feel this sluggish day after day. Cindy's husband was in A.A. He talked about being "sick and tired of being sick and tired." Now I understood what he meant. I could no longer remember how it felt to wake refreshed and eager for life.

I did a new Google search for post-traumatic stress and found a discussion forum. I put my feet up and skimmed through post after post. This was every bit as comforting as going in for an appointment with Dr. Marci and much easier because I didn't have to drive anywhere—or talk.

One woman, *timid1102*, shared a heartbreaking story of rape. She hadn't left her apartment in months. Her sister brought her groceries once a week, and she spent her nights longing for sleep but afraid of the nightmares. My fingers moved before I thought about it, and I posted a reply.

*I'm so sorry for what you've gone through. The world out there is very scary. But don't give up. I'll pray for you.*

And then I bowed my head by the computer and prayed, my heart aching for her pain.

My project notebook caught my eye, and my shoulders slumped. I couldn't go out today. Laura-Beth lurked outside waiting to drag me into her house to hang wallpaper. Teens roamed the streets. People died bloody, horrible deaths inside gas station convenience stores. And I was too tired to confront any of it.

I wrote the date on the top of the first empty page of my notebook. *Timid1102—sent her an encouraging e-mail reply.*

There. Maybe I didn't have to concede complete failure. I'd done something kind for a new person and never had to leave my chair. The victim support group would complain that an e-mail and prayer didn't count, but it was better than nothing. I stretched and wiggled my toes.

I surfed onward to another post-traumatic stress forum that Dr. Marci had recommended. Some of the screen names were becoming familiar. Colleagues in this crazy internal war we were all fighting. A new thread, started by Maria L., caught my eye

*Trapped forever.*

The theme of the post sounded devastating, but curiosity forced my finger to click the mouse. The words began poignantly, gently. A story similar to mine. A surprising horrific event, trying to cope by moving forward, denial, avoidance, and finally seeking help. I nodded, identifying so deeply with the description, with this mirror of my past weeks. I clung to this proof that I wasn't the only one.

Insomnia, flashbacks, nausea, panic attacks. Family and friends irritated when she didn't snap out of it. I continued to skim and rested my fingers over the keyboard. I'd write and let her know I'd felt the same things. The battle was daunting, but things would gradually improve.

Then my eyes caught the next words. *It's been ten years.*

My living room floor rippled. Ice burned in my chest. I wanted to turn away but the words seared into my brain—*divorce . . . lost custody . . . psych ward . . . disability . . . tried everything . . . never ends.*

I stood, shoving my chair back. It crashed to the floor. Bolts of adrenaline shot through my body. Hornets buzzed inside my skull. I fumbled for the mouse and shut down the computer, but it was too late. Despair blasted my soul like stinging sleet before a gale.

# chapter 20

DR. MARCI HADN'T GIVEN me any sort of timeline, but I'd assumed my goal was reasonable: be well by the time Tom returned. Sure, this morning had been a setback. I'd wanted to tell Mrs. Plimbott I'd be part of the school play—a task that even some normal people would find nerve-wracking. That achievement would have provided me with proof that I was fine, and it hurt to concede I wasn't ready for that yet. But deep inside I still held a morsel of hope that overall I was moving in the right direction.

But this anonymous woman online—she could be me. Ten years? Was this what the rest of my life would look like? Anytime, anywhere, out of the blue, these horrible attacks, long nights of dark horror . . . evil making my mind a playground? I couldn't live like this.

I'd had strep throat last year. It hurt like crazy, but once I started the antibiotics, I knew within hours I'd improve. Labor was tough, but I knew the baby would eventually be out of me and the pain would be a memory.

But pain that kept going with no end in sight . . . ?

I couldn't do it anymore. I'd jumped through the hoops. I'd tried to get better. Nothing had worked. I had been digging my nails into a crumbling cliff, scrabbling for hope. But nothing was going to stop the slide. I'd never be the old Penny. I was permanently broken. I'd never be normal, feel safe, or enjoy people again.

I stormed back and forth across the living room, trying to burn off some of my mounting anger. I ran my hands through my hair, tugging when my fingers found a snarl. Welcoming the smarting sting. Anything to distract me from the throbbing behind my eyes, the flashes of images.

My notebook rested on the coffee table, mocking me with its sunshiny optimism. I snatched it up and ripped the small bright cover right off the spiral binding. Why keep trying? My idea was a joke. I tore the cardboard cover down the middle, then tossed the yellow pieces in the garbage can next to the computer.

I cradled the stripped notebook, wire loose and bent from my attack, then dropped it in the trash as well—the exposed pages looking tattered and pathetic as they landed on top of wadded Kleenex and junk mail. My legs shook, and I braced my hands against the shelves along the wall. *Lord, I'm lost. The fear is eating me alive. Nothing is helping.*

Rows of cheerful movie cases and lighthearted CDs rattled. I pushed away from them, but then caught the glint of Tom's disc. With a desperate moan, I grabbed it and loaded it into the DVD player. My hands trembled as I hit Play and fast-forwarded through his first three messages. Today I needed something new. *Please, God, let there be something to help me.*

"Okay, I only have a few more thoughts for you." Tom smiled, more relaxed than in his first messages. I scowled back at him.

"But first, I want to tell you again. Thank you for supporting me so I can do this work. Thank you for your enthusiastic spirit, for caring so much about other people."

Didn't he get it? I wasn't that person anymore.

"I love you, Penny." His smile was soft and caressing. How did he manage that while looking into a camera?

My frown eased away and I sank to the floor in front of the screen. "I love you, too," I whispered.

"As I've been praying for you the last few days, I've missed praying *with* you. I know things have been hectic with unpacking and my deployment. But it's more than that, isn't it? It's something the other chaplains see all the time, I guess. When people are really hurting, they're afraid that if they pray, their words will bounce back at them and they'll feel even more deserted. Or if they crack open their Bible, the verses will be cold comfort. Makes sense. But, Penny, no one I know has a more vibrant faith than you do. It's one of the things that makes you so special. Even if you're confused by God right now, don't shut Him out, okay?

"I guess this could sound really simplistic, but use one of the best weapons we have. Dig into Scripture every chance you get."

He paused. "Maybe you're rolling your eyes. Maybe I deserve that for stating the obvious. But let's keep reminding each other, okay? Deal? And when you find a verse that comes alive to you, e-mail and tell me, okay? I'll do the same."

A shadow crossed his face. "I wish I didn't have to leave tomorrow." He tried a smile that came out crooked while the light caught a shimmer in his eyes. "Okay, I have time for one last message. Save it for later. I'll be home before you know it."

I hugged my knees and absorbed his words. Except for the one

Psalm I'd clutched at after my last crying jag, I'd avoided my Bible, secretly afraid the words would mock me. Numbly, I wandered into the bedroom, picked up my Bible, and carried it out to the couch, where I settled cross-legged. Last time I'd read, I'd found some deep comfort—at least for a while. Why hadn't I returned? I turned pages aimlessly and found myself in the Gospels.

Bits of familiar phrases flickered past as I skimmed. Then I stumbled across the story of the widow's mite and slowed down.

A woman in poverty. Empty, bereft, surrounded by others who flaunted their wealth and strength. A few copper coins. She gave from what she had. I read the chapters before and after, but kept coming back to the moment of Jesus' praise for the woman. *"She out of her poverty put in all she had to live on."*

The silence in my living room swelled with purpose.

*Thank you for giving me what you can.*

God whispered the words deep inside my heart, and goose bumps rose on my arms. My chest filled with a painful ache of hope.

"Really?" I breathed. "But I don't have anything to give you. I feel so worthless, so broken."

*Open your notebook.*

Swallowing hard, I walked the few steps to the computer table and reached into the garbage can, pulling out the battle-worn pages. I flipped a few pages and read the brief entries, page after page of notations from the past weeks. I read the names of Ashley, Camille, Henry, and Daniel. Their stories had stirred compassion in me and pulled me out of my misery. God was using our circle of broken people to help each other. Our tiny acts of kindness seemed pitiful in the face of the world's huge needs. To me they'd been a forced exercise. Hardly the great acts of love I wished they were. But He was using them anyway.

I hugged my notebook and closed my eyes. "Father, I didn't rescue the old couple. I'm not speaking at churches about how you protected me. I don't want to appear on *Oprah* and talk about how I've adopted the young man who almost killed me."

I'd concocted a daunting scenario of what recovery from trauma should look like. Could it be that He wasn't demanding all that from me? Could I stop demanding it of myself? Could I be patient while healing unfolded in my life by His timetable? My throat felt thick as I prayed.

"All I'm doing is getting through each day—and sometimes not doing that very well. My Penny's Project feels like the story—a few pennies. A widow's mite."

*She put in all she had.*

And He cherished the gift. Cherished her.

In the quiet of my living room with the dingy carpet and commonplace furniture, God's grace moved through me. Insisted that I hear the truth. Impressed it deep into my mind. My spirit rose up to respond.

"Yes. If it matters to you, I'll keep going. And please multiply the tiny kindnesses and meet the true and deeper needs that I don't know about."

The intense touch of His presence eased to a place where I could breathe normally again. I continued to sit for long minutes, murmuring occasional words of thanks and praise.

Later in the day, my lack of sleep began to catch up to me, in spite of the sense of peace that hovered around my heart. I needed to stay busy and awake, so that I'd sleep better at night. I managed a brief errand to the craft store for pom-poms and pipe cleaners. Bryan needed them for his science-class DNA model. Then I spent an hour slicing and sautéing and mixing up homemade spaghetti sauce. When that was simmering, I decided to tackle my voice mail.

"Penny, it's Cindy. Why haven't you called me? Isn't this wild? You should see Alex with my kids. It's so cute. Can you believe he's back?"

Muscles around my forehead tightened, and a dull ache pulsed at the base of my skull.

"Mrs. Sullivan? This is Dr. Marci's office. Would you like to reschedule your appointment? And Dr. Marci asked me to remind you of your group session on Tuesday night."

The headache sent tendrils across my temples and dug into my brain.

"Pen? It's Alex. Look, I got a call from some friends who want me to stop by, so I've decided to stay with them in Pennsylvania before I head down to your neck of the woods. Hope it's okay if I'm not there until the week after next. Let me know."

I drew a slow, deep breath, and the squeezing pressure around my head eased. At least I'd have a reprieve before seeing my long-lost brother and all the unknowns his visit would bring. Staying with friends? I didn't even know he had friends.

I didn't know anything about him, and right now I couldn't handle extra uncertainty.

Bryan arrived home in a good mood, and I sat on his bed while he fed sunflower seeds to Gimli. He'd found some books about hamsters in the school library and was full of new information.

"Hey, Mom, did you know that they don't like you to wake them up when they're napping?" He slanted a look my way. "Kind of like you, huh?"

"Oh, come on. How can they tell a hamster doesn't like being woken?"

Bryan faced me and crossed his arms in lecture stance. "The book says they sometimes bite when they're upset. And waking them up upsets them. So does dropping them or not feeding them."

I leafed through one of the books on hamster care. "That sounds reasonable. You get cranky when you're not fed."

He giggled. "And you better not drop me."

I grabbed for him and swooped him into my arms—not an easy feat now that his limbs were stretching into the gangly length of a schoolboy's. I hefted him up in a cradle carry and then pretended I was about to drop him.

He shrieked with delight, and I spun him around a few times and fell back onto the bed, joining him in helpless laughter.

For those blissful minutes, I was myself again. Warm. Witty. An energetic mom whose son adored her.

I needed to talk to Bryan about my e-mail to his teacher—about pulling out of the Thanksgiving play. But we hadn't had relaxed and happy times like this in so long, I couldn't bear to spoil it.

Throughout the evening, I waited for the right time, and it never came. I kissed his forehead at bedtime and decided to wait until the next day after school.

Big mistake.

---

Bryan stormed into the house Friday afternoon like a monster truck at a rally. He growled. He revved his engine and tore around the living room. Finally, he crashed against the couch in an explosion of fists.

"You promised!" he roared.

I wrapped my arms around his thrashing body and held on. "I'm sorry. I was going to talk to you about it."

"My teacher told us today that Brittany's mom is going to be the Pilgrim instead." He fought back tears.

What kind of stoic control had he needed at school when he'd gotten the bad news? No wonder his pent-up fury had built to meltdown levels.

"Sweetheart, I wanted to do the play. I wanted to so much. But remember when the doctor explained that I have panic attacks? I didn't want to ruin the play if I wasn't feeling good. I didn't want to do a bad job for you."

He squirmed away and faced me, breathing hard. "You don't have to be good at it. I just wanted you there."

"But I'm sure that Brittany's mom will do a better job than I could."

His skin flushed a darker red. "You don't want to do anything with me. Know what?" He took several rapid, shallow breaths. "I hate you!"

Shock hit his face a second after he said it, and he ran from the room. His door slammed, and my heart fractured into glass slivers that cut their way into every protected cubby of my soul. I deserved every morsel of the pain, and I let it lacerate me—holding perfectly still as the words sliced me again and again.

Sure, I'd gone through something traumatic, but parents all over the world pulled it together for their children. Maybe playing Pilgrim Mom in the school play was too big a leap for me, but I should have at least had the guts to discuss it with my son before he heard about it at school. He wanted some reason to be proud of his mother, and I'd provided precious little of that in the past month.

I forced myself up from the couch. He needed me. He needed to know his words were forgiven, and he needed an opportunity to forgive me for handling this badly.

I took two steps and froze. What could I say to him? How could I explain the terror that held me captive in the house, the exhaustion that followed every small attempt to reenter the world, the shame, guilt, and failure that pounded me with dull mallets every waking moment? I didn't know how to help myself, or Bryan, or our relationship.

*Give from what you have.*

The quiet reminder in my spirit made the skin prickle along my spine. I didn't have wise and well-spoken words to offer. All I had to give was my presence.

I stopped waffling and ran to Bryan's room, opened his door, and joined him on the floor where he hugged his knees, face hidden. I gathered him in my arms. "I understand," I whispered. "I really let you down."

Bryan's shoulders heaved, and he shook his head.

"I don't want you to die."

"Honey, what are you talking about? I'm not going to die."

He raised his chin and turned to look at me. His eyes were pools of misery, encircled by white fear. "You almost did. And Brittany said if you cheat death, it keeps coming to find you."

Where was my notebook? I wanted to write a reminder to call Brittany's mother and tell her to muzzle her daughter.

"Bryan, God protected me. He'll keep protecting me. He's stronger than death, remember?"

He adjusted his position but didn't pull away. "Mom, people die."

I seriously did not want to have this conversation.

"Yes. You're right. Everyone dies. But that's not the end, is it?" I asked. He swiped his sleeve across his runny nose. I decided this wasn't a good time for a hygiene lecture. "Buddy, after people die, then what?"

"If you believe in Jesus you go to heaven." He glared at me. "I don't want you to go to heaven."

I smiled. "I don't want to either. Not yet, anyway." I nestled him closer. "Have you been worrying about that?"

One small shoulder shrugged and he looked away.

"God didn't make us to be windup toys. He lets people make choices. The robber in the store chose to do something horrible and shoot people. I don't know why the gun jammed, but I'm really glad God gave me more time with you. It's a gift. I'm alive." A tingle of unfamiliar joy warmed my bones as I spoke.

"But what if he finds us? What if he shoots me, and Gimli, and you?"

I noticed that I ranked behind the hamster, but ignored that slight. "Honey, he won't. He's probably running far away because he knows the police are trying to catch him. He doesn't have time to come and hurt us."

Moms spend a majority of every day believing no one hears them. "Did you finish your book report?" "Don't leave your shoes in the hall." "How was your day?" Their words go out into a strange baffle that absorbs them into nothingness. Family members adopt selective deafness. Soon moms wonder if they've truly become inaudible to other humans.

However, there are times a mother's words ring with clarion power. Holding my son, I felt him draw in strength from my reassurance with a simple trust that both humbled and terrified me.

We talked until suppertime, and I even ventured into the backyard after supper to kick a soccer ball around with Bryan.

With inevitable radar, Laura-Beth slipped from her house and leaned on the fence. "How ya been? Hope you don't mind me saying, but you'll wanna clean out them gutters. We're due for some rain. They've been talking hurricanes on the news, ya know."

My shoulders sank as I turned toward her, and my son's errant kick sent the soccer ball ricocheting off the side of my head. Bryan doubled over with laughter. "Mom, you should see your face."

Apparently, his deep concern for my well-being extended to dying but not to being clocked in the jaw.

Laura-Beth's chuckle didn't help.

I rubbed my stinging face and sighed. "Thanks for the advice. I'll dig out the ladder tomorrow."

"And what about that border for my bathroom? You could come over tomorrow if you want."

"Whoops, there's my phone." I ran for my back door.

This time the phone really was ringing. I didn't want to risk missing a call from Tom when the communications blackout ended, so instead of keeping the ringer off, I let my answering machine screen calls. I needed to have a real conversation with my husband. Of course, I also needed to feel his arms around me and his hot kisses against my neck—but since that wasn't going to happen in the near future, I'd settle for a phone call.

My hand hovered inches from the phone, ready to grab it if the person who started to leave a message was someone I wanted to talk to.

"Mrs. Sullivan? This is Sergeant Stargill from the local precinct. We've arrested a suspect in the Quick Corner shooting. Detective Ramirez would like you to come in for an identification."

I snatched my hand away from the phone as if the receiver had burst into flames.

# chapter 21

"I CAN'T. YOU WOULDN'T do this, would you?" I searched the faces around the conference table for support. The room smelled like burnt dust. The victim center had turned on the furnace in deference to the chill in the air. From the lobby, pinging sounds carried from Bryan playing with his Game Boy. "Come on. Tell me I'm right."

Henry adjusted his tie and stared at the floor as if lost in thought. Ashley curled her lip—which probably hurt since it made one of her face rings pull upward. Camille shook her head gently, her face betraying disappointment in me.

Why were they turning on me? I shouldn't have come. My online forums had begun to serve the same purpose and were a lot easier. However, the call from the police station had sent me into a tailspin, and suddenly I needed the flesh and blood presence of the victim support group. I'd unplugged my phone and waited out Saturday, Sunday, and Monday. When Tuesday arrived, I raced to the victim center as if reaching for a life preserver. Why weren't they giving me the support they were supposed to give? Of all people, they should understand that I couldn't handle helping the police.

Camille reached over and patted my arm. Another week away from abuse and she carried herself with more confidence, although a haunted sadness still flickered across her eyes at quiet moments. "Penny, you can't run from your fears. Do they need you to testify?"

Tension tightened the skin around my mouth. "I haven't asked. I didn't call back yet." My breathing grew shallow at the thought of a mangy police station lineup, intimidating courtrooms, and a face-to-face encounter with the man who tried to kill me.

Dr. Marci leaned forward. "Take a deep breath."

I obeyed with a shaky exhale and inhale. "I was just getting over it. I've been able to shut out the memories more. If I talk to the police, it'll all start up again. The nightmares, the panic attacks."

"Someone from the victim center can go with you." Dr. Marci passed me a cup of water. "You don't have to do this alone."

"The guy was seriously whacked out." Ashley sniffed and rubbed her nose. "You don't want to be the reason he's running around free, right?"

My shame meter had been stuck on full for so many weeks, I hadn't even thought about the added culpability I'd feel if the murderer walked because of me. I chewed a cuticle and sent a beseeching look in Dr. Marci's direction. "Would you come with me?"

"We have another staff member who . . ." Sympathy washed over her face. "Sure. I can go in with you tomorrow morning. I had a regional conference that was cancelled."

"There you go, then." Henry grinned.

Camille nodded.

I wanted to scream. What right did they have to pressure me into this? Should I confront Henry about all the sugar packets he'd stuffed in his pocket from the tray of coffee fixings? How would Camille like it if I scolded her into dating someone new and used the whole "face your fears" argument on her?

"Any breakthroughs this week?" Dr. Marci asked. Perhaps she suspected the rebellion swirling in my mind and wanted to move the discussion along before I went on the attack.

Henry's fingers drummed the table. "I made a list of old friends I could do something nice for." He shot me an apologetic glance. "I figured I'd start with that. I'm not quite ready for helping strangers."

I shrugged. "There's no rule against that."

He nodded and tugged his watchband. "So each day last week, I called up a different old friend and met him for lunch."

"How did it go?" Dr. Marci asked.

A quick smile lifted his features, revealing a glimpse of the energetic investment broker he'd once been. "I heard a lot about grumpy bosses, insane workloads, cuts in benefits, and one guy is going through a divorce and another has a sick kid."

Henry's basset hound eyes looked compassionate instead of miserable. "I mostly just listened. But something weird happened. By the time we'd finished eating, they'd ask about me. I didn't say a lot, just that I'm out of work at the moment. And every time . . ." He swallowed and fought back some strong emotion. "They offered to ask around."

He lifted his eyes to the table. "They wanted to help." He looked at me again, as if confessing that he'd cheated on an assignment. "That's not why I asked them to lunch. I promise."

I wasn't the only one grinning.

Dr. Marci spoke for us. "Henry, what a marvelous experience.

There's nothing wrong with accepting the support and concern of others if it comes. You didn't go into those encounters with expectations. Ashley, how about you? Last week you were feeling frustrated by people's lack of appreciation."

A faint blush painted her ghost-white cheek. "Last Friday, I was sweeping the floor at work. A little girl was crying in one of the booths. I winked at her to try to get her to smile. Her dad didn't freak, so I came closer and asked her what was wrong. She said her mom was sick. So I used my employee discount and bought her a little ice cream sundae and gave her a couple extra kid's-meal toys we had in the back. When they left, she ran across the store to where I was wiping tables, and—" Ashley twisted one of the many bracelets on her wrist. "She hugged me."

She glared around the table, daring us to mock the sweetness of her story.

Camille spoke first. "You made her day."

Ashley shrugged. "But her mom's still sick. I didn't really fix anything."

A pall settled over the room. "She's right," I said, drooping lower in my chair. "All these little things we're doing . . . they don't really solve anything. They don't make people's problems go away."

"So your theory is that unless you can cure cancer, you shouldn't bother holding the hand of the woman battling it?" A smile sparked in Dr. Marci's eyes behind the calm, professional demeanor. "These small acts of love are changing things. They are changing you as they pull your thoughts from your fears, obsessions, and tragedies. They change the person you reach out to. Kind acts ease the level of suffering, even when they don't remove the source of the pain." She let her smile escape. "Give yourselves some credit. You can't fix everything. You're doing good work here."

"Like the fish and loaves," I murmured.

"Huh?" Ashley quirked an eyebrow stud at me.

Most of the group stared at me blankly, but Camille nodded. "The boy gave his few fish and a little bread to Jesus, and Jesus multiplied it to feed thousands."

Dr. Marci smiled. "I like the analogy of that story."

I wanted to point out it wasn't a mere story, but an actual example of God's miraculous provision, but I bit my lip and let her talk.

"If we help in little ways," she continued, "who knows how it might multiply?"

The discussion continued, and once again I was surprised by how much comfort this ragtag group brought me. The threads of painful experiences wrapped us into a strange sort of fellowship.

At the end of the hour, I stood to leave. "You can meet me here tomorrow morning," Dr. Marci said. "We'll head over to the precinct together."

*Shoot.* I'd hoped she'd forget about her offer. Of course if I continued to ignore calls, the police might show up at my door and cause more excitement for Laura-Beth.

"All right. I'll meet you here." I tried to sound mature instead of sullen, but my tone came out rather flat.

I couldn't do it.

That fact swirled around me as I drove home, stealing breath from my lungs and starch from my bones. Hadn't God asked enough of me? Tom's career change, a move across the country from family, handling single-mom status while he was on deployment, witnessing a double murder and nearly being killed myself. My mom's theory was that life's difficulties were sent to toughen us up, but I hadn't grown tough through this. I'd lost myself. I'd become one of the broken and frail, like the rest of the victim support group.

Now that I was a physical and emotional wreck, I was supposed to waltz into the police station and see the face of the man who had pulled the trigger?

"God, why?" I whispered the words through gritted teeth, hoping Bryan wouldn't hear me from the backseat over Go Fish blaring from the speakers.

At the next stop sign, I glanced back to check on him. His head was wedged against the window at an angle, his eyes were closed, and his mouth hung open. When I turned off the radio, his wuffling snore brought a soothing rhythm to the car. I pulled onto our block and parked in front of the house, tilted my head back, and matched the pace of my breathing to Bryan's.

"Okay, God. You won't tell me why. Can you tell me how? How am I going to do this?"

A memory of my brother surfaced, and July sunlight sparkling on unnaturally turquoise water. I could almost feel the tight pressure of my lungs as I had struggled to swim toward him at the city pool. I blew out into the water, turned my head, and gasped in a quick breath—and swallowed a mouthful of chlorine. My hands floundered for the rough concrete edge of the pool, and I hugged the side, coughing and sputtering. "I can't. I'm scared."

How young had I been back then? Seven? Eight? I still remembered the terror, the way the water lapped my chin and threatened to consume me.

My brother Alex treaded water ten yards away, his arms beckoning me. "I know you're scared. But do it anyway. Do it scared."

A whole summer of Guppy lessons at the pool, yet I'd never braved the deep end. A girl younger than me ran along the diving board and leapt into the air, squealing with joy. She surfaced and paddled to the ladder.

I stared at Alex, taking aim. Then I closed my eyes, puffed out my cheeks, and pushed off.

Sitting in my car, listening to the soft tick as the engine cooled, I remembered the feeling of flinging myself away from safety, water embracing my body, flying forward to safety.

I hadn't drowned.

"Okay, Lord. I'll do it scared," I whispered. "But I'm going to need your help." Then I set about hefting the deadweight of a second-grader out of the car and into the house.

---

The next morning, I pulled myself from bed and managed to shower and dress. Bryan eyed me over his bowl of Cheerios. "Why are you all dressed up?"

"I have to go in and meet with the police. They asked me to identify the man from the Quick Corner."

"Cool!" Bryan bounced on his chair. "Do you get to go in the room where they line everyone up? Do you get to see the jail? Will there be lots of bad guys? Maybe I can come, too. Do you need me to come?"

My lips twitched. "Thanks, buddy. I wish you could. But you have school."

"It could be a field trip." He blinked his wide hazel eyes and gave me his best pleading look.

"I'll tell you about it when you get home. Did you give Gimli fresh water today?"

He gulped a last spoonful of cereal and ran from the table to finish his morning chores.

After the bus scooped him up and carried him off toward school, I grabbed my purse and jacket and walked out to the car.

From the sidewalk, I glared at it. "You don't scare me. I've managed the trip in to the victim center each week. I can do this."

That's what I needed to do—pretend I was going to the victim center for the group meeting or my counseling session and ignore what came next.

My mental trick worked, and I was able to force myself into the car.

Dr. Marci met me in the lobby of the victim center and she studied my face, assessing. "Are you ready?"

I nodded, suddenly mute as my dry throat constricted. I adjusted my purse strap with a hand that trembled.

She smiled gently. "How about if I drive?"

Another nod, and I followed her from the building to her dented two-door Saturn.

"Oh," she laughed when we opened the car doors. "Sorry about the mess. Just toss everything in the back."

I picked up sunglasses, two empty Starbucks cups, and a few books from the passenger seat and set them in the back. It took three tries to fasten the seat belt with my fumbling fingers. Dr. Marci made small talk as she pulled out of the lot. I managed a few mumbled responses, but my knuckles grew white on the armrest. I closed my eyes and willed the car to stop. Could I conjure up a flat tire if I focused hard enough?

This was a mistake. It would set me back in my efforts to get back to normal. My neck began to ache from the grip of knotted muscles. My stomach churned.

"Breathe," said Dr. Marci.

My eyes popped open. "What?"

"You stopped breathing. Deep cleansing breath. Come on."

I struggled to expand my lungs, but the car was still moving, and we were still approaching the precinct office.

"This is such a bad idea." I labored to take in more air.

"Why is that?" Dr. Marci's counseling voice was switched on. She was probably thinking that if she kept me talking it would distract me.

"I'm trying to move forward. I need to put this behind me. Wasn't what I went through bad enough? Why does it have to keep disrupting my life like this? This is guaranteed to make the nightmares worse again."

The car's heater wasn't doing a good job of fighting off the chill air, and I shivered.

Dr. Marci turned on her wipers and washer fluid sprayed the windshield. The surrounding glass suddenly revealed its grime as two wide arcs of clarity appeared.

"I've worked with lots of folk who've gone through trauma," she said. "Most people want to shut out the experience or suppress it, but then it comes out sideways. Sleep problems, physical tics, health issues, depression, anxiety—"

"Okay, I know the list." This snarly, irritable woman wasn't me. Again, I mourned the loss of the real Penny—the fun gal who was bubbly and warm, who people enjoyed being with. "Look, I've started talking about it. I'm facing up to my feelings. But what if the guy threatens me? Or what if he smirks and makes me feel even more anger? What if I say something wrong, or can't be sure of the identification, and the case is ruined all because of me?"

"Breathe. Hey, look at that. They're opening a new Starbucks near the library. Have you visited this library? They have a really cute children's reading room."

We cruised past a cheerful building. Even though I knew Dr. Marci was trying to distract me, a spark of interest interrupted my panic, and I made a mental note to take Bryan to this library one day. My hands were shaking too much to pull out my actual notebook, though.

A few blocks farther, and we turned into a small parking lot.

The building in front of us looked more like a school than a set for *Law and Order.*

"This is it." Dr. Marci turned off the engine.

The innocuous building should have eased some of my terror. Instead I glared at it in suspicion. The Quick Corner had looked safe and innocent, too, and look what happened there.

# chapter 22

I HITCHED UP THE strap of my shoulder bag and marched toward the door. Though I was a wreck, I had too much pride to dissolve into a quivering puddle of jelly on the sidewalk in front of the precinct office. I yanked the door handle and stepped inside. Maybe this was my chance to take back my power. Confront the man who had tried to kill me and feel triumph that he'd failed. Maybe today would be the ultimate turning point.

The lobby was small and neat, like a dentist's office. I pulled up, confused. "Are you sure . . . ?"

Dr. Marci stepped past me to a counter. She pulled out a card. "Dr. Crown from Victim Support Services. We're here to meet with Detective Ramirez."

The young man in uniform at the counter carried himself with military posture. "Yes, ma'am. Have a seat, and I'll page him."

I perched on the edge of a cushioned chair and looked at the landscape print on one wall. Where were the screaming suspects wrestling against handcuffs or the world-weary detectives in rumpled coats? I heard the soft trill of a phone and murmured voices, way too benign to fit my image of a police precinct. Colorful characters arrested for nefarious activities should be slouched in a crowded cell nearby. When I threw a sidelong glance to the room behind the counter, I couldn't spot a barred cage anywhere—only bland desks.

Twisting my hands in my lap, I felt a rough edge on a fingernail and picked at it. Finally, I pried the thin line of white off and began nibbling the edges to smooth them.

"Mrs. Sullivan? I'm Detective Ramirez."

I shot to my feet. When had he walked into the lobby? I was really out of it if I didn't notice someone of his size enter the room. He was well over six feet and had a linebacker's bulk—pure muscle. The citizens of Chesapeake would sleep better at night if they all knew this guy was working to protect them.

"Thank you for comin' in, ma'am." His liquid drawl evoked the same melted honey and pecan as his dark skin.

I gave a halfhearted smile and nodded.

"I'm Dr. Crown from victim support." Doc Marci held out her hand. I suppose I could have done that. They shook hands and exchanged a little small talk. My feet still hadn't budged. I wasn't betting on his chances of making them move.

The buzz of the security door jarred me back into the present. The detective had swiped a keycard and was holding the door for us. "Let me bring you both back to my office."

Office? That didn't sound too frightening. I'd steeled myself to face the ravening suspect through cell bars, or imagined shivering behind a two-way mirror as hardened men lined up by a measuring-tape wall. Still, I stared at the open door and wavered.

With Dr. Marci's light touch on my back, I convinced my

legs to move and followed the man past desks and cubicles, then a short way down a hall that screamed grade school. The water fountain was even at child level. The only things missing were tempera paint art projects taped to the walls.

Detective Ramirez followed my gaze to the water fountain and sighed. "Saving tax dollars. When they okayed expanding the division's precinct offices, they bought a vacant elementary school. We haven't completed the transition yet."

A nervous giggle left my throat. Then he led us into his office, waved us toward some chairs, and settled behind his desk.

"How y'all doing?"

I murmured noncommittally.

His eyes softened. "It was a tough scene. I've had men in my department fall apart seeing the kind of thing you saw. I'm glad you're okay."

His quiet validation almost undid me. I cleared my throat and clutched my shoulder bag tightly. If we didn't get this over with fast, I might lose my breakfast. "So where is he?"

His eyes widened. "He's at the county lockup. I only need you to do a photo ID. The D.A. is working out a plea agreement, so it most likely won't go to trial. But we like having our ducks in a row in case anything falls through with that. We already have the security tapes and the clerk's eyewitness testimony. You're just part of dotting the i's."

No trial? Before I could absorb the relief, the page of six mug shots was in front of me. None of the young men looked particularly happy. I spotted the snub nose and hollow eyes of the boy from the Quick Corner right away.

"Him." I pointed.

I waited for rage, loathing, or fear to jolt me. Instead, I felt cold and empty—as dead and lifeless as the plain white sheet of fax machine paper with the row of faces.

"Okay. Sign here and date it." The detective pointed to a line on the page of photos.

I scrawled my name and suddenly Dr. Marci was ushering me down the hall and out of the building. As we stepped outside, I drew big, gasping breaths, as if I'd just escaped a burning building and needed to clear smoke from my lungs.

With a gentle hand on my arm, she guided me to a nearby bus bench.

I sat and doubled over, hugging my stomach.

"You did it. How does that feel?"

When the waves of dizziness passed, I laughed. "I was so worked up. Lineups and courtroom confrontations and defense attorneys badgering me. It's almost anticlimactic." I lifted my head. "Not that I'm complaining."

I waited for the splash of emotions to settle, so I could assess what I actually felt. Dr. Marci waited with me.

"Does this really count?" I said at last. "Do I have to see him face-to-face in order to heal?"

"Penny, only you can figure out what steps will help you move past this event. Do you want to see him?"

I shuddered. "No." I was uncertain about a lot of things, but I had great clarity on that issue.

"Then trust that instinct. I wouldn't be surprised if some of your anxiety begins to ease after today. You may have subconsciously feared seeing him again, as long as he hadn't been arrested. Now that you know he's going to prison, some of your hyper-vigilance might ease."

I did feel better. Calmer.

The achievement deserved a celebration.

Dr. Marci stood and smiled. "Well, I've got a meeting in a few minutes, so I'll drop you at the center. We can talk about this tomorrow during your appointment."

"Oh. Yes. Of course."

After picking up my car at the victim center, I decided to commemorate my courageous act with another. I stopped at a gas station to fill the car. That errand drained me, but I didn't have a panic attack. I'd probably always hate the smell of gasoline, but maybe it wouldn't always cripple me. On the way home, I took care to avoid the street that passed the Quick Corner where the crime had occurred. I'd been able to confront a photo of the man who tried to kill me, but I was never going to set foot in that store again.

More than anything, I wanted to drive to a friend's house to share my small victory. With a pang of loneliness, it hit home that I'd made no new friends. I'd been in Chesapeake for over two months. By now, I'd expected to be woven into the fabric of church, school, and Navy base.

Back at home, I prowled the empty rooms, and finally sat on Bryan's bed and talked to Gimli as he burrowed into his cedar shavings. Since telling him about my milestone didn't bring much satisfaction, I heated a microwave dinner and brought it over to the computer. While I picked at lasagna, I checked in on a Navy spouses' forum.

Loads of new messages since my last visit. I opened the most recent topic.

*It's my greatest fear.* One woman had posted. *I've tried to prepare for my husband being injured in combat. But I couldn't face this.*

I scrolled back to see what she was replying to.

*Helicopter Accident During Carrier Maneuvers. Three Injured.*

Pasta and cheese stuck in my throat, and I swallowed hard. The message quoted a news bulletin about a serviceman who was being lowered from a helicopter onto a ship's deck in rough seas. The deck rose unexpectedly and the man's spine was injured as he slammed into the deck. Two sailors on the ship were also injured as they ran forward to assist.

Tom had learned maneuvers like that at his basic training. He made lots of Holy Helo trips.

*Oh, Tom. Please be safe.*

Memories flooded me of the day he left for his deployment. I had pleaded a cold, and we decided to say our good-byes at home. I really didn't want to face the crowds or the drive home alone afterward. I wanted to get the whole thing over with before I fell apart.

Sitting tailor style in the middle of the bed, I drank in every detail: Tom's tawny eyebrows, his hazel irises with their flecks of amber; the stubble on the back of his neck beneath his too-short buzz cut; the small crease on his earlobe that I loved to nibble; the lean muscles that stretched as he reached for his bag from the top shelf of the closet.

He rechecked his kit as if he were a Boy Scout packing for his first camping trip. "You're sure you're okay saying good-bye here?"

I reached for a Kleenex and blew my nose. "As long as you don't mind. I wouldn't want to spread my germs to all the Navy families on the pier."

He zipped a pocket shut, tossed the duffle toward the door, and leaned down to hug me. "Okay. Look, I know we promised not to get all mushy, but can I just tell you what a great wife you are?"

I rubbed his back. "Sure. That's always allowed."

"You've had to give up a lot for this."

"Hey, it's what married couples do. Support each other."

He tightened his hug and lifted me.

I untangled my legs and let my feet find the floor. No more casual half hug. Standing in his embrace, the eagerness to get past this moment fled. Now I was desperate to make time stop. I squeezed Tom and memorized the scent of soap on his skin, the warmth of his breath near my ear, the way my head fit perfectly under his chin.

*Don't go. Please don't go.*

"You better get going." I eased away with a last pat on his back. "I'm betting the Navy doesn't approve of tardiness."

He snorted. "You got that right. It's a whole different culture. Not like working at our church back home."

I grinned. "When the youth volunteers would show up after evening farm chores—however long they took."

"And spit and polish meant a clean baseball cap with a tractor logo."

"Those were good years." I kept my voice bright, squelching any hint of nostalgia or regret. "But God's going to use your gifts here, too."

He stared hard into my eyes. "Do you think so?"

His disarming uncertainty was easy to handle, unlike the demons of my own self-doubt that I had to keep caged and out of sight. I met his gaze squarely. "I know so. Let's pray."

We hadn't prayed with each other much since arriving in Virginia. Too busy. Different schedules. We'd gotten out of the habit. Now we pressed our foreheads together in a huddle of three. God, man, and wife. We whispered our hopes and blessings for each other.

Tears began to run down my face, but they were clean tears, so I let them fall.

With a last kiss, Tom had grabbed his bags and headed out the door. Air had sucked out of the room as the front door opened and closed.

Thinking about Tom today brought the same hollow tightness to my lungs. The computer screen served up frightening statistics of Navy fatalities and stories from wives whose marriages were strained to the limit. I pushed away from the computer as if it had stung me. Loneliness was easier to handle than new sources of anxiety. Online chats might provide a sense of companionship, but I wasn't ready for the flood of information I stumbled across.

"Lord, I guess it's just you and me." I carried my plate to the sink and began tidying the kitchen. "Will you celebrate with me? I did it. I went to the police station and saw his photo. Thank you for giving me the strength. And giving me Dr. Marci's support. And thank you that it was much less scary than I expected." From a forgotten place inside me, a song welled up. The youth group kids used to love it. Tom would play bongos when we sang it.

" 'Every move I make I make in You. You make me move, Jesus. Every step I take, I take in You.' "

I sang loudly while cleaning the kitchen. The end of the chorus included a freestyle of "na-na-na's," and I boogied wildly around the space between the kitchen counter and our table.

A discreet tap interrupted me. Laura-Beth's face peered through the back door window, her gapped teeth flashing in a wide smile.

My skin heated as I opened the door. She didn't wait for an invitation, but sashayed right in. "Hey, what's the party about?"

I sighed. Since the floor wasn't going to oblige and swallow me—or better yet, swallow Laura-Beth—I forced an embarrassed smile. "I had to go down to the police station to identify the guy from the shooting. I survived the trip, so . . ."

"They caught him? Woo-hoo! This is a reason to party!" She marched over to my fridge and pulled open the door. "What's all this healthy junk? Juice. Juice. Milk." She shuffled through the contents.

I laughed. "How about if I make us some hot tea?"

"Now yer talkin'. Feels like it's gonna snow out there."

I laughed again. Since the time Tom deployed, two laughs in one minute had to be a record for me. "Back home, we're still wearing shorts when it's in the fifties. This is nothing."

She shivered. "No wonder you Yankees do everything so fast. It's the only way y'all can keep warm."

I unearthed some Fig Newtons, but when Laura-Beth frowned at them, I poured my secret stash of M&Ms into a little bowl and set it on the table. My neighbor kept up a stream of conversation, peppered with plenty of opinions and advice, while I made the tea.

When we both sat at the table cradling our mugs of apple-cinnamon spice, Laura-Beth fell silent.

I sipped and waited, confused by the sudden quiet.

"All righty. Guess ya' figured out I'm not here for a neighborly chat." Beneath her teased bangs, her face pinched, drawing wrinkles into her forehead and around her mouth.

"What's wrong?"

"It's you." Her tone held an edge of anger. "What have you been doing to Jim-Bob?"

I BURNED MY TONGUE on the tea and set it down. "What? What do you mean?"

With my only child, I'd had plenty of experience being the protective momma bear, and I recognized the raised neck fur in another.

Laura-Beth drummed her long nails on the table. "He's been telling me about the stuff you been saying before the boys go to the bus stop in the morning."

*Good morning? Have a nice day? Did you remember your lunch?* I was stumped, and my face must have shown it.

She leaned forward. "You know. Thumpin' their heads and incanting over them."

Incanting? Was that one of those southernisms I didn't know how to translate? "I don't know what . . . Wait. Do you mean when I bless Bryan each day?"

She crossed her arms and lowered her chin. "Mebbe."

I ran a hand through my hair. "From the time Bryan was little,

Tom and I decided to speak a blessing on him when he leaves the house. We pray for him at bedtime. We say grace at meals. It's the same sort of thing."

Laura-Beth lifted her overplucked brows and waited.

"I guess Jim-Bob got tired of waiting for Bryan at the sidewalk," I said. "So he started coming up to our door while I was saying good-bye to Bryan and blessing him. Jim-Bob wanted to get blessed, too." I touched Laura-Beth's arm. "I'm sorry. I didn't mean to offend you. I should have asked you if it was okay with you."

Mollified, she gave me a half smile. "Just so long as you aren't one of those hoo-doo women."

"Hoo-doo?"

She lowered her voice. "Voodoo. You know. Ain't ya seen the house three blocks over near the railroad tracks?"

"The one with all the stuff in the yard painted white?" I whispered without knowing why. Tom and I had noticed the house once when we were out walking. A woman wearing a white head wrap and long white dress had been working in her garden. Blood-red letters with snippets of familiar Bible verses were painted across her porch, and statues of various kinds dotted her cluttered front yard. We'd assumed she showed her faith in eccentric ways. I hadn't guessed that the candles, symbols, and warnings on small wooden signs were part of a dark religion.

"Yep. Folks go to her for magic. Spells. Potions. You know. If you don't mind my saying, that house gives me the creeps."

I shivered. "Believe me. I'm not into anything like that. I'm a Lutheran."

She scratched her head. "Are those Christians?"

I hid a smile. Back home, most of the town was Lutheran by default. Here in Virginia, we were an exotic breed. "Yes. That's why I pray for Bryan each morning."

"My momma was a Baptist, so I guess you'd say I'm one, too. But Ray works so hard that he's always tired on Sundays, and me with all the kids, 'specially the twins—I don't wanna go alone."

Once I might have jumped on her with arguments about the importance of fellowship, but I'd learned a little about the obstacles that could make it painfully difficult to attend a worship service. "I haven't gone very regularly lately, either," I said in a small voice.

"But at least you're doin' that prayer stuff for your boy. My twins are usually screamin' for breakfast when Jim-Bob heads out the door."

I tried my tea again, and let the warmth glide into my belly. "So do you want me to stop praying with Jim-Bob?"

"Nah. You keep it up. It's good for him. Fact is, he's even doing a little better in school lately. I guess a little religion is probably good for him. Now, tell me what you hear from that husband of yours."

Tightness pulled my shoulders. "They're on some sort of lockdown. We haven't been able to e-mail or call for a few days."

Her eyes gleamed with avid interest. "D'ya think that means he's doing something dangerous?"

"Not necessarily."

"Whoo boy." She shook her head. "I get worried when Ray's away for a couple days fishin' with his brother. Don't know how you do it. Do they stop in many ports over there? You know, men always stray when they're away from their woman for too long." She patted my arm.

A moment ago, I'd enjoyed the sense of connection with my neighbor and even felt a bit of tenderness for the open door to talk about faith issues. Now I resisted the urge to grab the nearest skillet and slam it on her head. Instead, I smiled tightly. "Tom and I have a firm commitment to each other."

She pushed away from the table. "Sure 'nuf. Besides, I can see why you'd be more worried about some bomb hittin' his boat. Thanks for the tea. And for explaining stuff."

She sailed out the door and I squeezed the mug in my hands as if it were her neck. "Lord, I know I was feeling lonely, but was that the best you could send me?" Then I chuckled. A hamster, a computer, or an opinionated neighbor without the gene for tact—none were exactly what I needed, but at least I wasn't feeling quite as empty.

A few petals of my old joyful nature uncurled inside me. Energy moved through my body like an old friend. I jumped up from my chair and finished cleaning the kitchen. Then I organized some cupboards, and gave the house a good cleaning.

As I picked up Bryan's room, I noticed Gimli wasn't moving. I tapped on the Habitrail a few times, and he finally lifted his head and gave me a bleary glare. He didn't look very healthy, but how would I tell? I didn't know anything about hamster vital signs. I'd keep an eye on him and see if he perked up for his middle-of-the-night burrowing and wheel running.

My burst of virtuous housecleaning wore me out, and I collapsed on the couch. My notebook rested on the sturdy wood coffee table. I opened it and pondered today's empty page. I slipped the pen from the spiral binding, and tapped it on my forehead, chewing my lip.

Then I wrote, *Wednesday, October 20. Detective Ramirez. Helped him dot his i's.* I doodled in the margin and then added, *Cities of Chesapeake, Norfolk, Virginia Beach, etc. Assisted in getting a criminal off the streets.*

I paged back and looked at my other kind acts. Many of the past days held notations about an encouraging e-mail sent to a stranger on a post-traumatic stress forum. I sighed. A valid way to show kindness, sure. But I had to agree with my support group. The point of my project was to interact with people live and in person—to show love while also challenging myself to reach out for human connections. When Lydia had prayed with me the first time I went to the mission, her warm hand squeezing mine had done more than a dozen pamphlets on dealing with anxiety. I could either shrink into more and more interactions online or break free from my inertia and get out of the house. Maybe tomorrow when I met with Dr. Marci, we could come up with some ideas.

SUDDENLY, I HAD TO check my e-mail again. I was desperate for news from Tom. How long would communications be on lockdown? How quickly would the Navy notify me if anything bad happened?

The computer took forever to boot up. No e-mail. No news on the forums.

I grabbed the phone and dialed Mary Jo, the ombudsman. It wasn't until she answered that I remembered how hard I'd worked to avoid the phone in the past few weeks.

"Penny, it's wonderful to hear from you. How's your cold?"

"B-better. Look, I'm wondering if . . ."

"Tom's fleet is okay? It's hard when they're out of communications, isn't it?" Her voice was warm with understanding and sympathy.

"Yes, and I . . ."

"Do you want to swing by the base? Some of the other wives are meeting—"

"No. I . . . I can't. But has there been any word?"

"Penny, this is nothing to be worried about. Trust me, the Navy makes it a priority to keep families informed. It's easy to let your mind create scary scenarios. Don't go there."

She had no idea how adept my mind had become at fearful Technicolor images.

"I know you've heard this before," she said. "Being a Navy spouse takes as much strength as serving at sea. This is one of those times when you dig down and stand strong. Then when you hear from him, you let him know how confident you are that he'll come back safely. How well you're keeping the home fires burning on your own."

She reminded me of my high-school gymnastics coach who coaxed me beyond my abilities. When she told me I was strong enough for a twisting back handspring, suddenly I was.

"I can do that." No more stammering in my voice. "Thanks."

"That's what I'm here for. I'd still love to go out for coffee sometime soon."

"I'd like that. I've got company coming into town, but after that, I'll give you a call." Alex's last message from his friends' in Pennsylvania had said he aimed to arrive in Virginia early next week. But I pulled out my notebook and wrote a reminder to myself to invite Mary Jo over after my brother's visit.

Not until I set down the notebook and pen did I realize how very normal and ordinary that action had been. Euphoria bubbled up and filled my chest like helium. I was becoming myself again.

I threw my arms wide and spun around, narrowly missing the kitchen table. My giggle whirled through the air. A tap on the back door window interrupted me.

Laura-Beth was back.

Heat flew to my face as I opened the door. Great. Now she'd go back to thinking I was a strange voodoo conjurer.

Her gapped teeth gnawed her lower lip, making her look even more like a prairie dog than usual. She thrust a baseball mitt out toward me.

She wanted to play catch?

"Bryan left this in our yard yesterday when he was playing with Jim-Bob. Figured he'd want it back right away. You know how boys are."

As soon as I took the mitt, she scurried down the steps and out the side gate of our yard.

I took a step forward, an explanation ready, but then stopped. If she thought I was a complete eccentric, maybe she wouldn't pop by quite as often. A slow smile pressed against my cheeks, and I closed the back door.

Bryan and I had a fun evening as he quizzed me on every detail of my visit to the police precinct. He was so disappointed that I hadn't been fingerprinted that I dug out an inkpad I used for rubber-stamping, and we fingerprinted each other. Then we took mug shots with my digital camera.

I was still smiling long after stories and prayers. Bryan slept, and Gimli didn't even squeak on his wheel. I changed into my red plaid flannel pajamas and crawled into Tom's side of the bed, where I settled down for sleep, ready for happy, hopeful dreams.

For once my subconscious cooperated. I snuggled deeper under the quilt, as flickers of sleeping scenes gradually took hold. Sunlight sparkled through mimosa leaves. I stroked one of the leaves and it curled up shyly. Wind brushed my skin and cool grass tickled my bare feet. I pushed past a wide lilac bush and crawled through a gap in the tangled greenery. Even while I enjoyed the whimsy of roses blooming on a lilac bush, and daffodils budding at the same time as mums, part of my mind acknowledged that the combination of plants was impossible, even in a botanical garden.

I touched a vibrant blue morning glory, and tendrils of the vine reached out and curled around my finger. Gently, I pried it away and continued through a tunnel of green. Before me, a glass door beckoned.

As I pushed it, sleigh bells bounced overhead, announcing my passage.

Fear began as a tingle in my chest. Cheerful sunshine tried to reassure me, but dark dread called its warning. "Get out. Go back."

I turned, but the door had disappeared. Through glass walls I saw gasoline pumps and cars.

A back door. Maybe I could find a back door.

I stepped into the store. Rows of shelves stretched into eternity, ten feet tall, leaning inward. Under my feet, the tile felt as wet and cool as the earlier dew.

I looked down and whimpered. There was no dew. Only blood.

The bright sunlight through the glass magnified the horror—made the blood stand out like vibrant red finger paint. My mind wobbled, and for a moment it was easy to believe children had played on the convenience store linoleum, smearing an abstract picture around the bodies.

An old man and woman sprawled across my path, playing dead.

"Sir? Ma'am?" I knelt near them, resting my hand on a shelf of beef jerky treats for support. "The game's over. You can get up now."

I touched the woman's shoulder. "It's okay. It was a mistake. You can get up now."

"Get back!" A figure loomed over me.

I skittered backward, trying to hide behind the magazine rack. Wild, bloodshot eyes found me. The man raised his gun.

*No. Not again.* I squeezed my eyes shut.

*Tom, I love you. Take care of Bryan. Don't forget to pack a cookie in his lunch.*

*Click.*

No explosion. No pain. No death.

I slitted my eyes open. The man was fumbling with his gun. I touched my forehead where the bullet should have struck. Sirens wailed in the distance. The man shouted a string of curses and ran from the store. Cheerful bells jingled as he rang out into the sunshine.

Bryan loved that song. "*Jingle Bells . . .*"

I crawled forward to the elderly woman. Lifeless eyes stared in the direction of the beverage machine, as if she were pleading for one last drink. I had come here looking for Coke, with lots of ice to ease the Virginia heat. Why hadn't I stayed home?

"Noooo." The wail tore from my lungs.

The bells jangled again. He was coming back to finish me.

I tried to scream but only moaned. Then I bolted upright, tangled in sheets and blankets. Sweat drenched my pajamas, and I clutched a pillow to my chest, shivering in the grip of the nightmare, like a rag doll in a pit bull's jaw. I concentrated on breathing until I could force myself to turn my head and find my clock.

Three thirty. Adrenaline coursed through me. It screamed at me to move, while the terror froze me in place.

I used one hand to pry the other free from its grip on the blanket. Slowly, painfully, I moved my legs over the side of the bed and found my footing. I stumbled to the bathroom and peeled off the damp flannel, then stepped into the shower. I let the water run so hot it nearly scalded my skin, but still the shudders came.

Hidden by the wall of water pouring over my head, I sobbed, letting the tears fall to spin down the drain.

*Why? Why now? This isn't fair. I'd faced my fear.*

Six hours later, I posed the same question to Dr. Marci at my appointment. "This was one of the worst nightmares yet. It was so . . . so *powerful.*"

Dr. Marci sipped her coffee. "I know it doesn't seem like it, but your unconscious mind is doing its job. It's trying to process things while you sleep."

I snorted. "Well, it's not going to get very far if I wake up screaming all the time."

"The nightmares have been less frequent, though, right?"

"I guess. But this was the worst ever."

She nodded. "A normal reaction after seeing the photo yesterday."

"Normal? Nothing about me is normal anymore." My voice sounded shrill in my ears.

"Have you reconsidered seeing your doctor?"

I yawned and shook my head. "What if word got out that the chaplain's wife can't cope? Tom tried to get me to go to the base shrink before he left, but I wouldn't. It's not a good idea."

"You're afraid that using a psych med would make you officially loony. But what if it gave you the biochemical help you needed to heal from a genuine trauma?"

"Never helped my brother."

Dr. Marci leaned forward. "Let's talk about that. How do you feel about his upcoming visit?"

I rubbed my eyes. "I don't know. My sister, my parents, they all sound so happy and excited. But where has he been all this time? He just disappeared. Why didn't he get in touch sooner? It's been twelve years. Twelve years! I don't even know if he's stable or if it's safe to let him into my life."

"Sounds like you have a lot of questions to ask him."

The suggestion plunked into my mind, like an uninvited guest on the couch. It hadn't occurred to me that I should direct some of those stormy questions at him. I'd planned to tiptoe, smile, and hide from a gracious distance. "Oh, that reminds me. I have to miss group on Tuesday. Alex is coming on Monday, so I'll be spending time with him."

"Why don't you bring him along?"

"To group?"

She smiled. "It's an open group. I suspect he has some experiences to share that could benefit others, even if they aren't directly crime related."

"We'll see."

She gave me the same knowing frown that Bryan always used when I resorted to momspeak.

I drove home with a dull headache at the base of my skull and familiar weariness weighting my bones. When I entered the house, the bedroom sang a siren song. Odysseus made his men stuff wax in their ears, but I doubted that would help me. Still, I had to fight this. I didn't want to fall back into the pattern of sleeping all day.

I made a pot of coffee and drank cup after cup while surfing the Internet. The caffeine helped me shake off fatigue as I chatted on forums. But the longer I sat in front of the computer, the more sadness crept over me like long afternoon shadows.

Summoning every ounce of willpower, I logged out and

pushed to my feet. Time to work on my project. Time to do something kind for a new person—a live person. I had a shopping bag full of baby clothes to donate to the mission. I should have gone right after my appointment with Dr. Marci. Pushing through the force field covering the doorway for a second time was almost too much to demand of myself, especially after the rough night I'd had.

With a deep breath, I surged down the steps and along the sidewalk. My feet followed the now-familiar path toward the storefront mission. When I reached the dented door of the mission, I didn't hesitate, but walked right in.

The room still smelled musty, although today there was no snoring old man in the armchair. Instead, a baby shrieked and two preschoolers raced among the folding chairs, knocking a few over while they made zooming car noises.

Lydia paced the floor under the painted cross, jiggling the baby at her shoulder. The infant howled all the louder.

She glanced my way, eyes wide. Then she smiled in relief. "Welcome back," she called over the noise. "If you want to pray, you might need to wait a spell."

"Your baby?" I set the bag of clothes next to the couch.

She shook her head and patted the small back. "Her mom had a job interview, so I said I'd watch these three—but it's taking longer than I thought, and this little gal isn't too happy."

Automatically, I reached out. Lydia deposited the baby into my arms.

She rummaged into a worn canvas bag. "I think there's . . . Here it is." Lydia unearthed a bottle, which she handed to me.

I settled onto the sagging armchair and chased the baby's tossing and twisting head with the bottle, coaxing her to taste a drop of milk. Finally the ferocious cries calmed to whimpers and then the sound of contented sucking. Wide brown eyes stared up at me, set in pale skin that was still rosy from the bout of crying. I smiled. "There. That's better, isn't it? Your mama will be back any minute. Aren't you an itsy-bitsy sweetie pie?" The cooing words slipped out like a reflex.

Lydia snagged the two boys as they zoomed by. They were fair and brown-haired like their infant sister and flushed with energy. "Story time," she said firmly. "No running in God's house."

One of the boys swiped at his runny nose. "St. Joseph's is God's house."

"Yes, it is. He has more than one house. Now come sit down."

Somehow she coaxed their fidgeting bodies onto the couch beside her, and she picked up a tattered children's magazine from the coffee table.

I fed the baby while she read the story of a girl who learned not to tell lies, interrupted by frequent questions by the oldest boy. Lydia answered each question and doggedly returned to her reading again and again, while I hid a smile at her exasperation.

Spit-up stains marred the lapels of her blazer, and one side of her conservative Afro jutted out where little hands had tugged. She looked as if she'd had a long day, and it was only two o'clock.

I stroked the cheek of the baby, whose eyelids began to droop. My own lids felt heavy. I hadn't gone back to bed after my nightmare, and even my earlier coffee binge couldn't hold back the sleepiness.

A shape moved past the tinted glass window and the door swung open.

"I can start Monday!" A curvy woman with a mass of dark curls swept into the room. She looked too young to be out of high school, much less the mother of three. Her eyes sparkled with the same excited energy of the two boys, who leapt from the couch and raced toward her with happy shouts.

The baby startled in my arms and let out an indignant wail.

The young woman stalked toward me and snatched her baby away as if I'd been sticking her with pins.

Lydia slowly rose to her feet. "Wendy, this is my friend Penny. She's a mother, too."

"Although mine is a little older," I smiled. "Bryan is seven, so he's in school. But I miss those cuddly days."

Unimpressed, she gave me a terse nod, then shooed her boys to the door. "Now I have to find someone to watch them every day." She gave Lydia a speculative look. "My aunt said she won't take them . . ."

Lydia shook her head. "I'm sure you'll find someone. And I'm always here for emergencies. But I have other people who need my help."

Wendy turned to me, and her frost became a cloying smile. "But what about your friend, Penny? She'd love to help, right?"

MY EYES WIDENED, BUT before I could frame an answer, Lydia guided the young mother firmly toward the door. "Penny has her own responsibilities. And you have yours. Talk to your aunt again." She pulled a folded paper from her blazer pocket and tucked it in the diaper bag, which she helped drape on Wendy's free shoulder. "I wrote down the names of some grandmas who might be able to help."

The young mother flounced out the door, herding her two toddlers ahead of her.

I ran a hand through my hair and sank back against the cushions. "Maybe I should have offered. I could help her watch her children. . . ."

Lydia crossed her arms and gave me a stern look. "Penny, I know you're looking for ways to help people. But don't help them in a way that hurts them."

"How would that hurt anyone?"

"Wendy would love for me—or you—to drop everything and

take care of her children. But they're her children. Her responsibility. I can support her, but I can't do it for her. Did God tell you to take over her parenting for her?"

"Of course not. I just—"

Firm nod. "Exactly. If He had, that would be different. But you weren't thinking about obeying the Boss. You were thinking it's your job to keep people happy. And it's not."

"But I know what it's like to feel overwhelmed. To need some help."

"Good." She straightened the magazines on the table and picked up the fallen folding chairs in the back row of the "church" area of the room. "Compassion is a good thing. Enabling isn't. I'm trying to help people be responsible for their choices."

More psychobabble. Had Lydia gone to the same school as Dr. Marci?

She must have noticed my wrinkled nose. "You don't agree?"

"I'm just trying to sort out how it could be wrong to help someone."

"Spoken like an idealist who's new to the neighborhood." Her grin was gently mocking. She sank onto the couch and pulled off one of her low-heeled pumps and rubbed her foot. "But it's good to see you. I was hoping you'd come by again. How are you?"

"Better." I realized it was true, even though pushing myself out my doorway today had been a huge effort again. I looked around the room and the evidence of Lydia's never-ending work. Would serving ever come as naturally to me as it did for her? I noticed the weariness around her eyes. "How do you keep going?"

She slipped her shoe back on and began rubbing her other foot. "Most days I want to run back to my comfortable apartment and give up."

"But you don't."

She finished massaging her foot before answering. "Honey lamb, you know how you felt when you were holding that baby?"

I nodded. Pure adoration. I couldn't stop admiring the sweetness and beauty of the clear eyes and the tiny fingers.

"Ev'ry morning I spend some time lovin' on God that same way."

I let her words soak in while I tried to pinpoint her secret. "You mean praying? I *do* that already."

She leaned forward. " 'Course you do. But how much time do you spend lovin' on Him? You know, like the way you were lookin' at that baby a few minutes ago."

She made it sound so simple. But the idea snagged me. Could my journal record more than a list of clumsy good deeds? Even more than a list of blessings like the gratitude journals that were so popular?

I rubbed my eyes. How would that help me get out of the house more? "I started my project to force myself to be more active, not all contemplative. But adoring God is—"

"Very active."

Before I could argue, Barney sauntered in from a back door, sorting through a stack of mail. He lifted his bushy brows and smiled at me. "Welcome back. Are you being penny-wise and pound-foolish?" He chortled at his own joke.

"And where have you been?" Lydia marched to him and plucked the mail from his hands. "I thought you were going to help me with Wendy's boys. If Penny hadn't stopped in, I don't know what I would have done." She tore open an envelope and frowned at the contents.

He rubbed his chin and studied the floor, casting glances toward Lydia. "I picked up those boxes from the Ladies Guild.

I've gotta take another trip to get the rest." He backed quickly toward the door.

"Mm-hmm." Lydia didn't look up until the door banged shut. She pulled her nose out of the mail and stared after him. She sighed, and softness touched her eyes. "I don't know how I'd manage here without Barney. He keeps this place running."

I crossed my arms. "Maybe you should tell him that."

She blinked. "He knows. The last thing I want to do is feed his ego. He doesn't think a woman can run this program. He's always sniping at me."

I fought a grin. "Kind of like Tom criticized my musical tastes when we met. And I teased him about the baseball cap he always wore."

"What are you saying?"

I lowered my voice. "I think he likes you."

A hint of burgundy flushed on her chocolate skin. "Honey lamb, the man can barely stand to be in the same room with me."

"That's not how it looks from where I'm standing."

"Gal, you're standin' in a funny place. That's all there is to it. Get on with you." She shooed me toward the door. But when I opened the door, she cleared her throat. "Thanks again for helping."

I laughed. "Anytime."

I got home in time to whip up some Rice Krispies bars for Bryan. Hardly gourmet delicacies, but he was impressed. Before heading to his room to play, he even gave me several sticky kisses. I savored each one, wondering how long it would be before he decided he was too old for open affection. I chased that sad thought from my mind as I cleaned the kitchen. God's gifts didn't need to be hoarded or clung to with desperate fear. He had new ones around each corner. Today he'd given me a seven-year-old with cheeks still round with baby fat, and soft downy arms, and mosquito bites peppering his legs, who tumbled through life with glee and loved seeing how hard he could hug me. One day my gift would look different: a coltish ten-year-old who showed affection with a macho punch to my arm, a pimply teen wavering between melancholy reserve and brilliant insights, an independent man making brave choices and giving me one-armed hugs from a height above me.

"Lord, I adore you," I whispered. "Your gifts blossom and grow and change shape. You are so lavish in your generosity."

Emotion thickened in my chest and throat. Licking marshmallow from my fingers, I grabbed my pen and wrote my realization about God into my notebook. In smaller print, I jotted down, *Fed Wendy's baby*—not sure if that good deed had been for Lydia, the baby, or Wendy. I flipped back through the notebook. The back pages held scattered tidbits of information and advice. The front of the notebook held records of awkward good deeds that gradually changed into entries about daily efforts to reach out to random strangers. Finally a few Bible verses appeared in the margins along with thoughts about what God might be speaking to me. Today's page felt even richer. I ran my hand delicately over the paper as if reading Braille, realizing I was touching another blessing. Was this what healing looked like?

"Mom! Mo-om!" Bryan yelled from his room. How did such a small body produce such a loud bellow?

I hurried up the hallway. "What's wrong? And what did I say about your indoor voice?" I tripped over his backpack in the doorway.

His chin quavered, and he pointed to the Habitrail complex. "Something's wrong with Gimli."

It took a moment to find the curled up body in the pile of

shavings. I tapped the cage lightly and Gimli lifted his little hamster head, eyes weepy and red.

Bryan was right. Something was wrong.

"Mom, do something!"

Hamster CPR? I couldn't even bring myself to touch the rodent. "I'll call the pet store."

The clerk I reached was disinterested and unhelpful. Gum snapping between words, she assured me that she couldn't imagine what was wrong, and they only sold healthy animals, and the best course of action would be to call a vet.

I jumped online and searched for the closest veterinarians. The first three I called didn't treat hamsters. Finally I reached a clinic that specialized in "exotic" animals. I'd never thought of a hamster as exotic, but all I cared about was that the receptionist said their vet was terrific with rodents.

Unfortunately, they were closing in thirty minutes. Yes, they could squeeze me in if I hurried. No, she had no guesses about the problem. The vet would need to see him to figure that out.

Bryan scooped his fuzzy friend out of the cage and into a shoebox. Shoeboxes were the classic coffin choice for small pets. I hoped carrying him in one wasn't a bad omen.

We raced to the car, and I followed the MapQuest directions to the Portsmouth Veterinarian Clinic twenty minutes away.

The parking lot outside the clinic was almost empty, but thankfully the clinic door was still unlocked. We rushed into the waiting room, assaulted by the smells of cat box and wet dog and antiseptic. The receptionist looked up from her computer and gave us a perky smile. She handed me a rainbow of different colored forms. I couldn't imagine what kind of medical history she expected me to provide for a hamster.

"Okay, it's thirty-five dollars for the office visit. Would you mind paying now? We normally take care of payment at the end of the visit, but I'm leaving for the day. Are you signed up for our pet-care program? It's only twenty dollars a month and includes a discount on vitamins."

I shook my head and glanced at the shoebox that Bryan clutched to his chest. Gimli was awful quiet in there. "No, that's okay." I pulled out my checkbook. Our five-dollar pet was becoming an expensive investment. Still, you couldn't put a price tag on little-boy love. Bryan was worried enough about death—between Tom being deployed and his mom nearly being shot. He couldn't lose a pet right now.

The vet was rotund and moved slowly. The various animals he cared for probably found his style nonthreatening. The molasses pace as he led us to an exam room set my teeth on edge. "So is this your first visit with us?"

Even by southern standards, his words came out painfully slow.

I gave short answers to his small-talk questions about weather, how many pets we had, how we liked Virginia. Finally he opened the shoebox and adjusted his glasses to study the hamster.

"What have you been feeding him?"

"Supreme Feed Mix, sunflower seeds for treats, and vitamins." Bryan answered with grave maturity.

The vet blotted his sweaty face, still moving slowly. But he won my heart when he looked Bryan in the eye and directed the rest of his questions to him instead of me. My heart swelled, and then twisted in pain as I watched my son carry the weight of parental love—even if it was for a rodent.

After peering at Gimli from various angles the doctor returned him to the box and leaned back. "Well, the good news is that he has a small abscess under his eye. We can treat that. The bad news is that the stress has also caused some wet tail. But you caught it early. He's not too dehydrated." The vet stood slowly and pulled a few boxes from a nearby shelf. Then he pulled out a receipt book.

"Okay, antibiotics." He paused in his scribbling to glance up. "Put that in water or hand-feed him with an eyedropper twice a day." He continued his calculations. "The eye cream is pretty expensive. You'll want to apply that each morning, and watch him to be sure he doesn't scratch at the sore."

How were we supposed to convince him not to scratch?

But Bryan nodded earnestly.

"Okay." The vet stuck out his tongue as he concentrated. "That'll be ninety-six dollars. And you already paid for the visit, right?"

Ninety-six *American* dollars? He had to be joking. "Um, yeah. I gave the receptionist a check for thirty-five."

"Okay." He tore the receipt from the book. "I can take your check for the rest. Now, Bryan, there's one more thing that Gimli needs."

I held my breath, wondering how else this animal doctor planned to bankrupt me.

"They should have told you at the pet store. Most hamsters get lonely easily. You know, Gimli had Legolas as a friend." The vet gave a wide smile. "You might want to get Gimli a companion. Just be sure it's another female."

Bryan gasped. "Gimli's a girl?"

"How can you tell?" I peered into the box.

The vet scooped Gimli up again and gave us a quick education—more than I ever cared to know about the nether parts of rodents. Then I wrote another check and thanked the vet for staying late.

Reassured that Gimli would most likely recover, Bryan bounced along beside me as we left the building. "Know what?

We should go to the pet store right away. Gimli could help us pick a friend for him. Her. Whatever."

"Maybe we better wait until Gimli is over this infection. Besides, you can keep her from being lonely. Only one more day of school and then you have the whole weekend to play with her."

He gave a dramatic sigh. "I s'pose. But you have to promise to play with him . . . her . . . when I'm at school tomorrow."

Great. My assignment tomorrow—get antibiotics into a transgender hamster and cheer her up. Not to mention revise our budget and find an area to cut to compensate for the vet bill.

Antibiotics: sixty-five dollars. Hamster eye cream: thirty-one dollars. Office visit: thirty-five dollars. Hopeful smile on Bryan's face—priceless.

FRIDAY MORNING, BRYAN AND Jim-Bob fidgeted on the top step near the front door. Cold, damp air made me shiver. The temperature was far milder than Wisconsin in late October, but the humidity seemed to soak the cold into my bones. I blew on my hands, then rested them on the ski-capped heads of the boys. "Heavenly Father, thank you for keeping us safe all night. Be with Bryan and Jim-Bob today at school. Thank you for who you are. For never forgetting us. For watching over the people who are precious to us even when we can't." A tear escaped one of my eyes, and I sniffled as I said, "Amen."

The boys stared at me. Jim-Bob shifted and gave Bryan a little kick.

Bryan rolled his eyes. "Mom, we're only going to school."

I smiled as another tear escaped. "I know. I just love you."

Both boys groaned and gave each other a very male look of disgust for weepy women, then galloped away.

I laughed and swiped away more moisture from my face.

After the bus came and went, I hurried to the computer. The emotions so close to the surface were more about Tom than Bryan. I'd still had no word. I tried to ration myself to checking e-mails three times a day, but self-control grew harder as each hour passed.

While the screen booted up, I grabbed a cup of coffee and swept cereal bowls into the sink. I wiped down the counters, then hurried back to the living room.

My fingers shook as I hit the icon to take me to our e-mail program. As the computer whirled and labored to collect e-mails, I cupped my coffee in both hands and took a slow breath in. "Lord, you love Tom even more than I do. You are able to protect him. You are perfect love and perfect strength."

This practice of adoring God still felt a little awkward, but I was determined to work on it. Lydia was right. I'd focused on serving, on trusting, on thanking, on listening. All good. But I often forgot how to simply love God. Or maybe I hadn't forgotten, but had been too angry and confused to try.

E-mails appeared on the screen. Forwarded jokes from a few friends, spam offering to introduce me to male enhancement products, a note from Cindy, and—

My coffee splashed as I thumped the mug down on the small table. I moved my mouse to open the e-mail and accidentally hit Delete. Then I rescued the e-mail from the deleted file and tried again. This time my nervous fingers managed to open it.

*Hi, my million-dollar Penny,*

*Sorry about the communications blackout. Hope you didn't worry. I miss you a ton. I'll try calling soon. Although I think Chaplain Mordai was right. Remember he said that he didn't call home very often when he was on deployment, because it made the homesickness worse? Somehow, e-mails don't rip out my innards quite as much as hearing your voice.*

*I got your e-mail about Alex. Wow. I wish I were there for you. I know it has to be hard. And Bryan must be learning so many new things. I worry that he'll be driving and holding down a job by the time I get home. I miss you both.*

*A hundred and one kisses. Your lonely hubby.*

Tears ran down my face, and I touched the screen with one finger, as if Tom's love and tenderness could seep from his e-mail and into my bloodstream. As I reread the words, a smile tugged my lips. He had a gift for understatement. Hard? Hard was seeing an old boyfriend at a high-school reunion. Hard was a tax audit. Hard was rubbing cream on a hamster's eye. Alex's upcoming visit was beyond hard.

Still, Tom's concern strengthened me.

His e-mail was too short. Of course, he'd never been garrulous, and out of concern for the men he served, he didn't share details of his conversations or experiences. He also couldn't say too much about where he would be heading next. All around, a frustrating situation.

*Don't be greedy, Penny. At least you know he's alive.*

I blotted up the splashes of coffee with the sleeve of my sweatshirt and hunkered down to write him a long e-mail. For those minutes, I could pause with my fingers over the keys and my eyes closed and pretend he was sitting inches away from me.

*Hi, hunky husband,*

*Of course I worried. You'd have hurt feelings if I didn't worry a teensy bit. Bryan talked me into a hamster that he named Gimli. It got sick and we found out Gimli is a girl and needs a roommate, so this weekend we'll head back to the pet store.*

*I went to the police station to ID a photo. I guess they caught the guy and he pled guilty, so there won't be a trial. Don't worry. Dr. Marci from the victim center went with me. She's been a big help.*

*I found a little ministry place within walking distance, and I really admire the woman who runs it. I think I'll start helping out once in a while.*

*Yeah, having Alex reappear after all these years has me feeling all mixed up.*

I paused. There were a hundred things I wanted to talk to him about. That mental illness might run in our family. That one day I'd have a breakdown and drop out of sight like Alex had. That I wouldn't be the woman he expected when he got home. Instead, I decided to sign off.

*I'm so proud of the work you're doing. Bryan and I are praying for you all the time. One hundred and two kisses. Your favorite wife.*

I sent the e-mail and sat back with a happy sigh. Even distant communication was better than none. Knowing Tom was within reach through my computer again gave me the courage to face Alex's upcoming visit.

---

Saturday, my brother called from a friend's house in Washington, D.C.

"I could drive down tonight, or should I come over Sunday?"

"Um, how about Monday?" I wanted to meet the first time while Bryan was at school. After that I could make a decision about introducing my son to his uncle.

"Sounds good. For you, I'll even get up before noon. Do you have a Starbucks near your house? I'll spring for some coffee."

I laughed. He sounded so normal. "Don't tell me you're a Starbucks addict."

Silence muted him for a moment. Then he sighed, and his

easygoing façade slipped. "The least of my addictions." Dark currents swirled beneath his quiet words.

I shivered. I really didn't know him anymore. I knew the warm-spirited older brother from my childhood. I knew the angry, despairing man battling serious illness from my teen years. I knew a dozen years of cruel, uncaring silence. Who was he now?

Then again, who was *I* now? Months ago I'd been confident, together, and blissfully unaware of how painful each day could be. Now I knew how it felt to be broken. I was best friends with brokenness. She wasn't a friend I'd wanted to make, but she brought some gifts along. She crumbled prideful independence. She had the power to stir compassion. Everyone suffered. Everyone made some bad choices. Everyone caught in the darkness held out a palm hoping for a touch of grace to light the next step.

Warmth pushed away my unease. "It'll be wonderful to see you, Alex. I've missed you. We have a lot to catch up on. And get me their breakfast blend with cream and sugar—the biggest they've got."

He chuckled. "It's a deal. I'll be there by ten."

"That's your idea of early?"

"Yeah, yeah. You and Mom both. Up at the crack of dawn, kids to feed, floors to polish, committees to organize."

I giggled. "Not lately." For some reason, that admission didn't bring the swoop of shame and depression I'd grown to expect whenever I glanced at how my life was looking. "I spend the days hiding so my next-door neighbor doesn't accuse me of voodoo or make me wallpaper her house, tricking the hamster into swallowing her antibiotics, checking for e-mails from Tom, getting pulled over by the police for crying while driving, and hanging out at a storefront mission with Popeye and Condoleezza."

Another silence from Alex. Then he cleared his throat. "Except for the hamster, I'm right with you. Sounds like a typical day in the life of a Norton."

"Except Cindy."

We snickered as only siblings could. "Yeah," he said. "She's got her life a little too organized for anything interesting to happen."

"Sometimes I wish I could go back to when things weren't interesting."

"No, you don't."

---

I was still smiling when Bryan and I ventured to the pet store to find a friend for Gimli. The teenage clerk had no idea which hamsters were females, so Bryan and I grabbed likely candidates and upended them to check. Frankly, I couldn't tell the difference, so we made a best guess and bought Legolas.

When I started the car up, the warning light flashed. Almost out of gas. My skin felt prickly with heat, then cold. I'd sailed through this errand, but at the thought of buying gas, panic throttled me. I glanced at Bryan. I could park near a gas station and sit there until Bryan turned sixteen. Then he could fill the car.

Or I'd just drive the car until it ran out and then leave it at the side of the road until Tom got back from sea. He could take care of it then. A much saner notion.

I pulled out of the parking lot. At least I didn't have many places to drive in the next few days. That gave me a little reprieve.

---

I even managed to get us to church Sunday morning and lasted through the service without rushing out in panic. The lector read strong, true words. I could read the same words in my Bible at home, but absorbing them along with a few hundred other people touched me with more power. The congregation spoke the creed with conviction. The pastor dug into the book of Galatians and explained how God creates fruit in our lives. Best of all, I shuffled my way to the altar for communion. Kneeling at the railing, hearing the words "The body of Christ, broken for you," I felt God's embrace. He understood brokenness. I suspected many of the others kneeling beside me understood it, too. I feasted on faith in ways I had missed by being home alone for so long. It's as if I'd been standing alone by the kitchen sink eating stale potato chips. Now I gathered with family and savored the banquet of grace.

Dr. Marci had told our group that growth isn't a steady consistent road. Two steps forward, one step back. I'd seen the pattern of improvements and setbacks in my own life. So the flare of horrible nightmares Sunday night wasn't too much of a surprise.

My dark imagination painted vivid scenes of mental hospitals. I wrestled against orderlies who dragged me toward the room where they gave electric shocks. I fought and screamed and tangled in my blankets. When I clawed my way to consciousness, I woke with a throbbing headache and stumbled to the bathroom for aspirin.

I must have been more worried about the visit with Alex than I'd realized. I'd talked myself out of my fear of descending into madness, but my sleeping mind hadn't gotten the message.

Alex hadn't sounded irrational when we'd talked. Why was I so afraid?

I crawled back into bed, but Bryan bounded into my room and leapt onto the mattress. "So will Uncle Alex be here when I get home from school?"

"I'm not sure what his plans are."

He trampolined on the bed, forcing a groan from my chest. I closed my eyes "Bryan, I've got a headache."

He flopped down alongside me. When a long silence stretched taut, I opened my eyes.

Bryan's bright hazel stare hovered inches from my face. As soon as he saw the whites of my eyes he laughed. "Cool. That always works."

I rubbed my forehead. "What does?"

"If I get real close and watch you long enough, you open your eyes."

I pounced and tickled him, even though his giggles shot pain through my head. "Okay, buster. Now make your bed. I'll get your Cheerios ready. If you hurry, you can send a message for Dad before school."

He tumbled over me and skidded from the room in his stocking feet.

"Bryan, wait! How's Gimli?"

He slid back into the doorway. "She's happier. Legolas likes her new house, too." He gave me an assessing look. "Maybe you should try some of Gimli's medicine. Works really good."

I threw a pillow in the general direction of the door and he scooted away, laughing. Despite the headache, I grinned and shook my head. "Lord, he's a charmer, that one. How did I get so blessed?"

I propped up and pulled my Bible onto my lap along with my notebook. Residue of the nightmare still twisted in my mind like a nest of snakes. Psalms would help. Those psalmists understood terror. My concordance didn't have an entry for post-traumatic stress or for fear of losing my mind. But I found a good chapter about God's protection and comfort. I read slowly and chose one verse to repeat again and again. If I could memorize one sentence to carry through the day, maybe I'd make it.

I copied the verse into my notebook along with a quick prayer. "Heavenly Father, your laughter lightens every heart. Thank you for making little boys and hamsters and giggles. Thank you for helping me laugh again. You are so tender and patient. I know you understand."

"Mom! I can't find my math paper."

My feet hit the ground and I gave my Bible a soft pat. In the corporate world, executives faced the tyranny of the urgent. In my world, I faced the tyranny of the missing homework. But the brief time with God had begun to unwind some of the snakes from my brain, and a few even crawled away to leave me in peace.

Once Bryan's bus pulled away, I poured myself a second cup of coffee. Alex might be bringing Starbucks, but I needed fortification sooner than that. I even brought the mug into the shower with me. That was a mistake. Jasmine shampoo did nothing for the flavor of Folgers.

Still, the caffeine and shower chased away my headache. Humming, I pulled on jeans and a sweater. I blotted my hair and ran a comb through it. Then my fingers took the place of the comb's teeth as I paced the house. Alex wouldn't arrive for another hour, and each minute gave me time to build anxiety. I scrubbed the kitchen, cleaned the bathroom, plumped the living room pillows, and played a few rounds of solitaire on the computer. Even that failed to hold my interest. Maybe I'd overdone it on the caffeine.

Finally, a car door slammed. I peered around the living room curtains. A thin man in a leather jacket walked up the sidewalk with two takeout cups. I pulled the door open.

"Penny?" His throat sounded thick, as if he were getting over a cold. "You look exactly the same."

I'd forgotten the copper glints in his mahogany-brown hair. Now I was surprised by the feathery accent of silver that joined them. His skin hung loosely over the bones of his face, as if he'd gained and lost weight several times. But when he smiled, the hangdog look disappeared and I recognized the brother from my childhood. He held a cup out toward me. "One large breakfast blend with cream. As ordered."

"Thanks." I finally managed a smile and took his offering, glad that with our hands full, I wouldn't be expected to hug him. Our family had never been huggy, and I definitely wasn't ready to throw myself into an embrace with this man I barely recognized. "Come on in."

Alex wiped his feet and strolled into the living room.

I closed the door. "You're taller than I remember."

He gave a surprised laugh. "I haven't grown. Maybe it's like going back to your childhood home. Everything looks bigger than you remember." He set his coffee on the table and shrugged out of his jacket.

We settled on opposite ends of the couch.

"So how *was* your visit to the childhood home?" I asked. "Was Mom playing Cleopatra?"

He smiled. "Queen of denial? Yeah. Some things haven't changed." He leaned back, at ease. No hint of apology or remorse.

My blood began to burn and veins in my neck throbbed. "So," I said tightly. "How was your drive? Good weather for it?"

He drew a deep breath. "I can see it's eating at you. Get it over with. Ask me the questions you need to ask."

*Hold it together, Penny. He knocked over your sand castle, but don't come up swinging.*

"Okay. I'll ask." The word caught and I cleared my throat. "Why did you leave? Why didn't you ever tell us where you were?" I stopped before the sting behind my eyes betrayed me with visible tears.

"Those were tough years." He picked at a thread on his jeans, a small tremor of his hand revealing that his own emotions weren't as placid as I'd thought. "I felt like a defective car part. Everyone kept trying to fix me. I . . . I resented it."

"But they only—"

"I know. They were trying to help. But I hated it. I did the only thing I could think of. I left it all behind. Escaped the weight."

"What weight?"

"Of causing so much grief. Of being the 'problem.' "

"But where did you go?"

He sighed and some of the weight he'd worked to escape pressed on his shoulders. "I made some stupid choices. Chased away my demons with drugs the doctors had never tried." He gave a crooked smile. "Not a great way to find sanity—but it held back the pain for a while."

"Drugs . . . ?" Instead of shock and contempt I felt sadness and a strange understanding. Hadn't I wished for something to muffle my misery in the past weeks?

He misunderstood my silence and raised his chin. "I've been clean for years. One day at a time and all that."

"Good for you. That takes a lot of courage."

He blinked and relaxed deeper into the cushions. "Don't put me on a pedestal. I have lots of regrets. But I turned things around about six years ago."

Six years? And even after that, he never let us know he was alive. My jaw clenched. "Back to my original question. Why? Why did you cut us all out of your life? Couldn't you have sent a postcard? Anything? Do you have any idea what it felt like?"

He looked away from my virulent words but didn't interrupt as I flung each question across the space between us.

"After you got clean? Why didn't you call then?" I hugged my knees against the pain in my stomach.

"By the time I got to a place where I might have been able to handle seeing the family, so much time had gone by I felt . . . ashamed. Ashamed of where I'd been. Ashamed of all the time that stretched between us. Does that make any sense?"

"Sort of." Some of the nettles of rejection and disappointment fell from my skin. I'd done something similar after the shooting. I'd been driven to the ground by fear, guilt, and anger, and I'd done all I could to pull away from people. He'd struggled for years before dropping out of sight. Coming back must have terrified him.

I reached for my coffee cup and hid behind it to take another sip. "Maybe I would have done the same thing. But still . . . all those holidays without you. You missed my wedding. You missed Bryan getting born, his baptism, all his birthdays." The nettles still embedded in my soul began to throb again, so I stopped talking.

"I know." His eyes met mine. They were clouded with emotion, but also held a dull tint of jaundice. He didn't look well. "I'm really sorry."

The coffee burned in my stomach and I swallowed hard. Is that why he'd come back? Was he seriously ill? Dad or Mom or Cindy would have told me if . . . Wouldn't they? "Why now?" A lump of dread tried to choke me while I waited for his answer.

# chapter 27

"NO, NO, NO." HE reached forward and touched my arm, then quickly withdrew. "Nothing like that. I know I don't look great. Hepatitis, among other things. But I didn't come back to stage some tragic death scene." He grinned. "Mom thought the same thing. I should have worn a shirt that said, 'I'm not dying.' "

I forced an answering smile, but it came out as a wince. "Not funny, Alex."

"Sorry. Look. I know I have a lot to explain. But it's your turn. I want to know how you're doing. I got some garbled version from Mom—just enough to make me worry."

My lips flickered upward without effort. "I can imagine." Suddenly, Alex slipped back into place as my older brother—the brother I'd always confided in when I was a little girl. I took another gulp of coffee and launched into my story of Tom's deployment, the challenges of moving to a new part of the country, and the shooting. He was easy to talk to, although I skated carefully away from my fears that I might break down one day as he had. A comment like that didn't seem very polite.

He listened with his whole body, focused like an English pointer on a duck. I finished my summary with the recent visit to the police precinct. He nodded with something like admiration. "Imagine: all my years on the street with no efforts at personal safety, but it's my cautious, reliable sister who's nearly shot. The world's a funny place."

"Yeah. Real funny."

He sobered. "Is it getting any better?"

"It was rough for a while, but I think I've just about got it licked."

Alex watched me. He didn't take my confident statement as a hint to brush aside the topic. Didn't hurry to a new subject. Didn't offer advice. Just waited.

A quiet voice nudged me. *Tell him the truth.*

He'd been open about his own struggles. I didn't need bravado with him. A fellow visitor to the dark valleys wouldn't despise me for admitting my fears. "I had a really bad nightmare after I went to the police station. And last night—" I clamped my lips together. Idiot! Don't bring up mental hospitals.

"Spiders? Snakes? Swirling down the drain at the neighborhood pool?" he teased.

I sputtered. "Those nightmares were your fault. You told me that if I didn't kick hard enough, the drain would suck me down. I had bad dreams for months."

He laughed. "Yeah, but you learned how to swim."

I stuck out my tongue.

"Watch out or your face will freeze that way. Come on, sis. It helps to talk."

A throw pillow captured my attention, and I fingered the

fringe along the edges. "In the dream I was in a hospital. A mental hospital." I glanced up.

His brow furrowed. "Ooh. Super deluxe nightmare. That's about as bad as it gets. What happened?"

"Some orderlies were dragging me to a room where they were shocking people. I couldn't get away. They were going to scramble my brain cells, and I kept fighting." I shook my head. "Sounds silly, doesn't it?"

"No. Electro-convulsive therapy is a scary idea." His voice rasped, and he reached for his coffee and drained it.

"Did you . . . did they . . ?"

"Yep. I should have known Mom and Dad never told you. They were horrified when the doctors recommended it. Appalled that neighbors might find out their son was that defective."

"Oh, Alex. You were never defective. You were brilliant and sensitive and so terribly sad. There were days when I wanted to yell in your ears—force happy thoughts into that sad place inside your skull."

He grinned. "It probably would have worked better than everything else they tried. But why were you having nightmares about ECT?"

I gnawed a cuticle on my pinkie finger. "Maybe because I've been so . . . unpredictable lately. I kind of figured it would be my turn next."

"Your turn?"

"To go . . . you know, crazy."

To my surprise he leaned back and laughed. "Penny Penguin, you are the sanest person I ever knew. You can't have changed that much in all these years."

I hadn't heard that nickname in decades.

"Oh, yeah? Well what about not being able to sleep for days, and then spending weeks doing nothing but sleeping. And the botanical garden—some guy bumped me and I thought I was having a heart attack . . ." Suddenly, my words couldn't come out fast enough. Alex had plenty of experience at the frayed edges of sanity. I told him each bit of evidence that I was nuts. No matter what I admitted, he didn't seem alarmed. He continued to nod, listen, and reassure.

When I ran out of proof of my frazzled mind, I rubbed my temples where my headache had reasserted itself. "You can see why I'm worried. I've even been going to a support group."

He didn't laugh. "Sounds like a good plan. I wish I'd accepted help sooner. But Penny, you're not crazy. You're having a normal reaction to incredible stress. You're already improving."

"I forgot to tell you about the tinfoil helmets I made so the aliens couldn't read my thoughts."

His eyes widened.

I grinned. "Gotcha."

He groaned and clasped his head, tilting back to look at the ceiling. "For this I drove all the way to Virginia?"

I giggled. "Are you hungry?" We'd been talking for over an hour, and lunchtime was creeping closer.

"Now you're talking." He surged to his feet. "Where's your bathroom?"

I sent him down the hall and hustled into the kitchen to whip up some fried-egg sandwiches. He'd loved them when he was living at home.

A few minutes later he meandered into the kitchen and sniffed the air with appreciation. "I should have gotten in touch a long time ago." Behind the breezy words, a shade of genuine regret colored his voice.

"Make yourself useful. Can you get out the iced tea?"

"Got any Coke?"

I stiffened. "I don't drink it anymore. I was at the convenience store to get some that day . . . when the . . ."

Instead of a murmur of sympathy, he tsked. He found two glasses and squeezed past me to open the fridge. "Sis, you're doing a great job healing, but you know there's something you still need to do."

"Drink Coke? Puh-lease."

He laughed. "No. But you said you haven't gone back. Where it happened."

A cold draft hit the back of my neck, and I whipped around to close the refrigerator door—but it was already shut. "That's not gonna happen. Do you want cheese on yours?"

"Of course. But, sis, you really—"

"Nah-ah. Your turn. No food unless you promise to tell me how you got better."

"Blackmail! Extortion!" He pulled out a chair at the table in the alcove.

"This from the guy who hid my diary until I convinced Mom we needed a swing set."

"It worked."

Laughing, reminiscing, and filling our mouths with gooey egg and cheese, the years fell away. He told me about Cindy's new baby, how much older Mom and Dad seemed to him, and revealed snippets of how he'd spent the preceding years. He nagged me to consider facing down the Quick Corner and paged through my photo album, admiring my wedding photos and Bryan's baby pictures. It wasn't until he glanced at his watch and pushed away from the table that I realized he hadn't explained how his life had stopped its downward spiral.

"I need to go, sis. I've got a meeting tonight, and my car's been overheating, so I wanted to take it in to get looked at first."

"Bryan is dying to meet you."

"I'm free again tomorrow. I could take you both out for dinner."

A generous offer. His car was rusty, and his jacket was worn. Wherever the years had taken him, a win on *Who Wants to Be a Millionaire* hadn't been one of his stops. "Sounds good. No, wait. I have my victims' group tomorrow night." I chewed my lower lip. "Dr. Marci said I should invite you. She thought you'd have some insights for our group."

"Insights?" His chuckle was warm. "Sure. Why not? But you still have to eat. What time is the meeting?"

"Seven."

"Okay. I'll pick you both up at five. Where do you like to eat out around here?"

"I haven't had time to try many places." Eating out didn't mesh well with agoraphobia, but I didn't bother reminding him of that. "I'll do a Google search for someplace close to the victim support center, okay? What do you like?"

"Anything I don't have to make for myself."

"Maybe there's a Cheesecake Factory around here. You could do with some fattening up."

"So could you," he shot back. "It's a deal. Major calories. I'll be here at five tomorrow."

He breezed out the door, and his car sputtered as it pulled away. I collapsed on the couch. Memories and emotions swirled like dust in a cyclonic vacuum, and I closed my eyes against their force.

---

"So, is he big? Does he play football?" When Bryan got home from school, his questions fired at me faster than I could follow in my post-nap fog.

"He's pretty tall. I didn't ask if he's played football lately.

Bryan, where's the costume information?" His classroom newsletter had warned parents to watch for the list of supplies needed for the upcoming Thanksgiving play.

"My backpack. Know what? He could stay here until Dad gets home. Then he could fix things, and play football with me, and lift heavy things. Stuff like that."

I couldn't wait to e-mail Tom about Bryan's description of the male role in the family. "Honey, Uncle Alex has his own life." Although what that comprised was still a mystery to me.

"Did he like Gimli and Legolas?"

"Go get me the costume list."

He scampered to his room and back in record time. "How many seconds did that take, Mom?"

"I wasn't counting."

He huffed loudly and planted fists on his hips. "Count this time."

"But I—"

Paper still clutched in his hand, he tore back up the hall.

"One-Mississippi, two-Mississippi, three-Mississippi . . ."

He skidded into me before I reached eight. Triumph flushed his face as he thrust the crumpled paper at me. "I'm fast, aren't I, Mom? Did Uncle Alex like playing with Gimli and Legolas?"

I smoothed the page, and my eyes crossed at the long list of suggestions for costume pieces. "He didn't meet them this time."

When the silence stretched, I tore my gaze away from reading. Bryan's arms were crossed, and his scowl was fierce. "Mom. Why didn't you show him my hamsters?"

*Think fast, Supermom.*

"I knew you'd want to introduce them to him yourself. He's coming over tomorrow."

Bryan leapt onto the couch, somersaulted across it, and

bounded up to stand on the cushions with one foot planted on the arm. "Yippee!"

Last time I'd watched nature shows on PBS, the silverback gorilla pounded his chest in the same stance.

*Time to stake out my own territory.*

"Bryan, no jumping on the furniture. We've gotta figure out this costume."

He plopped down to floor level. "You can just sew it. Can I play with Jim-Bob before supper? What's for supper? Know what? I don't think you should make grits anymore."

He charged through the kitchen and out the back door before I could answer.

I pulled out my notebook and grabbed my pen. *Reminder: shop for Pilgrim costume.* I finished reading the parent letter. *Bake brownies. Sign forms. Schedule after-school rehearsal.* Basic errands were still harder than normal, and I faced new challenges as we drew closer to the play. I also needed to go in to meet Mrs. Pimblott. We'd spoken on the phone, and she assured me that some of Bryan's attention problems had improved. But I couldn't keep avoiding the basics of parenting—teacher meetings, being a room mother, school events.

I sighed as I closed my notebook. First I had to face the immediate concern: supper. Next came introducing Alex to my support group. And soon I'd have to do something about my car that was running dangerously low on gas. Weariness pressed into me like the lead apron at the dentist's office.

I booted up the computer and ordered a pizza.

# chapter 28

Ashley sulked, arms crossed. "So who's this?"

Henry, Camille, and Daniel all stared at me, waiting for an answer. The conference table felt smaller with an extra chair pulled up to it. The air smelled like burnt dust again. The victim support center really needed to get the furnace vents cleaned, but considering the flaking pea-soup paint, I wasn't placing bets that it would happen anytime soon.

Dr. Marci placed her pen and steno pad on the table and folded her hands over them. "I asked Penny to invite her brother. He's in town for a visit."

Daniel tried a small smile, and then dropped his gaze to his corduroy pants. Camille ran a finger under the collar of her sweater set and glanced Alex's direction. "Well, isn't that nice. Where ya'll from?"

Alex leaned back in his chair. Wherever the years had taken him, he seemed to have acquired the ability to feel at ease in a new group. "I've been living in Texas. Working as a counselor at an in-patient treatment center."

My mouth gaped. I hadn't gotten that much info from him in a whole afternoon of probing.

Henry frowned. "This is a group for crime victims. What are you a victim of?"

Alex chuckled and rubbed his arms, probably feeling the chill in the room. "There have been a few traumas along the way. But crime? The worst has been what I did to myself."

"We're about specifics." Ashley's smirk wavered somewhere between grudging acceptance and challenge.

Alex turned clear eyes her direction. "Okay. My name is Alex, and I'm an addict. It's been six years since my last fix." He spoke calmly. Not defensive, not hiding in shame, simply stating his brand of suffering and failure.

And as simply as that, the group welcomed him into our club—Dr. Marci's Support Group for the Odd and Anxious.

"Your sister started us all on a project," Camille said.

He glanced at me. "Really? She didn't tell me."

"T-t-tell him," Daniel whispered without looking up.

I sighed. "It's not a big deal." I gave him a rundown of my plan to coax myself out of the house and into interactions with people as I battled PTSD.

"We call it Penny's Project," Henry said. He sneezed and pulled a paper napkin from his pocket. A few packets of ketchup and mustard fell onto the table from its folds. He must have stopped at McDonald's before our meeting and soothed his anxiety with a few hoarded items. "This week I stopped to help a guy with a flat tire, paid for the meal of the car behind me at the Taco Bell drive-through, and raked leaves for my neighbor. But the real test came on Friday." He stuffed the napkin back in his pocket, ignoring the condiments. His back seemed straighter this week, and his chin more firm. "I was waiting for an elevator on my way to a job interview, but a guy's briefcase had spilled his papers everywhere. I stopped to help him and found out he was on the way to interview for the same job. My interview was at ten, and his was fifteen minutes later."

All of us were leaning forward, waiting for the punch line.

"I helped him organize his files and pull himself together, and got to the office a few minutes late. But when I met the head of the department, the guy gave me a huge smile. He'd been down by the elevators and saw the whole thing. Said he was tired of workaholics so driven they don't even notice the real people around them."

His grin was so big I could see each of his teeth. "They hired me. I started yesterday."

I let out a whoop that was drowned out by the other cheers.

Color rose in his cheeks. "Thanks, everyone. I hope I'm ready for this. I won't be doing cutthroat brokering anymore. Just financial planning. But I think I'll like it."

"Of course you're ready." Camille touched her cheekbone, a reflexive gesture she'd used before, as if monitoring the healing of her bruise. The marks were gone now, but her fingers still found the place.

"Your ring!" Ashley pointed to Camille's empty finger, and the older woman quickly stuffed her hand into her lap.

"I haven't given up hope. He might get help one day." She ducked her chin. "But it was time to let go of believing I could fix him."

I wanted to cheer. Over the past weeks, she'd wavered between revealing horror stories of her abuse and blaming herself.

"I found an apartment, too. It's near my church, and I've started playing piano for the Sunday school."

She played piano? Our group focused so much on our wounds; I sometimes forgot that each person around this table also had talents, skills, and dreams. Week by week, we performed debridement like nurses in a burn unit . . . scraping away the dead skin and searching for signs of anything pink and healthy. But sometimes it was hard to see beyond the damage.

Dr. Marci smiled at the stories of her eaglets trying their wings. "Ashley, how was your week?"

She shrugged. "Same old, same old. But I picked up a brochure from the community college." She lifted her gaze and watched us, suddenly vulnerable and hungry for encouragement. "I'm sort of thinking I might try to take a few classes."

"Great idea," Dr. Marci said, with our backup chorus of murmured agreement. "What do you want to study?"

"Well, I sort of like kids. I keep doing Penny's Project stuff for the kids I meet at work. So I thought . . . maybe I'd wanna teach some day."

A few months ago I would have choked at the image of Ashley as a teacher. But she'd revealed more than her direct, fearless approach to life. She'd also shown us her tenderness as she talked about reaching out to hurting children. Any child would be blessed to have her for a teacher—although I hoped she'd cover up the tattoo on her shoulder before entering a kindergarten classroom.

"Daniel, how was your week?" Dr. Marci leaned back and pulled her notebook into her lap. Keeping her focus away from the older man seemed to negate any feeling of pressure the question might cause him.

Even so, he played with a button on his jacket and mumbled under his breath for a minute, rocking slightly in the chair next to mine. Matching myself to his slow movement, I leaned closer. "How is Sammy?"

He stopped swaying and pulled his awareness outward, giving me a smile as soft as his voice. "Good. I even took him to the park yesterday. Three whole blocks." He dropped his gaze again. "There aren't as many people as on weekends. Sammy doesn't like too many people."

I nodded. "I feel the same way sometimes."

"I sat on the porch one day, and said hello to the mail carrier."

"Daniel, that's wonderful." Dr. Marci kept her voice pitched low. Too much enthusiasm had sometimes driven Daniel from the room and back behind his four walls—the only safe place in his universe.

"Did he say hello back?" Camille asked.

Daniel nodded, looking a bit weary from this long conversation. "She. She said hello."

"Excellent," Dr. Marci said gently. "Alex, why don't you tell us more about your journey?"

"Yes, Alex, why don't you?" I muttered.

He grinned in my direction, then let his gaze travel around the table. "I suffered—and I do mean suffered—from depression when I was in my teens and early twenties. You know that expression 'I've lost my mind'? It's an accurate description. So I went looking for it. I traveled, did odd jobs, made friends here and there. For a while it helped to be away from the hospitals and the doctors and the medications that turned my brain to mush. But when the pain came back, I needed something to make it stop." He stared into his Styrofoam cup of water. "You know that part."

"So what brought the change?" Dr. Marci asked the question I'd been trying to get him to answer.

He rubbed his chin. "I was in a detox center in Chicago. Not by choice. Police had picked me up after a . . . disagreement in a bar. So I slept off the worst of it, and that morning anyone who wanted to could go to a meeting. I figured it would be the typical A.A. meeting. A chaplain with some volunteers to help lead it, you know?

"It's funny, 'cause I really only went for the coffee. But there was a family there—with a beat-up guitar and a couple kids. They sang this song, 'You Are my All in All.' One little girl with the sweetest voice sang about shame, and an empty cup, and Jesus."

Alex swallowed, staring at the table as if it were a plasma screen playing out the scene. No one moved, and the silence pulled at us.

"Hard to explain without sounding stupid." His voice rasped.

"Hey, man. Take a look at who you're talkin' to," Ashley said. "You don't have a corner on weird."

Alex nodded but still grappled for words to describe his experience. "God spoke to me in that song," he finally said. "In that room at the end of the hall in that smelly, noisy, detox center. In the voice of a little girl who probably didn't understand one atom about the kind of shame and emptiness I felt."

My eyes pricked in empathy.

"That's the moment that I started the road back." Still looking down, Alex began to sing. Gravel textured his baritone, and his voice was soft. But line by line he gave us the song a family had once given him. A family who probably never knew whether their volunteer visit to the detox center made any difference to anyone.

No one moved. No one interrupted. When he finished the song, the only sound in the room was the rustle of Kleenex catching tears and noses blowing.

"Amen," Camille whispered.

Alex looked up and smiled, bringing us back to earth as he settled against his chair. "Like I said, that's where it started. Long road, you know? God healed my soul, so at first I figured He'd fix everything. But I was still nearsighted, still had athlete's foot, and still had something wrong with the wiring of my brain. So I got glasses, some dry socks, and meds to help me with the physical part of the depression."

Dr. Marci scribbled a few notes in her steno pad. "But you didn't contact family right away?"

Alex's smile faded along with the warm color of energy in his cheeks, leaving a yellow tinge. He looked at me. "I wanted to. But I was scared. There was this weird connection in my mind between mental illness, psych wards, feelings of failure, and my family."

"You were afraid that if you went back home, you'd lose ground," she said.

"Yeah." He looked at me again, eyes asking for understanding.

I shifted and looked away. "You could have left a phone message. Sent a note. Something."

"Do you think Mom and Dad would have left it at that?"

He was right. One hint of his presence, and they would have pounced, pulling him back into patterns that he might not have been strong enough to resist. If he'd contacted me and not them, I'd have been snarled in secrets. Still angry at his choices, at least I understood his dilemma.

"What changed?" Henry asked.

"My work at the treatment center. I kept seeing how important it was for some people to face their past." His smile came back, a little lopsided, and he looked at me again. "Facing fears is an important step in healing, isn't it?"

My stomach knotted. Oh, he was a sly one. Subtle as a train

wreck. "I think moving forward is more important than looking back."

"Sure." Dr. Marci stood for a moment so she could pour cups of water and pass them around the table. "If someone has a fear of snakes, but never needs to spend time with snakes, it might not be vital to confront that fear. But if someone is a chef and afraid of vegetables, it might be important to take steps to desensitize."

Henry and Camille chuckled. Ashley rolled her eyes, and Daniel smiled.

I crossed my arms. "And I'm not a gas-station attendant. So it's not a problem for me."

"But you needed me to drive tonight because your car is out of gas."

"Penny, tell us about your fear," Dr. Marci said.

I loved the warm fuzzy part of this group. I wasn't so wild about the relentless probing. I shot a glare at Alex. "Sure, I'm a little twitchy about gas stations. I've tried a few times, but it always gives me a panic attack."

"Maybe it would help to have someone with you," Alex said.

"You want to come with me to fill the car with gas? Sure. Whatever." I pinched scallops into my cup's Styrofoam rim with my fingernail.

"I could come with you back to where it happened. Sis, don't you think this would lose some power if you faced it down?"

Excited murmurs around the table added momentum to his idea. I looked at my watch. "Wow, I need to get Bryan home. It's a school night, you know."

Dr. Marci smiled. "Penny, no one is forcing you to move faster than you're ready for. Maybe you can take that step after Tom gets back from his deployment."

Unfair. The one thing capable of tipping the scales in my inner debate. I wanted to push through this barrier *before* Tom returned. The scene of the murders continued to haunt my nights and cripple my days. Alex was right. Barriers to healing were serious things.

Sure, Tom would be willing to help me, but that wasn't what I wanted for his homecoming. I wanted to be ready to support my husband when he got home. And time was running out.

I squared my jaw and faced Alex. "You're on. I'll take you on a field trip tomorrow."

He nodded gravely.

Daniel slipped from his chair and ducked out of the room. Ashley gave a low whistle. "That'll be some story. I can't wait for next week."

Camille rubbed her cheek. "You could come to the mission tomorrow night." She smiled at me. "Are you coming again?"

I shrugged. One thing at a time. Though I did want another chance at nudging Barney and Lydia toward each other.

Camille turned toward Ashley. "Lydia is starting a morning Bible club for moms with preschoolers and needs some volunteers to play with the kids on Friday mornings."

Ashley chewed her lower lip, making her lip ring flicker. A hint of color rose on her pallid cheeks. "Yeah, might be fun. My shift doesn't start until the lunch rush."

Dr. Marci stood as the meeting broke up and then met me at the door. "I think visiting the site will be a good step for you. We can process it at your appointment on Thursday, okay?"

Did she sound confident or worried? I couldn't be sure. But the knot in my stomach left no doubt about which I felt.

# chapter 29

THE NEXT MORNING BRYAN ran in tight circles around the kitchen table as if he'd been taking lessons from his hamsters. He thought meeting his uncle last night had been "way cool," and his morning chatter reached new levels of energy. I sighed with relief once it was time to hook a backpack on him and open the front door.

On the steps, Jim-Bob swiped a sleeve under his runny nose and handed me a jar with a gingham patch tied over the top with raffia. "Mom made some gooseberry jam."

I knew as little about gooseberries as grits, but this gift of friendship fed my courage for the day's looming challenge. "Tell her thank you, okay?"

Jim-Bob pointed to his yard. Laura-Beth waved from her front door, her bleached hair flying around her head and a quilted robe hanging open over a flannel nightshirt. I grinned and waved back. "Thank you!" I hollered in good southern fashion.

"Welcome!" One of her twins wedged past her legs and onto the steps, so she pulled him back inside and closed the door.

Jim-Bob nudged Bryan. "She started blessing me now, too." He tried to sound annoyed, but his small chest filled and a dimple dented some of his freckles.

I knelt and gathered both boys close and squinted as I brought to memory a verse I'd read that morning. "Dear Father in heaven, 'everything you do is right and all your ways are just.' Thank you for helping these fine boys walk in ways that are right. Protect their steps, and give them courage for the work of the day. Amen."

They scampered off. "And give me courage for the work of the day," I breathed.

Jangled nerves fueled another cleaning frenzy as I waited for Alex to arrive. I gave Gimli the last of her antibiotics. Her eyes were clear and bright, and from the way she fluttered her scratchy little feet against my palm, she was clearly feeling feisty again.

When I finished my morning chores, and a few afternoon and evening ones as well, I stopped in front of the television and picked up Tom's disc. He'd told me there was only one more message. I should probably save it a little longer.

But when would I need some support more than at this moment? I breathed on the shiny disc and buffed it gently with an electrostatic cloth. I inserted the movie, but the screen remained blank. *This is crazy. Why is this one disc so finicky?* Or was it a problem with the DVD player? I pulled the television away from the wall to loosen and reattach the cables.

When he arrived, Alex found me in a mess of power cords, dusty stacks of commercial DVDs, and haphazard electronic equipment. "Did the hamsters get out?"

I shoved the TV back into place, and pushed hair off my face. "Stupid recording. Stupid stubborn recording."

"What?"

I settled back on the floor, tailor style. "Tom recorded some messages for me the day before he left. I know this sounds weird, but the silly thing only plays when it's in the mood."

He raised an eyebrow. "So you were . . ?" His wave took in the mess around me.

"Trying to see the last message. Something to make me feel better for today. For . . . you know."

He tossed his jacket on the couch and came to sit on the floor near me. "Let me try."

I gave him the disc.

He checked all the connectors for the system before inserting the movie. Nothing played. "Sis, this is a blank. Do you have a supply of these for backing up your computer or burning downloads? You probably grabbed one of those by mistake."

"No. This is the one. I keep it on the top shelf. And now it's not talking to me." I grabbed the remote and tried every button one more time. The screen remained blank.

"I'm sorry." His eyes were clear and guileless. Even better, no worry lines to indicate that he thought his sister was a sugar-sweetened, orange-dyed, vitamin-fortified Froot Loop. "Maybe God is letting the messages play when you most need them."

"Alex, I'm serious." I searched his face for any sign of mockery.

He met my eyes steadily. "I've seen some strange things since I left Wisconsin. It's better not to rule anything out where God is concerned."

A warm tingle spun up my spine and raised the hairs on the back of my neck.

"Well, if God is controlling the DVD, why won't it play today when I need it so much?"

He shrugged and stood, brushing his dusty hands off on

his jeans. "Maybe He knows you'll get more from it later. Now, quit stalling."

The visit to the gas station. My make or break moment. I'd either conquer this last hurdle and start moving forward or I'd have the proof that I couldn't cope and would never be normal again. A sensation very like morning sickness washed over me, and I heard someone whimper.

Alex suddenly shoved my head down toward the floor.

I wrestled against his arms. "What are you doing?"

"You turned white. I didn't want you to faint."

I knocked his hands away and came up glaring. "You idiot. I'm not going to faint."

"Okay, then."

"Okay."

"So get your coat."

The sick feeling swooped back in, but I marched to the closet for Tom's hooded sweatshirt. "You driving?"

"I could. But it might be better if you drive your own car. Re-create the event, you know?"

I crossed my arms. "You sound like you've done this before."

"Taken my sister to the convenience store where she witnessed a shooting and nearly got killed?"

I kicked the closet door shut. "Ha, ha. I meant, you sound like you almost know what you're doing."

He shrugged. "I got a social work degree along the way, and some of what I do at the treatment center involves counseling."

*I can send what you need.* God whispered quietly—a soft cashmere scarf wrapping around my heart. At a time when I had felt most alone, He sent me my brother, who just happened to understand trauma and just happened to be a professional counselor. And that wasn't all. He'd sent me Dr. Marci and her Troupe of the Terrified, and Laura-Beth, and Lydia and Barney, and . . .

I picked my purse up from the table by the door and looked for my keys, praying silently. *You never left, did you? I didn't recognize you all the time, but you've been here.* Gratitude gave me the push I needed to stride out to the car, leaving Alex scrambling to catch up.

The first few blocks were like a drive to the victim center, or church, or anywhere else. Low-grade anxiety buzzed inside my skull, but it didn't paralyze me.

Then I turned left toward the gas station and Quick Corner. An instant wave of heat scalded my skin, and my arms shook. The car slowed. A horn honked and someone passed me. I pulled over to the curb and stopped.

"So, have you driven down this street since it happened?" Alex asked conversationally.

I shook my head. If I opened my mouth to speak, my breakfast might end up all over the dashboard.

"That must have taken some creative maneuvering. Isn't this the shortest way out to the main road?"

His words peppered my nerves like sleet. I closed my eyes and went inside myself. *Breathe in. Breathe out. Stop shivering.*

"Penny, you did it. You're on this street and you survived it. You've taken a step forward."

I squeezed the wheel and opened my eyes. He was right. Until today, driving on this road had seemed impossible.

"So what do you think about going one more block?" Alex pointed to a stop sign. "Could you drive us that far?"

I swallowed hard. "One block?"

"Yep." He leaned against his armrest and smiled as if he had all the time in the world. "One block."

Checking to be sure the street was clear, I pulled out and drove to the next corner. From there I could see the traffic lights ahead that guarded the corner gas station. My car idled at the stop sign. Another horn tooted a staccato triplet. I flinched.

Alex twisted to look behind us. "Why don't you pull ahead, so this guy can go around you? Just across this intersection."

I nodded. After a check of the cross street, I wobbled through and pulled over in front of a house. The van behind me drove past, and the driver threw a curious stare our direction. Probably thought I was a student driver. A nervous student driver.

"Hey, Pen. Wanna pray?"

Alex's words triggered a grateful exhale. The knots in my muscles loosened. "Great idea."

We'd never prayed together before. Unless you counted "Come, Lord Jesus" at supper when we were kids. I let Alex's quiet petitions wash over me. When he stopped, I struggled to form words. "God, I don't think I can do this." Sweat beaded on my face. "But if you go with me, I'm willing to try. Help me take the next step. Amen."

My heart still tap danced against my ribs, but the sensation of floating above my body had disappeared. "Okay. What's next?"

"Can you drive up to the Quick Corner and pull into the lot?"

At this point, I was eager to be off the road, so I nodded.

Another block, a turn at the green light, and I pulled into the convenience store lot and parked. I turned off the ignition and squeezed my eyes tightly shut.

"What's your favorite song?"

"Huh?" I opened my eyes and stared at Alex.

"You looked like you were getting lost in there. I thought it would help to chat about something."

Past his tall form, I could see the glass doors of the store. I leaned back and closed my eyes again, fighting nausea. "I should have pulled up to the pump. The car is empty."

"Sure. Let's do that first. I'll fill the car for you."

I reached for the key, but my hand shook so hard, I pulled it back into my lap. Tears squeezed past my lids. *Oh, God, I don't want to be here.*

"Tell you what," he said gently. "I'll switch places with you, okay?"

*Yes. Take the wheel. But drive me to the ER. Maybe they can knock me out and make this throbbing terror go away.*

He got out of the car and walked around to the driver's side. I slid across to the passenger seat, and leaned forward laboring to breathe.

From somewhere far away, I felt the motor start and stop, heard the door open and close. Suddenly Alex was talking to me again. "Okay, time to go in and pay."

Already? Time had distorted. Moments had rushed by and disappeared. Yet, the current, pregnant second stretched into eternity.

*Just get out of the car and walk. You can do that. Walk into the store.*

Alex opened the passenger door and offered his hand. "Remember what I told you when you didn't want to climb up to the tree house?"

"Yeah. Your favorite line. You said it all the time. 'Do it scared.' But this is a little different than a tall tree, or a wobbly bike without training wheels, or the deep end of the community pool."

He nodded. "Yep. This is easier. No climbing, pedaling, or swimming needed."

"Anyone ever tell you that big brothers are a major pain?"

But his teasing had done its job. The latest wave of dizziness released me, and I stepped out of the car.

The smell of gasoline hit my nose, but in the cool autumn air, the note of sun-baked asphalt was missing—cushioning me from a full sensory flashback. A middle-aged woman hurried to the doors and set off jingling bells as she entered the store. The sound mocked me, but I squared my shoulders and followed her in.

The linoleum captured my attention first. Scuffed and gray, it could have used a good mopping. No viscous red crawled across the tile, but my memory filled that in. Blood clouded my vision.

A firm hand tugged my elbow, pulling me out of the way of another customer entering the store.

"You promised me a field trip," Alex said quietly. "Walk me through it. Where did you go that day?"

I tore my gaze away from the hallowed, cursed patch of floor. "I wanted a Coke." My shaky hand pointed toward the wall near the back with its beverage dispenser. I took a few steps. "I stopped in the candy aisle."

*The old man and woman were nearby. Teasing each other. Taking stiff, unsteady steps.*

"Then what?" Alex's voice pulled me back to the present.

"The bells." On cue, the door opened with a jangle. My chest moved faster as I panted, trying to find oxygen.

"Penny, look at the front of the store. There's no one scary in here today."

I turned to face the horrible doors. Sunshine streamed in, illuminating smudges on the glass. Out of the corner of my eye, I saw the man in the baseball cap. I snapped my head to the side, but no one was there.

"Alex," I whispered. "I'm not sure this was a good idea."

"Tell me what you see. Not what your memory sees."

I struggled to obey. "The doors. The checkout counter. The

floor. A lady in a green coat. A man in a jean jacket. Rows of shelves. Beef jerky. Snickers bars."

"Good job."

I nodded. "They moved the magazine rack where . . ." I stepped to the place where I'd held the woman's hand as life stopped flowing through it. I crouched and tied my shoe as an excuse to touch the floor. Cold. Dry. Death had touched this place.

*I am the Resurrection and the Life.*

My lungs expanded. She wasn't here. Her husband wasn't here. Death's power was no longer here. I rubbed my forehead, touching the place where the bullet would have entered. God protected my life on a late-August afternoon on this exact spot. And even when it was time to face death again, it couldn't destroy me. *When the time comes, He has new life ready for me.* I sank onto my knees as gratitude and hope pushed back another layer of pain.

"Lose something?" The shoes of a clerk came into focus.

I stood and stuffed my hands into Tom's jacket pockets, wrapping its edges around me more tightly. "No. Sorry. I was just . . ." My gaze traveled up to a name badge. *LaShaunda.*

"Girl, I remember you," she said. Dozens of small braids tipped with plastic beads framed a chocolate face. Alex hovered behind me. Another customer came in and set off the bells. "You were here that day."

A weak smile strained my lips. "You were, too. You're still working here?"

"Hey, my manager offered to have me transferred. But I figured, what are the odds of two shootings in the same store? I'm safer here than at a new place." She gave a sassy grin and tossed her braids. "Didja hear the guy's locked up?"

I nodded.

"Excuse me." The sour voice of a businessman carried from the checkout counter. "Is anyone working here today?"

LaShaunda hurried to her station and rang up his coffee and muffin. I drifted closer, and after he left I leaned on the counter.

She busied herself with replacing register tape but smiled at me. "How've you been? You had it worse than me. That creep stuck his gun right in your face."

I shuddered. "Yeah. It's been kind of hard."

Her eyes darkened. "People are slimeballs."

"Sometimes. Some of them." I managed a smile. "But then there are the folks like you with enough courage to keep going."

Her hands stilled on the roll of paper, and she looked at me in surprise. "Courage?" Her smile grew. "I never thought I was brave."

"Believe me. You are."

Her pleased expression rewarded me, and I turned back to Alex with a smile. "Okay. This was a good idea. I faced it. Let's go." I threw one more look around the store, absorbing the truth that I hadn't crumbled. Then I strode toward the door.

"Um, Penny?"

*Now what?* "Alex, this is enough for today. *Veni, vidi, vici.*"

"Yes. You came, you saw, you conquered. But you forgot to pay for the gas."

My cheeks warmed again, but not from panic this time. I stomped back to the counter and paid while Alex chuckled and LaShaunda giggled.

On the way out to the car, I laughed, too. And the laugh was as powerful as a shout of triumph.

ALEX STAYED IN TOWN for a few more days. He insisted on remaining at his motel, but came over each day. Long conversations filled in some of the gaps about his life journey, but left other mysteries. He didn't explain what kind of care he was receiving to manage his depression, and he didn't say much about how he had survived before that pivotal day in the detox center. I didn't press him. He'd face his ghosts when he was ready. And I'd be there for him.

Wednesday night, we went to the mission prayer service. Alex joined his throaty voice with Barney's and added a deep resonance to the old hymns. Even more uplifting, Ashley slipped in after the service started and spent some time talking with Lydia afterward. Maybe Ashley would volunteer to help with the preschoolers. Maybe she'd also find deeper help for her soul than Dr. Marci could provide. The support group was a blessing, but counseling only held pieces of answers. Good pieces. After all, the right medicine helped Alex manage his depression. But God also gave the profound gift of himself to reclaim broken spirits.

Saturday morning, before my brother headed back to Texas, he came over for a breakfast of pancakes. Alex shoveled food into his mouth, and held up his plate for more. Bryan copied him, and my brother grinned. "So are you and Tom traveling to Wisconsin for Christmas?"

"We hope to. If he can get enough time off. What about you?"

His eyes clouded. "Maybe. I don't want to make any promises. I hate letting people down." He stood up and stretched. "I better hit the road. Thanks for letting me visit."

"Thanks for helping me go back."

"Glad I could be there for you."

The second his car rattled away, Bryan tugged on my arm. "Jim-Bob and his whole family are going to the zoo and said I could go with. Okay? It's a good idea, right?"

I knelt and faced him. "Sweetie, you didn't invite yourself, did you?"

His eyes angled sideways, and his tongue poked out at an opposite angle. "I only said I like going to the zoo."

"Remember what I said about how it's not polite to beg for a bite when your friend is eating a candy bar? It's the same idea. You can't just ask if you can go along because it puts Jim-Bob's mom on the spot."

Bryan met my gaze firmly. "Jim-Bob wants me to go."

"Yes, but that doesn't mean his mom was planning on bringing extra kids."

"But, Mo-om, they have real tigers."

I sighed. "You're missing the point." I stood up and tousled his hair. "Let me call Jim-Bob's mom."

He beamed as I walked to the kitchen, dialed, and chatted

with Laura-Beth. She assured me she was delighted to take Bryan along, and that if I didn't mind her saying, I should try to get him to the zoo more often.

An hour later, I found myself alone in the house.

All the last boxes from our Wisconsin life were unpacked, and our new world was neatly organized. The rooms were tidy, and even the laundry pile was a foothill instead of a mountain. For a solid week, I'd stayed awake each day and slept through the night. Making a phone call caused only minor anxiety, and even short errands had become second nature again. In a few weeks, Tom would return, and I'd have something of myself to offer him again. He'd promised to love me through any struggle, but I was relieved to know I wouldn't be a huge burden on him—that my fears no longer consumed all my energy.

I wandered into the living room and picked up my notebook. I'd taped the torn yellow cover back together and reattached it to the spiral binding. I might be past the worst of my PTSD, but I wasn't abandoning Penny's Project. There were other enemies in my life besides trauma and panic attacks. Life was full of temptations to isolate and withdraw. Earbuds shut the world out. Instant messaging and Internet chat rooms substituted for human contact.

I grabbed my pen and wrote. *Lord, you are substantial. Real. Help me be more like you.*

When I looked up, the clutter of Netflix movies caught my eye. Time to cancel that subscription. Nothing wrong with an occasional movie, but I needed to cut back and leave more time for human interactions.

I slid discs into their return envelopes and put Bryan's scattered movies into their cases. As always, I came up with one extra disc. Silver, unlabeled, winking at me.

"Last try," I whispered. "Please show me Tom's last message."

Today, the DVD sprang to life. Afraid any movement would cause it to cut out, I sat immobile on the edge of the couch and let it run from the beginning. I slowly relaxed, convinced the disc was done toying with me.

"Message five." Tom glanced as his watch. "I just have a minute to get to a meeting, so it'll be short.

"I want to tell you one more time. I love you.

"I loved you when we met in college, and you debated our PolySci prof. You have more determination than anyone I know. And no matter how many papers you had due, you always had a plan to keep them under control.

"I loved you the day of our wedding. When you walked toward me, it hit me that you'd chosen me, over every other guy. I knew God had given me the best gift He'd ever given a human on this planet.

"And I loved you when Bryan was born. Watching you in pain was one of the hardest days of my life, and I wondered if anyone could survive what you were going through. And between every contraction, you smiled and squeezed my hand and told me you were fine. I wish I had your strength."

His sentences tumbled together. *Slow down, Tom. Let me savor this.*

He barely paused for a breath. "Tomorrow's the day. My first deployment. Don't know if I'll be able to handle the things that come up. And, hey"—he leaned forward and stage whispered—"that's for your ears only. As far as the chain of command knows, I am brimming with confidence."

I giggled and rocked back. "I promise not to tell."

"We're both facing challenges. This time apart is going to change us both."

He was right. Would I even know him when he came home? Would we feel like strangers?

He squared his jaw. "My love isn't going to change. And when I come home we'll catch up on the experiences we've had. We're going to come out of this closer than before. So hang on a little longer. I'll see you soon."

He stood and stepped around his desk.

He couldn't stop now. I needed more messages.

I caught one last flash of his sleeve as he stepped past the camera. Then the recording ended.

The couch cushions welcomed me as I sank back and closed my eyes. Instead of replaying the DVD, I reviewed the conversation in my mind. Emotions swam through me—tenderness, pride, yearning. Slowly, one thought flutter kicked to the surface.

I was the most blessed woman on the planet.

"Thank you, Lord." I reached for my notebook again. This prayer needed to be written down so I could share it with Tom when he got home.

*Thank you for Tom and his beautiful messages. Thank you for sending support every time I needed it. Thank you for staying beside me in the darkest places, and walking with me to places where the sun rises again. Amen.*

I paged back. Tom was right. This experience had changed me. I could read the change unfold on paper and ink. I held the notebook open at my goal of being in the Thanksgiving play. I'd blown that chance. I'd let Bryan down. But maybe there was still a way to serve the school and bring my son a little joy. A new idea sprouted to life, and I began to scribble, a grin growing across my face.

---

Tom came home in the afternoon. A brilliant, cool, amazing early-November afternoon.

We'd agreed I wouldn't stand on the dock with the crowds, because he still had responsibilities, and my presence would distract him as he provided reintegration care to the men and women from his ship.

Mary Jo called and let me know when the ship docked. From that moment I began to pace the house. Bryan was still in school, and the quiet made each minute stretch.

Using a curling iron on my hair one strand at a time filled an hour. By the time I finished, the spirals on the first side were straightening already. A futile effort, but it gave me something to do. My reflection blinked back from the bathroom mirror. Did I look the same? My eyes definitely had more life in them than back in September when Tom left.

I checked the roast I'd prepared and added a few more potatoes and carrots. The pan was ready to pop in the oven an hour before supper. I put candles on the table and stared at my watch. Each car that rolled by found me pressing my nose against the window, heart racing so much, I feared triggering another panic attack.

A distraction was in order. I flopped on the couch and picked up my little notebook. Somewhere in these past months, God had not only healed the effects of the crime, He had kindled love in my heart again. I lost myself in memories of friends and strangers, of smiles and moments of comfort. My days had filled with small efforts, sometimes wrenched from the deepest places of my soul, but always guided and supported by God's hands.

A car door slammed in front of the house. The notebook fell from my hands, and I sprang to my feet.

Suddenly I couldn't move.

Had he changed? Would there be an awkward gulf between us after so much time? Would we be strangers?

The door opened.

Tom shouldered his way forward and then tossed his heavy bag to the side.

His cheeks were windburned, ruddier than I remembered. His shoulders seemed broader, filling the entryway. He gave the room a quick scan. Bryan's bright handmade sign hung on the living room wall. Clusters of balloons dangled in each corner.

His smile acknowledged the decorations, but then his eyes locked on mine. "I'm home." The words were so low I almost didn't hear them, more a sigh of relief than a greeting. He took a step forward and paused. I realized he felt the same first-date shyness that gripped me.

"Penny?" He stared straight into my heart. All the swirling deep of oceans pulled me into his eyes.

I leapt across the few feet still between us.

Finally, finally, my husband's arms wrapped around me again. I clung to him and burrowed my nose into his shoulder as if I could be completely absorbed by him—his strength, his love.

"I missed you so much." My words were muffled against his shirt. I wouldn't dissolve into a puddle of tears.

He gave another squeeze, then eased me back and coaxed my chin up.

I met his gaze, unafraid to let him see my smile. Confident, strong, and utterly in love. "Welcome home, Chaplain Tom."

He kissed me, and I tasted coffee and smelled briny ocean breezes on his skin. His tenderness deepened to something more urgent, and his hands moved over me, leaving me breathless.

"What time does Bryan's bus get here?"

I glanced at the clock. "We've still got an hour."

Tom's smile grew, and he buried his hands in my hair and captured my lips again.

---

Several weeks later, I wrestled the squirming python in my belly into submission and stepped onto the Jackson Elementary School stage. "Good evening." The microphone hummed softly, and then my voice lurched up in volume as someone adjusted it. "Thank you to everyone who joined in our food drive. I'm happy to report that we were able to fill twenty baskets that the New Life Mission will distribute to families in our community who need extra support." The effort of squeezing the words out left me breathless. I forced my arm to lift toward the stage-left wings, trying to beckon Lydia forward with a graceful gesture. It probably looked more like the flail of a drowning swimmer.

Lydia marched out to join me and grabbed the microphone from the stand. "Y'all are welcome to come to our prayer service any Wednesday night. Don't know anyone that doesn't benefit from a little prayin', right? Thanks to all of you for givin' from your hearts. And thanks to Penny for organizing this project. Now let's get on with the play." She stuffed the microphone back into the holder and gave me a warm hug. Applause rose through the gym while she whispered in my ear. "They don't know what this took out of you. But Jesus does. And I'm thinkin' He's good and proud of you."

"I'm glad I thought of it. All it took was a few flyers and phone calls."

I caught sight of Bryan in the wings. His grin caught the light, and he gave me a thumbs-up sign.

Lydia released me. "A few phone calls and a bucketload of courage." She pointed her chin toward the handsome man in the third row, applauding more fiercely than the rest. "I'm thinkin' he's proud of you, too."

Six-foot-one of handsome Navy chaplain with fair hair and sea-flecked hazel eyes, Tom pushed out of the metal folding chair to lead a standing ovation. Warmth swelled under my sweater, stretching the cable-knit stitches. It was still hard to take in. *Tom is home. He's home!*

I had hoped that he'd return to find me playing a Pilgrim mom in the play, busy with loads of activities and completely free from any effects of the crime. My life hadn't followed that script. I still had nightmares sometimes, and I was easing back into life with tentative progress . . . two steps forward, one step back. But I had found a way to participate in the Thanksgiving play that worked for me. Satisfaction sighed through me like a deep breath as Lydia and I walked down the steps at the side of the stage. She went to stand beside Barney at the side of the gym. He put an arm around her and whispered something. She laughed and shook her head.

Another of my projects that was progressing well.

I took my seat next to Tom and he held my hand as the children jostled their way onto the stage for the production.

An hour later, pellets of frozen ice jitterbugged across the pavement outside the front windows of Jackson Elementary School. Not quite rain, not quite hail. Another example of Virginia's moderation.

Bryan tugged at the stiff white collar of his black Pilgrim costume. "Maybe it'll snow."

"Probably not, sport." Tom smiled at me over Bryan's head. "It's supposed to warm up, so maybe tomorrow we can toss a football around in the backyard."

"Football!" Bryan charged him in a fake tackling move.

Tom grabbed Bryan around the waist and hefted him up over his shoulder. Muscles bulged against the pure white of his uniform—a uniform that should have made him imposing and formal. Instead, Tom's laughter was boyish and full of mischief. He'd rarely stopped smiling since he'd arrived back home.

I joined their wild laughter. Other parents stared as they flowed past and out into the cold night.

Mrs. Pimblott maneuvered through the crush and headed our direction.

I ducked behind Tom, but she still marched straight toward us. Schoolmarm prim in a gray wool skirt and cat's-eye glasses, she gave us a wide smile. "Bryan did a terrific job with his song. You must be very proud of him."

I murmured agreement while Tom and Bryan continued to tussle.

"The food basket idea was inspired. And I love what you did with Bryan's costume."

I shrugged. "Just a little sewing." Since the boys were continuing to roughhouse, I stepped closer to her. "I'm sorry I wasn't more responsive when Bryan was acting up last month . . ."

She pulled off her glasses and let them dangle from the cord around her neck as she leaned in. "You don't need to apologize. Bryan explained that you were having trouble with the police."

"What? No. I mean—" I stopped stammering to elbow Tom, who was chuckling. Since I didn't want Bryan's teacher watching for my face on *America's Most Wanted*, I gave her a quick explanation. "But I'm doing better. In fact, if you still need a room mom to help the reading groups on Tuesdays, I'd love to help."

"This little Pilgrim of ours wants to get going," Tom said after Mrs. Pimblott scurried off to greet another family.

"Mm-hmm. I'm guessing the big Pilgrim wants to go, too."

Tom settled Bryan back on his feet to his right, and pulled me close with his left arm. "Good call. Your menfolk are hungry."

I giggled. "You could shoot a turkey or snare a rabbit or two."

Tom kissed my forehead. "Or we drive home and have some ice cream to celebrate our son's singing debut."

"Or that."

We laughed our way through the sleet and to the car. Driving home, we relived all the highlights of the play, assuring Bryan that his song was even better than the part where the Indian girl spilled a basket of corn and all the dancing deer slipped and fell.

"Tom?"

"Hmm?"

"I just remembered something. Can you pull into the grocery store?"

"Okay, but only one stop. Right, Bryan?"

"Yeah. We wanna go home."

"No place like it," Tom agreed. He pulled into the near-vacant lot and parked close to the door. "Want us to come in with you?"

"Nope. It'll only take a second." I slipped from the car and into the store. Up the aisle, I hurried toward the bakery counter. A stock boy dropped a can of soup with a loud crash. I startled but took a deep breath and marched forward.

Soon pastries and muffins stretched before me behind glass.

"Can I help you, ma'am?" The white-haired woman behind the counter smiled at me.

I looked her in the eye and returned her smile. "I need a cake. A chocolate cake."

# Acknowledgments

So many people have supported and encouraged me throughout my work on this book. I share my deep appreciation with all the wonderful folk at Bethany House, but particularly the stellar editors Charlene Patterson, Ann Parrish, and Karen Schurrer. Thanks as well to agent Steve Laube, and writer friends from ACFW, Mount Hermon, MCWG, Word Servants, my Book Buddies, and various critique partners, particularly Sherri Sand, Jill Nelson, Joyce Haase, and Chawna Schroeder, who dug into the complete manuscript.

Profound thanks to experts such as Rev. Randy Mortenson and Chaplain Richard Day—CAPT, CHC, USN (RET)—for their info about Navy chaplains; to the very experienced psych nurse and the gifted psychologist (who wish to remain anonymous) who offered terrific insights into group therapy and psychiatric disorders, as well as the many friends and readers who shared the details of their struggles with depression or anxiety and helped inform the story; and to Mark Mynheir for police procedural tips. Any errors in the story are not their fault. Blame my characters who sometimes sneak off to do their own thing when I'm not looking.

While my head is floating in story world, I treasure the friends in the real world who keep me rooted. St. Michael's, Life Group, Church Ladies, and even those brief acquaintances who have practiced random acts of kindness on me. Your example makes me long to pay it forward.

My family continues to go above and beyond in their sacrifices, love, and support. Joel and Jennelle, Kaeti, Josh, Jenni, Mom, and Carl, I'm so blessed you are in my life. Ted, I stand by what I said. Every novelist would benefit from being married to you. Love to you all.

Thank you, Father God, that you can work through weak and broken people, and that your grace often leaks out through our broken places to comfort others. Thank you for the many gifts you send when we are locked in places of pain—for laughter, for compassion, for wisdom, and for hope—often sent to us in strange packages.